D1257390

THE DEADLIEST SIN

Also by Jeri Westerson

The Crispin Guest Medieval Noir series

VEIL OF LIES
SERPENT IN THE THORNS
THE DEMON'S PARCHMENT
TROUBLED BONES
BLOOD LANCE
SHADOW OF THE ALCHEMIST
CUP OF BLOOD
THE SILENCE OF STONES *
A MAIDEN WEEPING *
SEASON OF BLOOD *
THE DEEPEST GRAVE *
TRAITOR'S CODEX *
SWORD OF SHADOWS *
SPITEFUL BONES *

Other titles

THOUGH HEAVEN FALL
ROSES IN THE TEMPEST

* *available from Severn House*

THE DEADLIEST SIN

Jeri Westerson

SEVERN
HOUSE

First world edition published in Great Britain and the USA in 2021
by Severn House, an imprint of Canongate Books Ltd,
14 High Street, Edinburgh EH1 1TE.

Trade paperback edition first published in Great Britain and the USA in 2022
by Severn House, an imprint of Canongate Books Ltd.

severnhouse.com

Copyright © Jeri Westerson, 2021

All rights reserved including the right of
reproduction in whole or in part in any form.
The right of Jeri Westerson to be identified
as the author of this work has been asserted
in accordance with the Copyright,
Designs & Patents Act 1988.

British Library Cataloguing-in-Publication Data
A CIP catalogue record for this title is available from the British Library.

ISBN-13: 978-0-7278-8971-3 (cased)
ISBN-13: 978-1-4483-0600-8 (trade paper)
ISBN-13: 978-1-4483-0599-5 (e-book)

This is a work of fiction. Names, characters, places and incidents
are either the product of the author's imagination or are used fictitiously.
Except where actual historical events and characters are being described
for the storyline of this novel, all situations in this publication are
fictitious and any resemblance to actual persons, living or dead,
business establishments, events or locales is purely coincidental.

All Severn House titles are printed on acid-free paper.

Typeset by Palimpsest Book Production Ltd.,
Falkirk, Stirlingshire, Scotland.
Printed and bound in Great Britain by
TJ Books, Padstow, Cornwall.

To Craig. Always Craig. You were there at the beginning and now at the end of this series. You read everything I ever wrote. You supported me when the thought of getting published seemed like a vanishing dream. You were there with a sweetness I probably didn't deserve. You told me to never quit. There is no greater love than that.

ACKNOWLEDGMENTS

A long time ago, in a manuscript far, far away, I typed out the name 'Crispin Guest' for the first time. This was the result of my former agent Kimberly Cameron suggesting I write medieval mysteries instead of historical fiction. And then came my original critique group, the Vicious Circle of Ana Brazil, Bobbie Gosnell, and Laura James. When I felt that first book was ready – *Cup of Blood* – I stumbled upon my fourth agent. Steve Mancino worked at JABberwocky Literary at that time, and we worked together on the manuscript for a long while before I said, 'So, uh, do I get a contract to sign, or what?' And we did. *Cup of Blood* didn't get picked up, but Editor Keith Kahla at St. Martin's Minotaur remembered it and, fourteen months later, he actually asked my agent, 'You know, I can't get these characters out of my head. Has she got another one in this series?' I did. I had the next two written, as a matter of fact, and I had just turned in *Veil of Lies* to my agent and it was signed by Minotaur fourteen years after I started writing for publication. It was a big deal to me to get a big New York publisher after all that time of working hard at writing book after book, honing my craft. Hector DeJean was my publicist then and I appreciated his working to get my name out there. I learned a lot from him. I mustn't forget that Minotaur best-selling author Julia Spencer-Fleming was kind enough to take this fledgling author under her wing, and I am ever grateful for all the help she's given me throughout the years, as well as the help and encouragement from author Cornelia Read-Reigert, who spotted me on a plane heading out to the same mystery fan convention she was going to. She noticed me because I wore a T-shirt that read, 'Read Banned Books'. She gave me my first blurb. And then the late, great medieval mystery author Margaret Frazer was kind enough to offer me another blurb at that same Bouchercon.

I've met so many helpful people along the way and I am so very grateful for all the support and friendships I have made writing this series. Joshua Bilmes, the owner of the agency who took over agent duties for me when Steve left, always oversaw this series even as it moved from St. Martin's to Severn House, and I thank my editors there in the UK, including Sara Porter.

Between publishers, I self-published *Cup of Blood* as a prequel, but it's really the first if you want to read it in that order.

Also, a very special thanks to my son Graham, who put up with his mom locked away in her office, writing, writing. Did you become a screenwriter just to get back at me when you could have had a normal job? And of course, huge thanks and much love to my amazing husband Craig. He's been through it all with me. He didn't even know I wrote novels when I suggested I should try and make a living at this writing nonsense. So, he gets the biggest cheers of all.

And finally, to my fictional medieval detective, Crispin Guest. We've been through a lot together. He patiently took all that I dished out. This is your last adventure, my friend.

It takes a village and one village idiot to have a writing career. Thank you to all the readers who stuck with me all along the way. I am more grateful to you than you can ever know.

For God's sake, let us sit upon the ground
And tell sad stories of the death of kings.

Act 3, Scene 2, *The Tragedy of King Richard the Second*,
William Shakespeare

GLOSSARY

Carrel – An alcove of high walls with a seat and a desk designed for a private reading space.

Cellarium – A storehouse in a monastery.

Chancel – The part of the church near the altar.

Chapter House – A room in which monastics met daily to hear a chapter of the monastic rule as well as to air grievances and get messages from the abbot, abbess, prior, or prioress.

Chatelaine – A decorative mounting hook with a set of short chains attached to a woman's belt. Each chain would carry keys or other items, such as a pin box and other accoutrements that showed her wealth and place in the household, castle, or monastery. Also the woman who carried those keys.

Ciborium – A form of chalice with a lid to contain consecrated hosts for distribution at the mass.

Cloister – A covered walkway in a monastery around a quadrangle of grass or garden, made up of a building wall on one side and a colonnade on the outer side. Sometimes carrels were built there, as the light was better for reading.

Clout – Diaper.

Divine Office – Seven or eight times during the day, monastics are exhorted to pray specific and regimented prayers, at, roughly, these times of night and day. They are:

Matins – midnight

Lauds – dawn, or sometimes immediately after Matins

Prime – six a.m.

Terce – nine a.m.

Sext – 11 a.m. or noon

None – 3 p.m.

Vespers – 6 p.m., twilight/sundown

Compline – 9 p.m., night

Dorter – A dormitory for the monks or nuns.

First Sleep and Second Sleep – It should be a relief to insomniacs that humans used to have a 'first sleep' when they would retire after sunset and naturally awaken between midnight and two a.m. This awake time was used for prayer (as in monasteries when, in the Benedictine Rule, 'At midnight, I rose to acknowledge to thee; on the dooms of thy justifyings . . .' Psalm 119, Wycliffe Bible), or chatting with one's neighbors, or snacking, or having sex. Then, after an hour or so, they would retire again for their 'second sleep' till dawn. This was a common enough thing that it was barely ever mentioned in writings. It wasn't until the days of the industrial revolution, working in factories, and harsher artificial lighting, that humans forgot about this two-tiered natural sleep cycle.

Garderobe – A lavatory in a medieval building.

Girdle – A woman's belt.

Infirmary – Part of the monastery which housed the clerics who were too sick or too old to take part in the normal monastic life.

Jesu – Middle English from Old French. In the sixteenth century, 'Jesus' became the common spelling but '*Jesu*' was often used in Bible translations, harking back to the Latin. Pronounced JAY-zoo.

Lavatorium – A place either outside or within a room which contained a trough with running water where monastics washed.

Lychgate – A covered structure as a gateway to a church, usually leading to the church graveyard.

Nave – The long, central section of a church in which the laymen pray. In the Middle Ages, there were no pews, no seats.

Necessarium – A communal latrine.

Night Stair – A staircase used by monastics to enter a church directly from their dormitory in order to attend late night and early morning services.

Prie-dieu – A kneeler for private devotion with a flat surface above the kneeler part for a prayer book or prayerful hands.

Pyx – A small, portable container with a lid for a consecrated host.

Quire or choir – Situated in a church between the nave and the chancel, with rows of seats facing each other across the aisle for monks or nuns to gather for the Divine Office, mass, or other ceremonies.

Rectory – Living quarters for a priest at their parish church.

Refectory – Dining hall in a monastery.

Religieuses – French term for female persons bound by religious vows in a monastery.

Seven Deadly Sins – A concept – not specifically found in scripture – but defined by a fourth-century monk, Evagrius Ponticus, and later expanded on by the fifth-century saint, John the Ascetic, into the familiar Deadly Sins we are familiar with today. They are 'deadly' in terms of one's soul:

Lust

Gluttony

Greed

Sloth

Wrath

Envy

Pride

Tonsure – Clerks (part of the clerical class), priests, and monks shaved the crown of their heads as a reminder of humility and chastity.

Watching Loft – A second story in a church or hall, as big as a gallery or as small as a narrow passage, where watchers could look down onto a shrine or other important area below.

Wimple – A head and neck covering for women from the early Middle Ages and continued in some nuns' habits even to the present time. In the medieval period, it was made of white linen and covered the entire head and neck, leaving only an opening for the face. Veils were pinned to it.

ONE

3 February 1399, Leicester Castle

He'd waited a long time in the anteroom until he finally heard the words, 'Let Crispin Guest come forth.'

He didn't know who said it and he cared little to know. All his concentration centered on putting one foot in front of the other.

The chamber was dark and close. And there, before him, stood the duchess, Lady Katherine.

She said nothing. Her solemn face and red-rimmed eyes told him all he needed to know. He held her hands for but a moment and bowed to her. In her long veil and wimple, she seemed like a holy sister . . . or the visage of the Holy Mother, but he knew she would not like the comparison.

She gestured toward the immense bed with its four robust posters more suited to a castle's foundation than a bed. But it well-matched the status of the dying man within it. And yet, he seemed a small, weak figure among the white linens. Crispin could scarce believe that this was his mentor, his friend; the man he had known all his life. A man now surrounded by solemn clerics and lords, whose shadowed faces looked on at Crispin with a mixture of puzzlement and distaste. Crispin once had a place beside these lords, but no longer. He had lost that place decades ago. He was not fit to stand in the presence of the dying Duke of Lancaster.

He ignored the men, their soft murmurs of disapproval, and stepped up to the platform, kneeling beside the bed. Throat swollen with misery, eyes full of unshed tears, Crispin managed a raspy, 'My lord.'

John of Gaunt slowly turned his head. His hair was covered with a cap and his beard was shot with gray. Cheeks sunken, eyes peering out from deep, bruised hollows, he recognized Crispin with a flash of life in his eyes.

'Crispin,' he said slowly. 'Am I truly seeing you or is it a vision?'

'It is me, my lord.' He reached up and took the man's hand. It was soft and papery like that of a weakling.

'God is good. I wanted to see you. I wanted . . . to ask your forgiveness.'

'My lord, you have it. You know you have it. You've had it for years.'

The thin fingers squeezed his hand. 'A man in my current position must make certain,' he said softly. He smiled but he could not seem to hold it. After all, it had been John's scheme to ferret out traitors to the king when Richard was given the crown as a child of ten. John couldn't have known that Crispin would be swept up in the false conspiracy to put Lancaster on the throne. He couldn't have imagined that Crispin would have been in danger of his life and was banished from court instead.

'Crispin, who are all these crows around me? I've told them to go away but they will not seem to leave.'

'These are the lords of the court, my lord. They . . . they are in attendance . . . because . . .'

'They want to make certain I'm dead when they are called by the king.' He chuckled, a hollow, rattling sound deep in his chest.

Crispin said nothing. John knew the truth of it. At least his mind was as sharp as ever.

'But look at you, Crispin. You're old.'

'I am.'

'My children have come to say goodbye to me. All my lovely children. All except . . . for Henry.'

'He . . . he couldn't come, my lord . . .'

'I know.' He patted Crispin's hand. Henry had been banished by King Richard some months ago. He wasn't allowed to return even to be at his father's bedside. Crispin scowled. He hadn't realized he was doing so until Lancaster squeezed his hand again. 'Not now, Crispin.' His yellowed eyes flicked from one figure to another around the bed. 'Not while these crow-lords look on. They're waiting to peck away at all the corpses before them. Me . . . you . . .'

Crispin had promised himself to be strong, had promised himself not to weep. But, with a harsh lump burning his throat, he knew he couldn't keep that promise. The tears fell and he could not speak. All the things he had wanted to say were now forever imprisoned in his mouth, unspoken. He'd forgotten them all anyway.

John squeezed his hand again. 'It is a foolish thing to tell your loved ones not to weep for you. For we have all enjoyed each other's company and desire that it continue, even knowing full well it cannot. I've had a good life, Crispin. And my lady wife, well . . .' His eyes lifted. Lady Katherine's shadow was suddenly cast upon the bed, and Crispin felt her presence behind him. 'It is good to have one's love at last.' He blinked and let his gaze fall upon Crispin once more. 'You will pray for me, won't you, Crispin?'

Crispin nodded, still unable to speak.

He patted Crispin's hand and finally let it go. There was a rosary in his other hand, likely given to him by Lady Katherine. John did not allow for such things, normally. His Lollard heart rejected them. But Crispin supposed it was a comfort, to hold the cross at least.

Lady Katherine's hand lightly touched his shoulder, and with a jolt, he realized he was being asked to leave. It wouldn't do, what with the circumstances of Henry's banishment, for the traitor Crispin Guest to linger at the duke's deathbed.

He rose, his heart heavy. He supposed his tears told John all he had wanted to say. He hoped they did. He clutched one last time at Lady Katherine's hand, and left the chamber and the castle to head back to London.

TWO

August 1399, London

After nearly seven months had passed, Crispin still brooded. In those early days of February, he could do little else. He had skirted the sorrowful gazes of his apprentice Jack Tucker and Jack's wife Isabel by simply staring into the fire, watching the latter cook their meals at that hearth, and ate of them in silence.

His apprentice and family lived with him in the old poulterer's shop . . . or did *he* live with *them*? Sometimes it seemed the latter was true, for it had been twenty-two years since he had been banished from court, and Jack had walked into his life over a decade ago as a scrappy young thief and become closer than any apprentice could have been. Almost as close as a son. Their shared arrangement – with Crispin in his own chamber across the gallery upstairs, and Jack and his family in the other – suited them both.

Jack's children, though they were schooled to be judicious and leave their master alone, were, in the end, just children, and so it was Gilbert, at four, who did not ask but simply climbed into Crispin's lap as he was accustomed to doing, only a fortnight after the duke's funeral.

'Why are you sad, Master Cwispin?'

Crispin, without thinking, had slipped an arm around the boy to keep him close. 'Well, I'm sad because someone very dear to me has died and gone away. And I shall never see him again.'

'Oh. But you pway for him?'

'Yes, I do.'

'Mother says that if we pway, the people we love will go to God and that's a happy thing. He's with God, isn't he?'

Crispin turned and gazed at the face of the small boy who had his father's flaming red hair and freckles, a pudgy face where one plump cheek was smeared with a blot of butter. He held the boy tighter. 'Gilbert, your mother is very clever. Because he *is* with God. And that *is* a very happy thing. And . . . I *shall* see him again.'

Gilbert put a hand to Crispin's cheek. 'Then you don't have to be sad.'

He smiled, the first time in days. 'No, I don't. You are most wise.' Crispin put a hand to his cheek where the smaller hand had been. 'And most sticky.' He wiped at it but then let his hand drop. 'You are quite the philosopher, Gilbert.' He kissed the boy on the top of his head, lifted him from his lap, and stood, watching Gilbert scuttle across the room and run out the front door that lay ajar, letting in the busy noise of the Shambles, the butcher's district of London, with all its commensurate smells and bustle.

And, seven months later, Crispin could finally breathe deep. That little boy, in his innocence, had made his heart lighter. Still, Crispin sometimes felt melancholy for the death of his former master.

The chatter that followed hadn't helped. When Lancaster died, there were rumors that King Richard had cancelled the documents – fair and legal papers – that assigned the lands automatically to the exiled Henry, Lancaster's son. And if that were true, the king had disinherited Henry Hereford, not only from the lands and chattels rightfully his, but from the title 'Duke of Lancaster.'

Crispin had done his own listening in clutches of men when they discussed the matter, and finally sought out his old friend Abbot William de Colchester, the Abbot of Westminster Abbey, to ask what the truth was. And reluctantly the abbot had confirmed Crispin's fears.

How would this sit with the angry young man Henry had been when exiled by Richard? And Henry had made Crispin swear he'd watch out for the duke. And he had, to the best of his ability. Which wasn't much, being that he was still considered a traitor by Richard. There was only so much Crispin *could* do.

What would *Henry* do now?

Crispin felt the itch of the summer heat and humidity at his neck, and pulled his collar away from his throat. Casting about for his apprentice, he bellowed, 'Tucker!' into the rafters.

Jack poked his head over the side of the gallery above. 'Master?' His ginger curls fell over his forehead, and his cultivated beard – equally as red as his hair – flamed from his pale face.

'Just wondering where you were.' Crispin stretched. It seemed he had been immobile during these warm days of summer. 'Have we any clients to attend to?'

'Er . . . no, sir. None have come our way as yet.'

'Let us go to the Boar's Tusk. I feel like a little walk.'

'Aye, sir.'

Jack hurried down the steps and joined his master at the door. They each eschewed their hoods and cloaks to walk out into the humid streets.

'I suppose I should tell you, sir, that we, er . . . Isabel and me, that is,' Jack began as they walked, side by side. 'We've been paying the priest at St Martin's Le Grand to say prayers for His Grace the duke, in your name, sir. I mean, it wasn't much, but I hope that was keeping with my place, master.'

Crispin slowed to a stop and turned to the man. He eyed Jack carefully. Jack was actually worried he'd overstepped the line, when nothing could be further from the truth. But Crispin wasn't able to speak the words. He closed his hand over Jack's shoulder instead, squeezing.

Jack's lips crinkled into a smile before they continued on.

When they reached the Boar's Tusk, it was full of men of all stripes; merchants, clerics, travelers, all crowded in the little space whose rafters always looked as if they'd buckle in, whose smoky fires never seemed to relieve the room of their dense murkiness, and whose smells of smoke and wet woolens were as familiar to Crispin's sharp nose as his own person.

They found a table so that Crispin could keep his back to the wall with a view to the door . . . as he liked it.

Gilbert Langton, the stout tavernkeeper and the eponym of Little Gilbert Tucker, came to their table with a slower gait than he used to, and laid out cups and a jug of ale. 'I thought I'd see you here sooner. I didn't think summer was usually your time to do your "tracking".'

'Ah, but Gilbert, it *is* one of my seasons. The heat makes a man's blood hot. And murder is most often on a man's mind. It is the winter that is the bleakest for my fees.'

The big man huffed. 'You speak like a farmer.'

'Should I sow discord to grow my crop of coins?' He laughed and Gilbert joined him.

'Jack Tucker,' said the tavernkeeper, 'when will you bring your brood again to visit their aunt and uncle?'

'Whenever you can rest yourself enough for it, Gilbert,' said Jack, after drinking from his cup. 'You know how much vigor it takes.'

'Aye, I saw them just yesterday in the market. That namesake of yours, Crispin. Looks like he's taking after his master more than his father.'

'Eh?' said Crispin.

'Oh, it's true,' said Jack. 'The lad is becoming a serious boy. And studious. He'll be a scholar in no time at all.'

'He takes to his tutoring,' said Crispin, proud of Jack's firstborn. 'He's as quick with languages as you, Jack. He'll be speaking Greek soon.'

'I was never good at Greek,' Jack admitted.

Crispin took a drink and licked his lips. 'You wouldn't study.'

'I studied French, Latin and English. That's enough for any boy.' He lifted his cup, saluted Crispin, and drank.

Gilbert laughed as he walked away. Crispin followed his progress and noticed a gangly young lad in a slightly dirty tunic peering here and there by the door, looking for someone. He reminded Crispin mightily of the lanky boy Jack used to be. He watched him for several moments, idly wondering who the boy might be looking for, when the lad's eyes finally rested on Crispin's. The boy's face lit up and he pushed his way forward.

'Harken,' said Crispin, elbowing Jack.

They both watched the boy as he squeezed through the patrons and finally stood before their table. 'Am I in the presence of Crispin Guest and Jack Tucker?'

Crispin glanced sidelong at Tucker, who seemed to sit a little straighter at being mentioned. 'You are.'

The lad bowed messily. 'I was told I might find you here, my lord.'

'I am not a lord,' said Crispin. Saying it hadn't made his heart rumble like it used to do. Strange how one could become accustomed to almost anything.

'Oh.' The boy bowed again. 'My apologies, my lord. I've come to fetch you.'

Crispin leaned forward. '*Fetch* me?'

'Aye. To my Lady Prioress at St Frideswide Priory, at Old Dean's Lane and Thames Street, sir.'

'Is she expecting me?'

'Aye, my lord. I've been instructed to take you there.'

'Are you certain you want *me*, boy?'

'Oh aye, my lord. You're that Tracker they talk of, aren't you?' He got in close to Crispin and whispered loudly, 'My Lady Prioress says she wants to hire you. It's on account of all them murders, sir. At the priory.'

THREE

'I beg your pardon?' asked Crispin.

'*Murders*,' hissed the boy.

'At the priory?'

The boy looked over his shoulder. 'I'm not supposed to know about them, but I do. The Lady Prioress is at her wits end, and she wishes to hire you.'

Crispin glanced at Jack. 'Then . . . lead on, lad.'

They rose and followed the boy as he boldly shoved his way through the crowd – regardless of whom it might be, rich or poor – and led them to the door.

At that moment, a man pushed his way through, bare-headed with his clothes spattered with mud.

'Henry of Lancaster is back!' he cried.

Crispin whipped around, forgetting all else. He jerked forward and grabbed the man by his arm. 'What did you say?'

The men in the Boar's Tusk began to gather to him. 'Henry of Lancaster made landfall in Yorkshire and moved with his army through the Midlands.'

'His army?' asked a man in the back of the crowd. 'What's he doing with an army?'

'He's come to regain his inheritance by the point of a sword. But harken. The only ones who have died have been the king's councilors. Chester surrendered to him peacefully.'

Crispin's throat was suddenly so thick – his heart clattering against his chest – that he couldn't even ask his questions.

Henry found no opposition? None? Where was Richard?

'What of the king?' he finally managed to croak.

The man turned toward Crispin. He appeared to be a grizzled veteran of a soldier. A scar ran the length of his face from the left eyebrow to the right side of his chin where the gray beard hair would not grow, and his ear had a nick out of it. It could have been that Crispin fought side by side with this man who appeared to be ten years older than him. 'He was in Ireland. He heard of Lancaster's coming, but he didn't even start his journey south for three months. They say he's in Wales now.'

The man was taken to a table, urged to sit, and given ale. They gathered close about him as he drank and talked of the detail he knew, which wasn't much. And all the while, Crispin stood like a lump, unable to think clearly. Henry was back. With an army. What was he planning? Richard would not countenance this.

'You're Crispin Guest, aren't you?'

He woke from his musing and jerked his head toward the messenger, who had foam on his beard from the ale cup he had lowered from his mouth.

'Yes,' he said cautiously. Though thinking on it, it was foolish of him to try to be cautious. After all, everyone in the Boar's Tusk knew who he was and his history.

'Take heed, then. I don't doubt that Henry Lancaster will move south from the Midlands.'

Crispin couldn't help but slide his gaze to the surrounding men . . . who were all looking at him expectantly.

It was on his lips to refute association with Henry, but his mind flitted to Saint Peter's denial of Jesus. He said nothing instead.

'Hadn't we better follow the boy?' came the urgent voice of his apprentice at his ear.

He wanted to listen more to the old soldier, but the wisdom of leaving was the better part. Reluctantly, Crispin left the Boar's Tusk with Jack at his side.

The boy was still waiting for him on the street with an impatient lilt to his brow. Crispin vaguely gestured for the boy to lead on.

He hardly noticed how the muddy streets smelled of horse dung. Or how flies lazily circled, for even they were more lethargic in the sunshine. The sky was a deep blue and streaked with swathes of clouds. Each day brought sun but each afternoon seemed to bring on steamy rain. Yet none of that reached his consciousness. He thought only of Henry and his miraculous journey through England. What was he going to do? And what would it cost England?

'Sir,' said Jack's persistent voice.

He glanced at the concerned countenance of his apprentice. He'd probably tried to get Crispin's attention more than once.

'Best to be at the business at hand, Master Crispin,' he rasped.

That damned man could read his very thoughts. His first impulse was to snap at him, but he relented when he saw the sense in what he said. He couldn't wallow in his thoughts. And he couldn't help Henry. Crispin was no one. He had no funds, no retainers, no army *he* could muster. He *had* best get down to his own business and earn his keep for his family before war reached their doorstep with shortened provisions.

They took Newgate Market to Paternoster Row and then on to Old Dean. Crispin must have passed the high walls and steeple of the priory all his life and scarce noticed it. He had little to do with a nun's priory, after all, though he was a frequent visitor to Westminster Abbey and to the two abbots there he had befriended, what with it being so enmeshed with court politics.

They passed through the lychgate before the squat church, with its bell spire reaching upward. Its lead roof shone white in the sun's glare, though its windows were dark. Beyond that and the gate to the priory grounds, he could barely make out the long row of arches of the cloister, and the rest of the outbuildings of the monastery hidden behind trees. To their left was the churchyard where the gravel ended and became a muddy path. They saw three recent graves with freshly mounded earth atop them. A man with a rake – with only one full arm and another down to just the elbow – stopped his work to watch them through his salty gray hair and grizzled beard.

The ashen stone walls of the priory shone in the sunshine and stood well over seven feet. A gate of iron to their right kept the inhabitants from the world beyond. The boy stepped up to the gate and pulled a chain that rang a bell.

They stood together, occasionally flapping their collars. In the Boar's Tusk, Crispin had unbuttoned the top several buttons of his cote-hardie and now reluctantly buttoned them again as he peered through the ironwork to the gravel path. He elbowed Jack to do the same.

Presently, a tall nun in black habit and white apron hurried out along the path to the gate. When she arrived, she looked them all over with expressive brows and brown eyes, and nodded to the boy. She reached through the gate and handed him a farthing. He bowed to her, bowed to Crispin, and scurried off.

The tall nun, face pale and round beneath her white wimple and dark veil, studied Crispin with curious brown eyes. 'You are Master Guest?'

He bowed. 'I am, Dame.'

'Then you must enter.' She cast aside her apron to withdraw her chatelaine from her girdle and chose one key to unlock the gate. Crispin squeezed through the narrow opening she had made and Jack followed. Once they were in, she wasted no time locking the gate again.

'Please follow me.' She did not wait for them, but began a more sedate pace back up the curving gravel path, the rocks crunching under their boots . . .

They next entered through a shaded, windy passage between the cloister and the church. Crispin didn't mind the cool respite, the swaying of the trees.

It opened to the long, arched gallery of the cloister garth to their right as they followed the wall of the south transept of the church. They headed toward a long passage with a path made of flagged stone, through the night stair to the dorter, and on to an octagonal structure Crispin assumed must be the chapter house. He doubted they would be taken to any prioress's lodgings.

The nun stood before the oaken door and drew out her chatelaine again, unlocked the door, and stood aside for them to enter. There was a fire grate in the center of the tiled floor, but it stood unlit, surrounded by a few benches with high backs, like a quire. Obviously, St Frideswide had fewer than fifteen or so nuns in its company, if the seating were to be used to count them.

The nun gestured for them to sit nearest the tall-backed chair on its raised platform, reserved for the prioress, and there she left them, walking back through the quire to the door and closing it behind her.

Jack's eyes dithered all over the room. 'This place gives me the shivers.'

'Don't like monasteries, eh?'

'Not since you made me play the monk when I was thirteen, sir.' Jack gingerly sat, rubbing his palms on his thighs.

'That was some time ago,' Crispin mused. He recalled it well. Jack had done an exceptional job on that score.

'I still remember it,' said Jack, running a hand over his scalp where the brothers had tonsured him. It had taken a long time for his curls to grow back in.

Crispin sat back, running his gaze over the chapter house, with its curved plaster walls – a crudely painted scene on one wall of the Visitation of the Holy Mother to Saint Elizabeth – and up to the arched windows of clear glass that filled the room with shafts of light.

'That boy had said *murders*,' said Jack, cracking the stony silence.

'I had noted that. You saw the graves.'

'By the saints, what must be happening here?'

'We shall find out presently.'

'I'm wagering poison,' said Jack. 'That can wipe out an entire monastery, I'm thinking.'

Crispin bristled. 'I will not wager on the cause of death.'

They were both startled from their seats when the door opened.

A dark figure was momentarily framed in the doorway before she closed it after her. She walked without urgency down the aisle until she was standing before Crispin. She was short and her figure was robust, with cheeks full and round pressing against her linen wimple. Her small mouth made no expression, but her lively brown eyes seemed to spear into Crispin's soul, trying to discover what manner of man he was. She could be forty. She could be fifty. There were only the merest creases at the outer edges of her eyes, but otherwise, no wrinkle betrayed her exact age, and, of course, her hair, being completely hidden by wimple and black veil, gave no indication.

'Do I have the pleasure of addressing Crispin Guest?' she asked sharply. It sounded like no pleasure at all.

Crispin bowed. 'Indeed, my Lady Prioress. And this is my apprentice, Jack Tucker.'

Jack bowed, and she acknowledged him with a nod. She moved around the cold fire grate and proceeded up the dais to sit on her chair. 'Please be seated, gentlemen. I am Prioress Drueta Rowebern. I have dreaded calling upon you, sir. But your reputation throughout London made it impossible not to. I will get to the point. Some of our number . . . well. Two nuns died under mysterious circumstances.'

Crispin leaned in. 'By misadventure, Lady Prioress?'

'Yes. There can be no other interpretation.'

'I beg your mercy, Prioress Drueta, but I noted *three* graves when we entered.'

'Our apothecary died of natural causes before these others occurred.'

'Can you relate the circumstances?'

'Yes.' She shifted in her chair, finding a comfortable spot. 'A sennight ago, Dame Marion was found near the pigsty . . . strangled. When we examined her, there had been bones and scraps of food stuffed down her throat. And then, a few days ago, Dame Katherine was found wrapped within the blankets of all the others from the dorter and smothered with a pillow.'

Jack crossed himself with a gasp of surprise.

Crispin was equally shocked by the severity of the crimes. He shook his head. 'Lady Prioress, these are horrific. What did the sheriffs have to say?'

She sniffed. 'I did not call the sheriffs.'

He and Jack exchanged scandalized expressions. 'But . . . Lady Prioress, these were crimes. Did you not call out the hue and cry?'

'This is a monastery, Master Guest. It is not right to call the hue and cry. And to whom would we call it? The sheriffs did not need to disrupt our priory with men tromping about.'

Crispin took a long breath. 'Lady Prioress, I and my man Jack here will be "tromping about", as you say, in order to investigate.'

'Yes, but from you, Master Guest, the Tracker of London, I expect results.'

He glanced about him at the empty chapter house. 'Well, I do so for a *fee*, Lady Prioress.'

'Yes, I understand. Six pence a day. Do you have any idea how long it will take you to investigate, Master Guest? We are not a wealthy house.'

'I cannot begin to say, Dame. I will do my level best to be as quick as possible.'

She sighed. 'Very well, then. I suppose you would like to go about it immediately?'

'With all haste. Can you tell me the particulars?'

'We buried poor Dame Audrey, our apothecary, ten days ago. How we shall miss her expertise. I seem to recall the first death was discovered three days after she was buried. *Requiescat in pace.*' She crossed herself.

'And the second death?'

'Another day after that.'

'Curious.'

'I see you have already begun your work, Master Guest.'

'It seems rather urgent, Lady Prioress. What did your apothecary die of, if I may ask? You said natural causes.'

'It was a fever. She was being cared for in the infirmary for five days before she succumbed to it. And one so young, too.'

'You had no sense that it was foul play?'

She shook her head. 'No. It wasn't sudden. She became ill, and even her own herbal concoctions could not break her fever. There was nothing sinister to it, Master Guest. I have seen it many times in my years here.'

'I see.'

She rose from her chair, straightening out her girdle with its rosary, keys, pouch, and eating knife. 'You have the run of the priory, then. I shall so inform the sisters. Of course, you will wish to speak with them and I will allow it. The only caveat is that you may not interfere while the nuns conduct the Divine Office.'

'Understood.'

'And, of course, you are forbidden entry to the dorter.'

'It . . . might be necessary to—'

'It is *forbidden*, Master Guest,' she insisted.

He bowed his head and hoped that would appease . . . for now. For if someone from within the priory was killing these women, he knew he should eventually have to go to the dormitory.

'Then . . . you are dismissed.'

She moved to leave when Crispin stopped her. 'Lady Prioress, may I have a list of the workers and the nuns within the priory? This information will be most important.'

'I've already had my chaplain make up that list.' She pulled a folded parchment from the pouch at her hip and handed it over. She swept the end of her veil over her shoulder, as if sweeping long hair, and strode away down the tiled floor.

Jack laid a hand on Crispin's arm. 'These deaths, sir. Strangled with bones and scraps shoved down her throat. Another smothered. What does it mean?'

'These would seem to be the murders of an angry individual. Someone who was wronged, perhaps.'

'They're horrible, sir. I can't even imagine such things.'

'Yes, the world is filled with the unimaginable. Let us look at this list to see what we must contend with.' He unfolded the paper and Jack looked over his shoulder to read along:

Lady Prioress Drueta Rowebern

Dame Emelyn, chaplain

Dame Cecille, cellarer

Dame Sibilla, laundry overseer

Dame Joan, bakery overseer

Dame Petronella, apothecary

Dame Elizabeth, apothecary apprentice

Dame Mildred

Dame Jemma

Dame Margaret

Father Roger Holbrok

Edgar Crouch, caretaker

'Only ten living nuns, then,' said Jack.

'So it would seem. A caretaker – perhaps that one-armed fellow we saw in the churchyard – and the nuns' priest. We shall have to see if any other men have been inside the priory to repair or otherwise serve the monastery.'

'What would you have *me* do, sir?'

Crispin rubbed the parchment between his fingers. 'Yes, it might be best to split up. Perhaps you could seek out this Father Holbrok. Talk to him. See what he is about.'

'Aye, sir. He would be on the grounds.'

'Look for the rectory.'

Jack nodded, and moved away swiftly to comply.

Wistfully, Crispin watched him go. There was little of the frightened boy Jack had been when Crispin had first taken him in. He shook his head at all the years that had seemed to storm past him.

With a jolt, he suddenly remembered Henry again. He was grateful this work could keep his mind away from thoughts of Henry. *Let us keep it that way*, he thought sourly. After all, he could do nothing for Henry. But he *could* do a great deal for this priory and its inhabitants.

He folded the paper and stuffed it in his money pouch. Turning on the path, he tried to get his bearings. One monastery was laid out much like any other, with a few distinctions to each. Naturally new structures were built as needed, but church, cloister, dorter, refectory, necessarium would all be where expected. He knew this priory made their living by baking bread and by taking in laundry. Those would be the busiest buildings during the day and a place he could question the nuns without getting in the way of their Divine Office.

And what *of* the church? Crispin cast his eyes toward the larger structure, with its buttresses, ornate colored-glass windows, and square bell tower. Instead of following the path from which they had come, he chose to find the night-stair between church and dorter. The dorter seemed to be just beyond the chapter house. He slipped through the narrow passage of chapter house and dorter and found the small entry. It was merely a covered passage that allowed the nuns – in any sort of weather – to traverse between their dorter in the mid of night to the church for their prayers of the Divine Office. He ducked into the passage and nearly upended a nun.

She screamed and he recovered hastily to grab her before she fell. She looked down at his hands on her and shrieked again, and other nuns came running.

He stepped away from her and bowed. 'Forgive me, Dame. I am Crispin Guest. I was hired by your prioress to investigate the dread goings-on in your priory.'

The nuns, standing like inquisitive magpies, glared at him, embracing the plump nun he had first startled. She calmed herself enough to look him over. 'Crispin Guest, you say?'

'Yes. I am called the Tracker of London. I solve crimes.'

'Then . . .' She took in the others, cheeks flushed with embarrassment. 'We must not interfere with Master Guest's task. We will pray for you, sir.'

'Thank you. I will be speaking to all of you in the following days.'

She stopped and turned. 'Why?'

'To see if I can reckon why these murders occurred.'

'It is no secret why they occurred, Master Guest,' she said, raising her chin and looking down her snubbed nose at him. 'Because of the sin of our sisters here.' She turned abruptly and stomped away, the others in the passage moving out of her way.

Crispin raised a brow, hoping the others would enlighten him, but they all scattered in different directions, leaving him alone.

FOUR

Crispin listened as the nuns' footsteps receded. 'Monasteries,' he muttered, and moved forward toward the church.

He entered in the south transept by an oaken door, with its bands of iron and squared iron studs set in a grid pattern. The church was small, as expected. He couldn't imagine more than the nuns and a few patrons ever attending masses and festivals here.

The floor was set in small, glazed tiles, each of different design, with crosses on some, animals on others, and simple patterns on still others. He walked out onto the floor and gazed down the brief nave. A font and arched doorway in a foyer were positioned on the west end, and above it the bell tower. He walked down the nave, stopped at the font, and looked upward. A bell rope hung at the side, and the tower was open all the way to the top, with exposed rafters upholding the stone. The bell hung above in its headstocks, headframe, and wheel. It was silent now, but Crispin knew it would be a loud claxon in that narrow space.

Before he returned up the nave, he dipped his hand into the cold font water and absently sketched a cross over his head and torso. As he walked toward the high altar, he couldn't help but be taken aback by the striking painting – chipped with age – on the eastern wall behind the altar, curving around it with the shape of the wall. Executed by the same – he assumed – long-dead and unskilled artist who did the mural in the chapter house, Crispin's mouth fell open at the ghastly apparition of characters depicting each of the Seven Deadly Sins.

Lust was a woman, a nun, now that he had better look at it, tearing at the breast of her clothes and attempting to accost what appeared to be a priest. Gluttony was a figure sitting in a pigsty along with the pigs, stuffing its face with food, its over-round cheeks bulging with it. Greed was a figure – whether man or woman, Crispin could not tell – drowning in a sea of gold coins. Sloth was a woman asleep in her bed while her children wailed with empty bowls. Wrath was a man, red in the face, with his hands raised into fists, stomping the ground, while his servants cowered around him. Envy was a woman so fixated on the fine clothing of a noblewoman on a horse, that she draped herself in layer upon layer of filthy finery. And Pride seemed to be a man standing on a castle, while beneath the castle's walls lay the corpses of those who had built the structure.

He had seen murals aplenty in churches. It was to remind the viewer of the Bible stories, the lessons to be learned. True, they were sometimes frightening and grotesque, for Hell *was* frightening and the masses needed to remember that fact, especially those who could not read. Skeletons often danced across those walls in the *Danse Macabre*, reminding the viewer that death could be imminent and salvation was at hand.

But this mural . . . Its colors were vibrant, and the figures painted with such abandon of hasty brushstrokes that the effect was grotesque and garish at the same time. That it surrounded a large reliquary seemed unholy.

He found himself standing within the quire, whose high-backed seats of carved wood were polished to a high sheen, glowing in the light of a lit candle on the high altar's dais.

Crispin wondered what would be in such a reliquary that, were it not for the overwhelming imagery above it, would be in pride of place at the altar. It was gold and was fashioned as a church façade, complete with spires and arches. Behind its glass doors, he could see several objects within. Clearly, he'd need the help of the nuns to explain to him what was inside. Presumably relics of Saint Frideswide.

He took one last look at the ghastly painting and decided he did not like this church. How could one do any amount of prayerful contemplation with that vision of Hell on Earth glaring down upon them? *No wonder they are mad here*, he mused.

He supposed he'd go first to the bakehouse and ask the nuns there what they might know of the murders.

This time, he exited by the west door, passing under the bell again, and trotted down the steps. He searched for the outbuildings and saw most of them to the south, following well-worn paths through the unevenly cut grass between the buildings. Upon nearing the bakehouse, he could follow his nose toward the structure, where the blessed aroma of baking bread flowed outward. It was nearest a gate in the wall, where a few women had gathered to make their purchases. He wondered, vaguely, if Isabel Tucker got her bread for their household here. She could be purchasing it from anywhere, he supposed. He didn't pay attention to such things these days.

The laundry seemed to be just on the other side of the bakehouse, for he could smell that too, and its steam and odor of lye also rolled along the rooftops.

But he decided to see what lay beyond, for he heard the sounds of animals to the east. There was a wooden gate with a simple latch that he lifted and locked behind him. A sow and piglets nuzzled the scraps in the fenced enclosure, and they grumbled at him as he passed. Two goats were on leads behind a fenced yard. They looked up at him hopefully, but he passed them by. Chickens, too, wandered in this area where a vegetable garden – also fenced – warmed its green leaves in the sunshine. He recognized fennel, cabbage, onion, garlic, leeks, radishes, parsnips, and pease on a trellis. All looked well ordered, but it seemed strange that no nun was there to tend to it. He supposed that three deaths in succession stretched the limitations of the priory's inhabitants. After all, the laundry and the bakehouse brought in funds that could be used to supplement any losses in the garden.

Back he went to the nearby bakehouse, stepped up the carved granite steps, and pushed open the door. One nun, her sleeves rolled up with a flour-dusted apron tied around her waist, worked at a table kneading dough. Another was placing chopped wood near the domed ovens that he could see through two wide-open doors in the yard beyond the building.

The nun who had placed the firewood took up a long, wooden peel, pulled out the round loaves and placed them on a board. She hefted that board and went to the gate, taking the coins and handing each woman a loaf. One woman, behind the gate, stood off to the side. She didn't seem interested in the bread, and looked on anxiously, appearing to wait for all the customers to dwindle.

Two sisters that he could see were occupied with the bread. Perhaps three or four more were at work in the laundry, for the apothecary had her own apprentice and the two of them likely tended to their own garden.

Crispin watched their busyness for a several moments before he cleared his throat.

Both nuns looked up toward him.

He bowed. 'Ladies. I am Crispin Guest. Your prioress hired me to look into the recent murders.'

Neither of them spoke. Their rounded eyes seemed to speak for them. He recognized the tall one who acted as porter and let them into the priory. 'I would like to start with you, Dame, if you have a moment.'

She scraped her palms back and forth across her apron before glancing at the nun beside her and girding herself. 'Of course, Master Guest.'

'Let us go outside for our talk.'

A narrow bench stood against the bakehouse wall and he directed her there. She sat gingerly and placed her hands in her lap while he sat beside her at a respectful distance.

'Dame, what is your name?'

'Dame Emelyn. I am the prioress's chaplain.'

'And porter.'

'When necessary. We all have many roles here, by necessity.'

'And naturally, because of the deaths, it has left you all short-handed, no?'

She merely gazed at him.

'Dame Emelyn, do you have any idea who might have murdered Dame Marion or Dame Katherine?'

'None whatsoever.'

'Is it your thought that this might have been done by someone from outside or someone from within the priory?'

She stared at him suddenly and scrutinized him like a governess about to mete out justice with a switch. 'Is there any proof that it was perpetrated by our numbers *within* the priory?'

'That is what I am trying to determine, Dame.'

Her hands found each other in her lap. The fingers tapped, tapped. 'I can't imagine anyone that . . . that . . . *angry*.' And then she stilled. Crispin watched the shade of something pass over her expression before it blanked again.

'Dame? You had a thought?'

She shook her head. 'No. No, nothing.'

Something, Crispin thought but didn't say so aloud. He had the sense that to contradict this woman would get him nowhere. 'If you do think of anything . . . anything at all . . . do contact me. I will be in and out of the priory. But a private message can always be sent to me on the Shambles.'

She nodded distractedly.

'Very well. Could you send out the other—'

His words were cut off by a sudden and startling scream. It was coming from the direction of the laundry. Crispin leapt up and ran. He skidded around the corner and stopped. Some of the sisters were comforting one of the nuns. Her chapped hands covered her face; her sleeves were rolled up past her elbows.

'What's happened?' Crispin demanded.

A short, older nun, who appeared to be the laundry overseer, had a look of disgust in her gray eyes. 'It is nothing, Master Guest.'

'I'll be the judge of that. Dame?'

The young nun who had screamed pulled her hands away from her reddened face. 'I'm . . . I'm sorry, Master Guest. I was being foolish.'

'Foolish about what?'

They were calling her Margaret in reassuring tones. She had a thin face and was short of stature.

From the list from the prioress, he recalled the laundry overseer to be called Sibilla; she seemed anxious to get them back to work. 'It was nothing,' said the overseer. 'She thought she saw the resident ghost, of all things.'

Before Crispin could answer, there was another scream from far off. They all turned in the direction of the church.

Crispin whirled and ran ahead of the nuns. He arrived before them, pushing open the doors at the south transept entrance of the church, and rushed in.

An older sister stood over a supine figure on the floor, just before the quire. Her hands were on her lined face, and her mouth was still open from her scream. She stared at the body beneath her.

Crispin reached her and grabbed her arms, spinning her around. 'Dame! Dame! Look at me.'

Her eyes, locked on the figure, slowly edged toward him. Dame Emelyn came up beside her and took her hands, turning her even farther away. 'Dame Petronella! Calm yourself.'

She calmed for but a moment before she twisted in the nun's arms, looking back again. Her face seemed to be winding up to scream a second time when Dame Emelyn, years younger than this older nun, shook her hard, forcing her gaze back to her. 'In the name of Jesus Christ, becalm yourself.'

Crispin left her to Dame Emelyn and knelt by the dead sister, her head aimed toward the high altar, her arms lying at her side. There was blood on the wimple at her forehead where she was likely struck. But the worst of it was not her head. Her mouth was overflowing with coins, stuffed within. So many that some smaller pennies stuck to the side of her face, her chin, and had fallen around her black veil like rose petals.

FIVE

'**S**end Dame Petronella for the priest. And you, Dame Emelyn,' said Crispin, 'fetch the prioress.'

He watched them comply before his sharp eyes scanned the scene deep past the chancel, the quire, and into the nave. Some of the nuns stood all about the church and, like sticking pins in a map, he tried to identify each person, at least by sight. And once that was burned into his memory, he looked down at the body and could not help but raise his eyes again into the dim light to the frenzied mural behind the high altar and spied the figure of the deadly sin of greed . . . and marveled at the same appearance of the nun lying before him.

A dreadful thought began to form in his mind. At first, he swept it away as the fancy of desperation, but it would not abate, and he set his mouth into a grim line at the certainty that had taken hold of him.

It seemed to take little time for footsteps to return. This time it was those of the priest, Jack and Prioress Drueta.

He rose and faced the priest, a young man with dark hair and gray eyes, fair of face and slight of form. A priest of this kind situated in a nun's priory would seem to test logic . . . as well as the man's determined celibacy.

Crispin snatched a glance at Jack, whose expression was solemn and tempered to silence, but Crispin could well see that the man longed to tell him all that he had learned. They both knew that this would have to wait.

The priest, Father Holbrok, knelt beside the nun. 'Why, it's Dame Mildred,' he whispered. He offered what benedictions he could but, since she was dead, she could not receive the last sacrament. He suddenly looked up at Crispin. 'Who has done this?'

'That is why I'm here, Father.'

Holbrok rose, dusting off his cassock. 'Lady Prioress, I think a meeting is in order.'

But instead of rushing to comply in obedience, Prioress Drueta merely folded her hands together. 'There is no need for a meeting, Father. I have already discussed the situation with Master Guest and his man. That was my intention when I hired him. I think it is for us to leave him to it and allow him to investigate undeterred.'

'But . . . Lady Prioress!'

'Do you have some objection to Master Guest doing his job?'

'Of course not, but—'

'Then I think he should be allowed to do so.'

The priest closed his mouth and bowed his head. Father Holbrok was obviously used to being cowed by the prioress and made no more objections. Crispin felt slightly rankled at this, but he, too, was accustomed to a strong woman in his household and understood that the priest – like Crispin himself – saw it as the better part of valor to let the woman have her way in the name of peace.

'Jack,' said Crispin, 'you'd best go to the sheriffs to bring the coroner.'

'Young man,' said the prioress, 'you will do no such thing.'

Crispin girded himself. 'Madam, it is the law to call the coroner when there is a body discovered. Your nun, Dame Petronella, was the first finder, and by law—'

'These laws have no sway here, Master Guest, as I thought I had made clear. We are under ecclesiastical law as a religious society. We are not under the king's jurisdiction.'

'Prioress. You stretch the laws too thin, I think.'

'Nevertheless. I will not have the sheriff and his men *and* the coroner creating havoc. This is our chapel. Our prayers of the Divine Office cannot be interrupted.'

'I'm afraid I must agree with the prioress on that point,' said the priest.

Indeed, thought Crispin. *And do you have something to hide?* He glanced toward Jack, who had a suspicious glint to his eye.

In the end, he couldn't go against them. He signaled to Jack to stand down.

The prioress must have taken this as a sign that she was free to go, and as she strode down the nave, she gave her own silent signal to Dame Petronella, now decidedly paler, and another nun whom Crispin did not yet know, stood by. They both made their way, in a sluggish and reluctant fashion, down the nave toward them.

The priest lingered and Crispin told Jack with a mere look to delay him should he try to leave, while Crispin crouched again at the corpse and looked her over. He examined her hands to see if she had fought. Her nails seemed relatively clean and free of skin and hair. They wouldn't have been had she defended herself from her attacker. Instead, she was likely come upon unaware and struck down before she could react. Or she knew well her assailant.

He peeled away as much of her wimple at her forehead as he could, sliding it past the bloody stain that was quickly turning to a crust. There was a bruise that had had little time to form, and a tear in the skin where the murder weapon had struck. There might possibly be brain matter with the blood. She was struck hard, with a vengeance. He wondered what the instrument could have been and found himself scanning past the quire and to the high altar. A candlestick, perhaps? A floor chandler? The latter might be too unwieldy.

He left it for now and turned to the coins in her mouth. All silver pennies. Perhaps from an alms box. He turned her head and allowed most of them to spill out, tinkling on the tiled floor.

He was only interrupted for a heartbeat at the noise of objection the priest made, but he continued. A mere handful of coins. But enough to make a statement.

'Father Holbrok,' said Crispin, still peering into the nun's mouth. 'What do you make of such a display of the corpse?'

'Horrific,' he gasped. 'Unholy. The Devil's influence, surely.'

'Yes,' he drawled. He pushed the coins around with his finger, but he could find nothing unusual with them. 'But . . . do you see a reason for positioning the corpse in such a way?' He wiped his finger on his coat and turned. 'Or for Dame Marion to have been strangled and left by a pigsty, her mouth also stuffed with pigs' scraps? Or Dame Katherine to have been wrapped in all the bedclothes of the dorter and smothered with a pillow? Does any of that remind you of anything?'

'Remind me?' He wrung his hands and shook his head. 'It reminds me well of the evil in the world.'

Crispin tried not to roll his eyes. 'Yes, but of something more . . . palpable.' He rose and walked forward through the quire. When he reached the foot of the raised altar, he turned back and gestured with his head toward the mural.

He saw the moment Father Holbrok understood. The priest slowly raised his eyes to the curving painting and a look of horror crossed his face. A hand went to his mouth, muffling his gasping prayer.

The nuns behind him, too, saw and crossed themselves.

'Do . . . do you mean to say, Master Guest, that the nuns who were killed were murdered in the style of . . . of . . .' He couldn't seem to speak and raised his arm to the painting.

'Of the Seven Deadly Sins, yes. Father Holbrok, can you tell me about the relics here at the altar?'

'Oh, I am no expert on the matter, Master Guest,' he said. He did not move toward Crispin but stayed as he was and raised his voice to carry up the brief nave. 'I came to this parish only four months ago. But I believe . . .' He turned to look at the nuns cowering together at the west entrance. 'I believe Dame Petronella can tell you – she oversees the relics.'

'Very well, Father. I will talk with you later.'

The priest seemed most happy to be allowed to leave. He ducked his head when he approached the nuns and said nothing to them as he left.

'Dame Petronella?' pronounced Crispin from the altar.

She seemed reluctant to come near, to pass the dead nun. The sister with her, though younger, gave her hands a squeeze and nodded her reassurance.

Dame Petronella seemed to gird herself before moving down the nave. She glanced down at Dame Mildred, where Jack was standing guard over her, and crossed herself.

When she reached Crispin at last, he greeted her. 'I know this is all very difficult for you and your sisters, Dame, but any little thing could help me understand why this is happening and how to stop it.'

'I understand, Master Guest.'

'Good. You are doing very well. You heard what I told Father Holbrok?'

She nodded. Her green eyes darted here and there. She was older than some of the others. He thought she was about his age, in her middle forties. Her face was thin with a narrow nose and no chin to speak of. Her wimple cupped her face at the jaw and seemed to stay there from will alone.

'And so, you understand that these murders copy the Deadly Sins . . . as you see in this mural.'

'God help us all.'

'Indeed.' He glanced back once to the reliquary. 'I wonder, Dame, what is in the reliquary here. Is it to do with Saint Frideswide?'

She took a deep breath and seemed to calm herself enough to speak. 'In a way, sir. Some of the objects belonged to her and some to her contemporaries. Because this priory was founded on a crusade to fight the Seven Deadly Sins, it was thought that the relics of the saint remind us of those sins and to repel them.'

Crispin found himself thinking like a Lollard in that instance; that a relic should be from the saint, something *of* them – a bone or hair or blood – not a poor substitute like a cup or a piece of cloth. Of course, Lollards disagreed with the veneration of saints at all . . .

'And what is here?'

The nun did not step up on the dais, but merely gestured. 'Within is the girdle of Saint Frideswide to fight the sin of lust,' she began. 'A wooden bowl she herself used to represent the sin of gluttony. A coin purse for greed. A pillow of hers that represents sloth. A broken staff used by her as abbess for wrath. Her ring for envy. And a velvet cloak given to her but never worn, for the sin of pride.'

'And all of that is in that small reliquary?'

'Why, yes. You see . . .' She took a step up onto the dais. 'It is sometimes my task to care for the reliquary and the relics within. You can plainly see through the reliquary glass . . .' She cocked her head. 'That's strange.' She genuflected to the crucifix above it, and then took a key from her own girdle, unlocked the door and looked inside. 'But . . . there is something amiss. The . . . the cloak. The ring. The girdle. Oh blessed saints! They're not here.'

Crispin came closer and peered in with the nun, who rummaged through the strange belongings of the saint who had lived nearly seven hundred years ago. 'Are you certain?'

'They are not here.'

'Could a sister here have removed them to . . . well, clean them?'

'No! We would never do such a thing. They were placed here not long after she died. They were sent to this chapel upon her death from the abbey in Oxford. This priory was founded for her.'

Crispin sighed deeply. It was plain that those items were now missing.

SIX

Crispin entreated Jack to come to him. His apprentice glanced over his shoulder at the dead nun, who was being borne away on a litter, Dame Petronella with them. 'No coroner,' he said.

'It appears not, Jack.'

'So now relics are missing?'

'Yes.'

'Why is nothing straightforward? Can't people kill anyone in anger no more?'

Crispin almost laughed at the sentiment, but didn't think it proper under the circumstances. 'Apparently not. I still have nuns to question.'

'Then let us both get to it. It's like a ghost moves among them, killing when everyone's back is turned.'

Jack was right about one thing: this nun was slain under everyone's nose in the light of day. This murderer didn't seem to fear anyone. That was troubling.

He walked with Jack back to the baking house. 'You can tell me of Father Holbrok now.'

'Aye. He's a nervous fellow, is our priest. He intimated that he never wanted this assignment amongst nuns. I think he suffers from the sin of lust, for he would not stop talking about all them "young, pretty nuns", as he would say.'

'Well, that *is* interesting.'

'It's worth remembering. Perhaps he killed these nuns because they spied him in an . . . impropriety.'

'It's possible. But the staging of them in the form of the Deadly Sins. That seems too much for a needful murder.'

'Not if he's obsessed with it himself. And he is. Besides talking about the nuns, he said he's striven to make them Deadly Sins his . . . how did he call it? The "pillar of his mission". Or some such.'

'"Pillar of his mission"? That *is* worth noting.' They turned the corner and reached the shade of the trees along their path. 'But the staging. That takes valuable time. And preparation. He would have to have known that a nun would be coming to the church alone and he would have to have lain in wait with his bundle of coins.'

'That does seem like too much planning. And what if more than one had come across him?'

'He could claim he was praying. And the coins wouldn't take up too much space in a pouch.'

'Except for one thing, sir. He was with me at the time.'

He glared at Jack for a moment. 'Damn.'

'There's that Crouch fellow. I didn't see him about. And where was he when all the screaming was happening?'

'Yes. He wasn't in the church with the others, was he?'

When they arrived at the bakehouse, all the women buying bread were gone, save the one anxious woman he had seen before.

He scrutinized her out of the corner of his eye as he walked by and entered the bakehouse again.

Instead of attending to their duties, three nuns had gathered in a tight circle, talking in excited tones.

Crispin cleared his throat and the talking ceased abruptly as they turned.

He bowed and Jack did so too, belatedly. 'Forgive the further intrusion, ladies, especially at this horrific moment when one of your sisters has fallen this day. But it makes it that much more urgent for me to conduct my enquiries.'

Dame Emelyn, the chaplain, stepped away from the others. 'You already spoke to me.' She gestured to the other two. 'Dame Joan, our bakery overseer, and Dame Jemma can speak to you now.'

'Before I do, I noticed a woman waiting beyond the gate. Who is she?'

Dame Emelyn walked to the window, pushed open the shutter, and stretched to see beyond the wall. She pulled back in and folded her hands together. 'I do not know her.'

'I think she awaits Dame Petronella,' said Dame Jemma, the younger and plumper of the other two nuns.

'And why does she await her?' asked Crispin.

Dame Jemma shook her head. Her veil rippled. 'Dame Petronella is the apothecary. That was Dame Audrey's position. Women went to Dame Audrey to cure their complaints, and now this is Dame Petronella's task.'

'I see. Have *you* a moment to talk with us?'

Dame Jemma blushed, lowered her eyes, and nodded. Crispin motioned for her to leave the building.

Crispin entreated Dame Jemma to sit on the bench beside him, while Jack stood off to the side. The day was growing warmer, and it was a relief to sit in the shade with the pleasant sounds of birds overhead. But it was also near the gate, and the dust of the road made his throat dry and hot.

'Dame,' he began, clearing his throat. How he wished for a cool cup of ale at the Boar's Tusk now. 'When we first encountered one another on the night stair, you seemed to indicate that God's justice was being done to the murdered women. That it was the "sin of our sisters", you said, that killed them. Can you elaborate on that?'

Her face, made plumper by the tight wimple, reddened. 'I . . . regret those words, Master Guest. I was not in a holy frame of mind.'

He waited, saying nothing.

As he hoped, she could not refrain from speaking. 'You see, none of us comport ourselves as we should. And I include myself, for we are all sinners, even the holiest of us.'

He continued to say nothing.

'It is merely foolish gossiping. It is nothing, Master Guest.'

'I see.' He waited a bit longer but she would speak no more. 'Can you enlighten me on anything unusual you might have seen or heard in the last sennight or so?'

'Anything I've seen or heard?' Her brow furrowed.

'Anything that might have struck you as unusual. Or anyone who should not have been where you saw them.'

'I . . . I don't know. I don't know if it is unusual.'

He offered a brief smile. 'Why don't you tell me, and I can judge for myself.'

'Very well. The . . . the night before Dame Marion was found by the pigsty in the morning, I thought I heard footsteps outside the dorter.'

'And what time was this?'

'Late. After the first sleep and Lauds. They seemed to be coming from the cloister and then down to the walk above the refectory.'

Crispin glanced over his shoulder toward the dorter. There were windows that faced in that direction. It *was* possible for her to have heard it.

'Are you certain you heard this?'

'Oh yes. It was strange for anyone to be roaming at that hour, so I rose from my bed and looked out the window. I saw no one, but I heard them continue and open the gate.'

'Which gate?'

'The gate to the outbuildings.'

'And does that include the pigsty?'

She nodded.

'Is there any way for you to note who was or was not in their cell?'

'No, Master Guest. For I was in my own cell. And we are not allowed out of them until right before Prime.'

'You saw no lamp, nor light anywhere? Under your cell door, perhaps?'

She looked off to the side, concentrating. 'I . . . I don't think so. I did not hear any steps *within* the dorter. Only outside.'

'I suppose it could have been your ghost.'

Jack made a sound in his throat, but Crispin ignored it and continued. 'One of your sisters seemed to have seen this apparition only moments before Dame Mildred was found.'

Dame Jemma's brow creased. 'The ghost is said to be the spirit of one of our sisters. She has been seen here for decades. Centuries, likely. And she has been seen in the gardens of late.'

'Come now, Dame Jemma,' said Crispin mildly. 'Surely you do not believe in such spirits. Have *you* seen it?'

'I thought I did the other night. It was late, before the work day was done and I was returning to the dorter. I thought I saw her there.' She pointed toward the gate.

'And what was she doing?'

'Nothing. Merely walking, I think. It was only from the corner of my eye. The hem of a skirt disappearing through the trees.'

'Then it might have been another of your sisters here.'

She shrugged.

'Very well. Where were you when Dame Mildred was killed?'

'Here, in the bakehouse.'

'Can the other sisters corroborate that?'

'Of course.'

'Very well. Can you send Dame Joan out to us?'

She rose, bowed, and moved back into the bakehouse.

'Jack? You have something to add?'

'A *ghost*, Master Crispin?'

'Jack, there is no ghost.'

'I thought you'd say that,' he muttered. 'Well then, if these foot-steps belong to our murderer, then they weren't in the dormitory. That means it wasn't a nun. And that puts it back onto Crouch.'

'If she is telling the truth. Or if the nun had already left the dorter. Or if they remained out of the dorter after Lauds.'

Jack's shoulders sagged. 'Oh. God's blood, Master Crispin, you're right. They could have snuck away and then simply joined in with the others back to prayers at Prime. It's diabolical, that's what it is. And how you think of them things . . .'

'Perhaps I have a diabolical mind as well.' He winked and Jack smiled, but soon dropped that expression when Dame Joan appeared.

He asked much the same of her, but she did not recall hearing any footsteps or any other peculiar thing. 'Does your cell face the path? There.' He swiveled and pointed toward the windows.

'No,' she said. 'My cell is on the other side.'

Crispin flicked a glance at Jack and the man knew instantly that their enquiries must also discover if any of the other nuns on Dame Jemma's side of the dorter had also heard footsteps in the night. 'Who are the nuns who have cells on this side?'

She pressed her eyes shut tight and wrinkled her nose. She pointed toward the ground with her finger as if reciting something by rote. 'Dame Jemma, Dame Sibilla, Dame Margaret . . .' She stopped to cross herself. 'Dame Mildred, bless her soul, and Dame Petronella.'

'I see. Thank you.' The nun made to rise when Crispin said, 'One thing more, Dame Joan. You were in the bakehouse when Dame Mildred was struck down?'

Her lip trembled and she crossed herself. 'Yes, Master Guest.'

'And what of Dame Jemma?'

'She was not in the bakehouse at the time.'

'Indeed. Could you send her out once more, please?'

She rose, bowed, and left him. Presently, Dame Jemma hurried out the door again. 'Truly, Master Guest. We are all in a fit state, and with much work to do with fewer hands.'

'Just one thing, Dame. The witnesses say you were *not* in the bakehouse when poor Dame Mildred was killed, as I myself were a witness to that. Then, where were you?'

She frowned. 'But that's absurd. Of course I was.'

'Shall I bring Dame Joan to tell you so?'

She paled. 'Oh. No, of course not, Master Guest. That must have been when I went to fetch a sack of flour. Then I ran to the church when I heard the scream and joined the others. I'm afraid these deaths have mixed us all up.'

'Did anyone see you go for the flour?'

'I don't know. But the others can attest that there was more flour available where there wasn't before.'

'That will have to do for now. Thank you.'

Crispin watched her go. He felt Jack standing directly behind him. 'You can't trust no one these days,' said his apprentice.

'No, one can't. Especially when murder and thievery are involved. It's the hangman either way. We'll have to see which nuns were missing from the laundry as well.'

'That must include the prioress.'

He didn't like to think it, but he nodded. 'Of course, you are right, Jack.'

'Do we trust what Dame Jemma said about hearing footsteps?'

'For now. Dame Mildred cannot answer, of course. But the other nuns on this side of the dorter can. Though the rest could have slept through it.'

'Or lied. If it was one of them nuns who killed Dame Mildred, then they had to have the biggest bollocks to do it during the day while you were here investigating. And so far, Dame Jemma was missing when the others heard the cry in the church.'

'And the prioress, as you said.'

'God save us.'

The anxious woman was still at the gate and, as he tried to pass her, she called out to him. 'Sir! I have been waiting for Dame Audrey for some time. She has not come to the gate.'

Crispin approached. She was in the garb of a merchant. Not poor, not wealthy either. There were lines of worry stepped up her forehead. A young woman with a plain face. 'Demoiselle, I regret to report that Dame Audrey died more than a sennight ago. Dame Petronella has taken her place.'

'Died?' She frowned and shook her head. 'More than a sennight ago? That's not possible.'

'I'm afraid it is true. Shall I send someone to fetch Dame Petronella?'

She worried at her finger's knuckle before she finally nodded. 'If you please, sir.'

He nodded to Jack. 'I'll be in the laundry area.'

Jack hurried off, and Crispin bowed to the woman before walking around the bakehouse to the acrid-smelling laundry.

Steam and lye made for an unpleasant atmosphere, but he stood nigh anyway. There were steaming vats and paddles and sticks, and some of the clothing was already drying on the dewy grass. Some of the nuns were absent, likely due to helping with the body of the murdered Dame Mildred. He was about to ask it of the single nun remaining when the bell started to chime. It was Sext, one of the hours of the Divine Office set aside for daily prayers. All the sisters would leave their tasks to go to the church to pray, but would that be proper when a murder was committed there? Would it not require re-consecration? And after that, the sisters were supposed to have their midday repast. There would be no talking to any of them for two hours or more about this murder.

He watched the nun walk by, offering him the slightest of glances.

Hands on hips, he stood alone on the grassy area and decided – with watering eyes – he didn't have to stay.

Jack came around the corner. 'I nearly got there before the bells rung. How I hate them bells.'

'I suppose if you are devout, the sound of the bells is a relief rather than a chore.'

'I suppose. But it reminds me that we were invited to sup with Master Christopher and his mother today.'

How had he forgotten that? Crispin had agreed nearly a sennight ago to have a midday meal with his son, the son he could not acknowledge, and the mother of that son who was the wife of another man. 'Why did I agree to that?' he muttered.

'Because you love your son,' he said quietly. Jack had the discretion to *not* say aloud that Crispin also loved the *mother* of that son. Jack wore the truth of that knowledge in his eyes. It was a sad look, a look that said he was sorry for his master, who had been too stubborn to marry Philippa Walcote himself all those years ago.

'Well, I suppose it will be a welcomed respite from all this death.

Will, er, Master Clarence Walcote be joining us?' He thought he had framed that as casually as he could. But when he glanced at Jack, he found he hadn't.

'Master Walcote is on another buying journey, Master Crispin. Have you forgotten?'

'I suppose I did,' he grumbled.

They passed the woman at the gate. She seemed resigned to having to wait again, and sank down onto a tree stump for the nuns' Divine Office to be over. Crispin wondered that the nuns could simply go about their business as one of their own grew colder wherever it was they put her. But it was the way of it. One's life could not come to a halt simply because someone had died. Food still needed to be put on the table. Fires still had to be laid. Bread had to be baked, and laundry done for their fee. It was really no different inside a monastery from outside one, as much as he might like to think it was.

Crispin and Jack walked through the priory and left by the church facing Old Dean Lane. It was only a little walk along Thames Street to Bread Street and thence to Mercery and the Walcote estate.

It seemed strange to go about his tasks, both pleasant and unpleasant, while the drama of Henry and King Richard played out somewhere in the Midlands. Even if Henry had acquired an army, Richard already had one. How could Henry ever find an advantage?

He walked on distractedly, almost missing the Walcote gatehouse, when Jack stopped him. 'I know, sir. I'm thinking about Lord Henry, too.'

Crispin nodded and turned toward the gatehouse. The gatehouse arch had a new porter, who barely gave them a glance, since most of the household seemed to know that Crispin Guest was not to be stopped at the Walcote door.

Crispin paused.

'Something amiss, Master Crispin?' Jack asked.

He sighed and studied Jack, half a hand taller than himself, blazing red hair and beard. He didn't look like anyone's servant. He was as broad and tall as any knight in the realm. Jack had cultivated his body into fighting form, as well as working at cultivating his mind. Crispin always supposed he'd need these skills as a Tracker's apprentice if he were to take over those duties someday.

Crispin cleared his throat. 'I wonder if it is wise, this visiting the Walcotes.' It was only a year since Clarence Walcote had revealed to Crispin that he had known fairly early on that Christopher wasn't his. But he'd promised to keep it to himself. Clarence had said he loved the boy as his own and didn't intend to disinherit him. Crispin had been relieved. Christopher was safe. And so was Philippa for, as Master Clarence had said, he might not be clever but he could count. And the months between their marriage and when the boy was born was too brief a period. He rightly reckoned that she had become with child before their wedding.

Though Crispin and Philippa still burned for each other, they had not sinned. Not against Clarence, at any rate.

All this he hoped Jack could read in his eyes, for he had not told Jack or Christopher or even Philippa that Clarence knew.

'You promised, sir. And it isn't good going back on a promise. Besides, *I'm* here.'

That was Jack's way of saying that his presence served propriety.

'Very well. Perhaps I'm merely being foolish.'

'Aye, sir. Very likely.'

He narrowed his eyes at Jack's glib reply as they passed under the arch and made their way to the front entry.

SEVEN

They were expected and ushered into the dining hall. Philippa came forward to greet him, taking both of Crispin's hands in hers. 'Crispin, it's good to see you.'

The sight of her never ceased to take his breath away. She might have grown a little plumper with the years, but Crispin found it pleasing; rounded cheeks and . . . rounded everywhere else as well. Her hair was never the gold of wheat fields, but of brass with slightly reddish tones. She had a sleepy cast to her eyelids that gave her a sly mien, which Crispin had found was no mere expression. She *was* sly, and clever, and . . . No, he mustn't think about it too closely. To him, despite her lowly accent like Jack's, he found her the most compelling woman he had ever encountered.

Fortunately, that accent hadn't stopped her from being one of the most respected mercers in London. For though Clarence had the name and the familial traditions of a mercer family, it was a bit of an open secret that it was Philippa who was the shrewd one in their business.

He melted a little inside at the touch of her hands in his. 'Madam Walcote. The pleasure is mine.'

'Crispin!' shouted a young man.

It was still a shock encountering Christopher Walcote, the young man, at fifteen now, who looked remarkably like Crispin, with his same sharp nose, gray eyes, and black hair. It didn't help that the boy often wore clothes just like Crispin's, with his scarlet cote-hardie and blue stockings . . . as he was arrayed today.

Crispin glowered but couldn't maintain it and greeted his son with a smile instead. 'Master Walcote. One wonders why a mercer, with many a bolt of fine cloth at his fingertips, still manages to dress as *any* man on the street.'

Christopher had the grace to lower his eyes, but his burnished cheeks and secret smile were still evident.

Philippa leaned in between them. 'It is a blessing to have you and Jack grace our table. There is much good food to eat and conversation can be better made joyful with a little good wine.' She gestured toward the white linen-clad board. She seated Crispin across from her and Jack opposite Christopher, leaving the head of the table noticeably empty.

Crispin tried not to stare at the food that was laid out. There was roasted lamb still sizzling from the fire, a platter of steaming chicken and raisin pasties, carrots and greens pooled in butter, white loaves of bread, cheeses both hard and soft on a wooden plate, and a cheese pie with strawberries.

The servant brought the aquamanile and basin first to Crispin, who allowed the fragrant water to pour over his fingers and wiped them dry with the towel the servant offered.

When all had washed their hands, Christopher led the prayer of thanks before they crossed themselves.

'Wine, Crispin?' asked Philippa. She directed the same servant to pour the golden and fragrant libation into a rare glass chalice.

He took it up, looked at the wine through the glass as it caught the light like amber, and took a sip. It was slightly sweet.

He recognized the flowery flavor from the Spanish wine Lancaster used to import.

The Walcotes were wealthy. Not quite as wealthy as his former lord, but they could obviously enjoy the finer things on their table. He was glad of it. Christopher had been raised almost as he would have been if he had been in Crispin's former household. It satisfied.

'Holy saints!' said Jack, wiping his mouth with the tablecloth. 'That *is* good wine, Madam Walcote.'

She chuckled at his enthusiasm. 'I'm glad you enjoy it.' She took her own sip, smiling as the glass reached her lips.

Christopher speared a piece of lamb with his knife, tore it into bits, and fed himself. After he'd chewed and swallowed, he glanced up at his companions. 'What are you and Jack working on, Crispin?'

Crispin ate a slice of carrot. It had been cooked with honey, leaving his palate sweet. 'What makes you think Jack and I are working on anything?'

'There's a look about you. As if you're always thinking, even when you're saying naught. Half-listening to the others around you and mulling the puzzle over while you sit there. And Jack too.'

'I do not,' said Jack.

'But you do. You no doubt got it from your master. The two of you are conspiring even now and saying not a word in exchange.'

Crispin glanced at Jack and Jack looked at him. A slow smile crept up Crispin's lips. 'That's too close for comfort, Master Walcote.'

'You see. I could easily be a Tracker if I wanted to.'

Philippa only made a soft sound in warning to Christopher. He lowered his eyes and set to eating.

'It is most gracious of you to have invited us,' said Crispin to fill the silence.

She cut a pastie in half and began to delicately nibble on it. 'I felt it was time. You've been so solicitous to Christopher, teaching him arms practice and horsemanship. Clarence don't think it's important, but there are the guild processions. And I always said that the lad could be more to our clients. He could be a part of their lives. For example, what if our clients' sons invited him to a hunt? He'd be ready. And then they wouldn't even *think* of going to another mercer for their wares.'

'That *is* wise. And far-sighted, madam.'

'Crispin.' She leaned toward him. 'You don't have to stand on ceremony with us. You can call me Philippa and him Christopher. We're old friends.'

Crispin flicked a glance at the servant standing by. 'I prefer a certain level of formality.'

Christopher snorted, but when Crispin shot him a look, he hid it in his wine glass.

Crispin ate, cleared his throat, and wiped his lips on the tablecloth. 'Well, since your observations are so astute, Master . . . Christopher, it so happens that Jack and I *are* working on a new task. At St Frideswide Priory.'

'Relic or murder?'

It annoyed him that the boy would even ask the question, but he supposed it was warranted. 'Well, both, but I am more concerned with the murders.'

His wine glass stopped midway to his mouth and he locked gazes with Crispin. 'Murders?'

'Yes.' He waited till the servant left the room before he said, quietly, 'Several of the nuns there . . . have been murdered in a most foul manner. One was even killed today, right under our noses.'

'Christ God,' gasped Philippa, crossing herself.

'I apologize Mada— Philippa for my indelicacy. It is not fit conversation at the table.'

Christopher leaned toward him. 'Several murders? That sounds terrible.'

But he didn't look as if they were terrible to him. Crispin looked down his nose at the boy. 'It is sinful to look upon these tragedies as merely an intellectual exercise, young man.'

Christopher didn't appear the least contrite. 'Do you hear that, Mother? He called me "young man". I'm sure to be in trouble with him now.'

'Christopher!' she admonished. 'You are to treat Master Guest with all the dignity he deserves. He's been at this longer. And may I also remind you that his skills have served to save your miserable hide *twice* now . . . as well as mine. Have a care.'

Now he *did* look contrite. 'I'm sorry, Mother. And I apologize to you and Jack, Crispin. It is out of turn. These are souls we are discussing. And I confuse the puzzle with the souls sometimes. I promise. It won't happen again.'

'See that it doesn't,' said Crispin. 'A certain level of empathy is needed in a wealthy man. He should be charitable at all times. And treat the weak with dignity and concern. We are all God's creatures, after all.'

'Even the murderer?'

Crispin finished his lamb and moved on to a pastie. 'I have found that some murderers are weak-willed, succumbing to their greed and the evil that man is subject to. Most are worthy of death. But yes, they too are God's creatures. And He will deal with them at the final judgment.'

Jack wriggled in his seat as if he couldn't contain himself, and finally blurted, 'It may be the ghost of the priory.'

Wide-eyed, Christopher looked from Jack to Crispin. 'A ghost?'

Sighing heavily, Crispin tore a piece of bread. 'We will not entertain any talk of ghosts. Let this be the end of the subject.'

Philippa cut a slice of the strawberry pie and put it in front of Crispin. 'But Crispin, could it be a ghost vexing this priory?'

'I don't believe in any idea of ghosts. A ghost cannot kill, nor in the manner of the nuns' demise. Let us have no more talk of ghosts. This was the work of a mortal with evil intent.'

'I'd rather fight a ghost for all that,' she said. 'For a ghost can be dealt with by the power of Christ. Alas, a man – who has been instructed all his life about God's kingdom – is far more dangerous. For he has ignored his good instruction. But Crispin, how can a *man* investigate in a nunnery?'

'Though Jack and I have been given free passage, it is still a delicate thing. I fear the one place I have not been allowed to go will hold some of the secrets I seek.'

'One place?'

'The dorter, the private cells for the nuns. The prioress has forbidden me to go there. But I can't see that I must obey her.'

'You are a rascal, aren't you? Wanting to look into the *private* places of the nuns.'

He sputtered, trying to think of a reply, when he saw that she was jesting with him. That gleam in her eye told him much. She was, after all, a bawdy woman, and did love to tease him.

She concentrated on her meal and asked, 'What of the sheriffs?'

He sighed and shook his head. 'The prioress has pled that the king's justice has no jurisdiction there and have not called them in, nor the coroner.'

'That seems suspicious to me,' said Christopher. He looked a little too eager and suddenly seemed to realize it. More sheepishly, he offered, 'It . . . it seems to me . . .'

'Clerics do not like interference by the king. They prefer the sovereignty of the pope. This is drummed into them from their bishops. I see nothing suspicious in it. Unless . . . I suddenly do.' He smiled and took a bite.

Christopher shook his head. 'Just as I think I understand how to be a Tracker, you throw something like that at me, like a caltrop, and I'm stopped dead.'

'It is my age and experience. Jack, though very skilled, is still learning too, and he is nearly twice your age.'

'It's true, Master Christopher,' said Jack, cheek bulging with food. He sawed on a piece of lamb with his eating knife. 'The things Master Crispin discovers and puts together in his head . . . I tell you. There's an angel beside him whispering in his ear, I think.'

'No angel. Merely an abundance of common sense tempered with a little . . .' He bobbed his head, looking for the right word. 'Audacity,' he finished. 'But I tell you,' he went on, gesturing with a crust of bread, 'I wish I had a spy. Someone who could be in the monastery with the sisters and go to the places I cannot go. I can't trust any of them.'

'Oh no, Master Crispin!' Jack threw down his cheese. 'You dressed me as a monk all them years ago, but I'll not put on a *nun*'s gown for you. I'd have to shave me beard.' He rubbed his hand along it. 'And that would be a great pity.'

Crispin sighed. 'A great pity. And I'd not have you do that.'

'Oh!' said Christopher. 'I long to hear that tale, Jack.'

Jack took a drink from his cup and smiled. 'It was a long time ago. I was about your age, come to think of it.'

'What you need is a woman spy,' said Philippa.

'Aye,' said Jack. 'But where's he to get someone who could do it? Oh, there's Eleanor Langton.'

Crispin sat back and pursed his lips. 'I don't know. She's getting on in years. And your wife would never allow it.'

'That's true.' He sat in thought, staring at the ceiling, until he turned to Crispin and said carefully, 'There's . . . there's the *other* Eleanor. Eleanor . . . Cobmartin . . .'

Crispin's hands clamped into fists on the table. 'I'll not have John Rykener go into a nunnery,' he said tightly.

They argued back and forth for a moment before they were both brought up short by a piercing whistle.

They turned toward Philippa taking her fingers from her lips. 'Now that I have your attention . . . how about me?'

Crispin shot up straighter. 'What? No!'

'You said you needed a spy.'

'Philippa, this is dangerous work. There's a murderer there.'

'Why murder me? They don't know me.'

'Philippa, it is absurd.'

She lifted her nose at that.

'No, it's not,' said Christopher, excitement creeping into his tone. 'Put me in there as a laborer and I'll keep watch over her.'

'The two of you are mad. I will not entertain such foolery. And what of your business while you play the spy and the guard, eh? Who will run it while your father is away? And what could I possibly say to him if either one of you got hurt?'

'It's only for a few days,' Christopher insisted.

'And just how do you suggest you pose as a laborer? You've never done such work.'

'I can learn. I've a strong back.'

'You know, sir,' said Jack, 'they've never seen either of the Walcotes.'

'Not you too!'

Philippa moved her chair closer. 'But Crispin, it's perfect. I can do it. You know I can.'

'But . . .'

He looked at all the eager faces and suddenly the walls felt as if they were closing in on him. He *knew* this meal had been a bad idea.

Crispin paced in the Walcotes' parlor. 'It's absurd,' he muttered once again, for what seemed like the twentieth time. 'It's not wise, Philippa. I can't guarantee your safety.'

'That's what *I'll* be doing there,' said Christopher, thumping his chest once.

'But you can't be watching her all the time, neither,' said Jack. 'What would *that* look like to the others? You, always there, peering around corners at her. They'd beat you.'

'I'd like to see them try.'

'Christopher,' interjected Crispin. 'It would be their right and their duty to protect one of their own. And then you'd be dismissed for indecency. The prioress would have no choice, even if I tell her the truth of the matter, for surely I would have to in order to get you hired and to place your mother there as a false nun.'

Philippa wore a satisfied grin. 'Then you *will* do it?'

Had he talked *himself* into it, even as he was trying to talk *them* out of it?

He dropped his head to his hand. 'God save me. Very well. I tell you both true: when I give an order, you obey it. If I tell you to run, you run. If I tell you to hide, you hide. Do you understand me?'

'Yes, Crispin,' they said in unison.

Jack grinned. 'You've done it now,' he muttered, folding his arms over his chest.

EIGHT

They returned home to the Shambles where Crispin penned a note to the prioress, telling her to make ready the clothes of a nun and that Christopher would be there as a servant. He explained all the reasons it was necessary, whether he actually believed them or not, and he gave it to Jack to deliver and await her answer.

In the meantime, he decided to spend time with the children and the horses while he waited for Jack's return, which seemed to be taking longer than anticipated. He placed all four children on Tobias's back while he led the beast around the garden. He felt badly for the horses, for the space wasn't as big as they would have been used to and they needed their exercise, but the beasts were older and received a lot more attention from the children than they would have otherwise, and they seemed to enjoy it, taking to following them about the yard, looking for treats and cheek scratches.

The children laughed and giggled. Baby Johanna was too little to ride at barely a year old; she was properly with her mother by the hearth.

Finally, Crispin pulled the wriggling children from the horse's back. They ran off in different directions, and Tobias wandered to graze, hopefully not on Isabel's vegetable patch.

Little Crispin didn't run away with the others and stood beside Crispin, watching the horse nose around the grass in the yard. He was seven years old, and though sometimes quiet, his mind always seemed to be buzzing with thoughts.

'Did you have a horse when you were a child, Master Crispin?'

'I did. Several.'

He seemed shocked. 'More than one?'

'I used to be a very wealthy lord, living as I did with my own lord, the Duke of Lancaster.'

'I remember you said so.'

'Yes, he was quite the wealthiest man in all England. Even wealthier than the king.'

'You were sad when he died.'

He glanced down at the boy. Crispin was about that age when *he* was orphaned and taken into the Lancaster household to live and learn to be a knight. 'Yes, I was. I am sad even now when I think on it.'

'He was like your father. That's what *my* father says.'

'Yes, very much so. I learned everything I needed to learn to be a knight and lord from him. I learned my languages and how to ride a horse and to fight.'

'Like Christopher. When he comes, you teach him.'

'Yes, as I will do for you when you are old enough. As you are now old enough to learn your letters and languages. And you do very well at that.'

'Why do I have to learn languages?'

Crispin trotted forward slightly to discourage Tobias from nuzzling at the vegetable patch. 'Because some of the world's greatest histories and philosophies were written in languages other than English. French, Latin, Greek. Your father speaks and reads those.'

'He said you taught him.'

'Yes, I did.'

'You don't seem like a great lord to me.'

Taken aback, Crispin crouched to look him in the eye. 'Oh? Why not?'

'Great lords are frightening. They don't look at the people when they ride by. They wear very fancy clothes and they don't look like they have any fun at all. You're very friendly and you have fun all the time.'

A smile stole across Crispin's face. *I'll be damned. Out of the mouths of babes, eh?* 'Well, I used to be like those lords, and you're right. I didn't look at the people. I was always thinking of the things I had to do, the responsibilities I had to fulfill. I was very serious. And . . . I *didn't* have a lot of fun. Not like I do now with you and Helen and Gilbert and Genevieve and Johanna. So, I supposed I've learned.'

Little Crispin kicked at the grass. 'What's treason?'

Crispin stopped. He felt the blood drain from his face and he slowly turned. The boy's expression was entirely innocent as he chewed on his thumb's cuticle. He truly didn't know what the term meant but must have heard it on the streets. Surely people still talked of Crispin and his past and it wasn't something that could ever quite be forgotten.

He led Little Crispin to the garden bench – something little better than a few pieces of wood pegged together – urged him up onto it, and sat beside him. 'You must have heard people talk of treason and that I was a traitor to the king, eh?'

The boy nodded solemnly. He may not have known what it meant but he had reckoned rightly that it was something bad.

'Well, I suppose you're old enough to learn the truth.' He took a deep breath. 'Long ago, well before I met your father, I was a knight and lord. And I loved the old king, King Edward, the one before King Richard. King Richard was only three years older than you are now when he came to the throne. And I did not want to be ruled by a boy who could be influenced by bad men. And so . . . I joined with others who tried to put my mentor and lord the duke on the throne. He was the king's uncle, after all, and a man who knew how to lead armies, how to negotiate with other men, how to run a kingdom. But . . . because I made oaths to the boy king, that meant I had to break those oaths, and it is a very serious thing to break an oath.'

'Mother tells us we mustn't lie. Is it like lying?'

'It is. Because you swore to God you would follow one man, and then you didn't tell the truth about it, and followed another instead. I broke my oaths because I wanted Lancaster as king, and a knight mustn't ever do that.'

'Did you get into trouble? I always get into trouble when Mother catches me in a lie.'

'Little Crispin, I got into the most trouble a man can be in. They captured me and I was going to die for it.'

The boy gasped. 'But only bad men are put to death, my father says,' he whispered.

'And he's right. But I had done a very bad thing and so, at that time, I *was* a bad man.'

The boy shook his head furiously. His eyes glazed with tears. 'No, you weren't. You couldn't have been!'

God's blood, that boy can hit a target.

'Well, at the time, I did not listen to my conscience, you see. I was to be hanged. But my lord Lancaster begged the boy king for my life. And, as it turned out, that king had loved me too for all the things I had taught *him* and for making *him* laugh and for riding with him, and he was glad that Lancaster had given him an excuse not to kill me – that as a favor to Lancaster he should spare me. But he did have to punish me, so instead he took away my lands, my wealth, and all my titles. And I was given my liberty in London and had to make my way on my own, without ever asking the help of my friends and relatives, for they, too, would have been punished for helping me.'

'I see why you loved Lancaster,' he said with a sniffle. He dragged his sleeve across his wet nose. 'Now I love him too.'

Crispin put his arm around the boy and squeezed. 'Yes, I was grateful to him. But it was a bitter lesson, for I wasn't allowed to see him anymore either, and I had no money to live on. I was afraid.'

'You, afraid?'

'Oh yes. I thought I'd have to become a beggar on the streets, you see. But then I remembered I had skills.' He emphasized by gently poking Little Crispin in the chest. 'I could read and write in many languages. I became a scribe for a while and did some other jobs, until I became the Tracker.'

'And then my father joined you!' He bounced up and down on the bench.

'It was a bit after that.' He touched the boy gently on the nose. 'He was nearly twice your age . . . nearly. I am ever so grateful that he came into my life, for if he hadn't, I never would have met you and your brothers and sisters.'

'I'm glad too.' He gazed at Crispin for a moment before he opened wide his arms and leapt upon him, embracing Crispin. 'I'm sorry all these things made you sad,' he said into Crispin's ear, 'and I promise that I will not break my oaths. You must promise not to ever break yours again.'

Crispin hugged the boy back and nodded, even though Little Crispin couldn't see him do it. But he also thought of Henry, for he had been the same age as his cousin Richard and they often played together under Crispin's tutelage. If Henry asked him, would he commit treason again?

He felt the warmth of the child in his arms and closed his eyes. 'I promise. I shall not break my oaths again.'

But he wasn't certain that he wouldn't be compelled to.

NINE

Jack returned at last and he sat down hard in his chair at the table. 'Well, Master Crispin. Our Lady Prioress was not best pleased by this news, and it took some convincing, but she agreed at last.' He took a bundle from his scrip. 'She said it would be best if Madam Walcote arrived in her nun's weeds, and so here they are. They should both be there tomorrow morning after Prime.'

Crispin could tell Isabel had half an ear open as she swept the hearth. 'Isabel, perhaps it would be wise if *you* were to take the clothes to Madam Walcote.'

She turned, glanced at the both of them. 'Very well, sir. Shall I go now?'

'It would be best if you do.'

Jack scooped up his youngest. 'And I'll take care of this little imp until you return.' He leaned in and gave his daughter a loud kiss just under her cheek, and she giggled and squirmed in his arms.

Isabel was with child once again, but not too far along. She didn't seem to mind the task. Perhaps she even relished the brief respite from her household duties. She took the bundle under her arm, gave a nod to Crispin, and departed.

Jack offered Crispin a smile. 'This should prove interesting.'

The man seemed to actually enjoy Crispin's misery.

They stood outside St Frideswide Priory early in the morning, just before Terce, but it was the one-armed servant who let them into the gate when they had rung the bell.

He wanted to arrive after Philippa and Christopher. It wouldn't do for the others to think they knew one another.

After the man had locked the gate, Crispin blocked his path. 'You're Edgar Crouch, the caretaker.'

'Aye. What of it?'

'These murders. What do you think about them?'

'It must be sin.'

'Of the nuns? Do you think God's wrath is killing them?'

'Might be.'

'But in such horrific ways?'

'Who can know the mind of the Almighty?'

'Have you heard or seen anything unusual before the murders?'

The man scowled. 'You're trying to make it *my* fault. You're going to tell the sheriffs that *I* done it.'

Crispin smoothed his expression. 'Did you?'

Crouch pointed with his one hand. 'Now there! That's the evil in you. Blaming a poor, innocent soul like me. With me only having one hand and all.'

'How did you lose the other?'

His face reddened, and he looked as if he was ready to spew a diatribe, when Father Holbrok came upon them.

'Here now! What is all this? Master Guest? Are you harrying this man? Has he not suffered enough?'

'If he is a murderer, we must know it.'

'Nonsense. Edgar Crouch is no murderer.'

Crispin looked them both over. Was he to be like other men on the street and mistrust Crouch for his deformity? 'Very well. One thing more. Where were you, Crouch, when Dame Mildred was murdered in the church?'

'I was working, mending a fence.'

'Can anyone verify that?'

'Father! You see what he's doing? He's trying to blame *me* for this!'

Crispin rounded on him. 'Stop your grumbling, Crouch. Did anyone see you?'

'No! Why would anyone see *me*? I'm just the caretaker.'

'Truly, Master Guest . . .' warned Father Holbrok.

Crispin waved the man off. 'That's all for now, Crouch.'

Crouch puffed and muttered his vitriol as he stalked away.

Holbrok watched him go. 'God bless the man. Such a miserable existence.'

Crispin watched him too, briefly, before he turned back to Holbrok. 'How *did* he lose his arm?'

The priest sent him a scathing look. 'Very well, Guest. It is no doubt what you expected. He was a thief, and the sheriffs cut off his hand. And they did a miserable job of it. The arm festered and had to be severed to the elbow. He had paid well for his crimes and so the sisters took him in. We believe in forgiveness in the Church.'

Crispin scowled and pulled his cote-hardie taut. '*I* do not.'

'Then that is the difference between us, sir. My holy orders beg us to follow our Lord Jesus Christ's teachings; to turn the other cheek, to forgive our enemies, to love one another.'

'And so you would vow on your soul that he is innocent of any crimes within this priory, would you?'

'I would.'

'That is indeed a testimonial, Father.'

'Yes. I am grateful that the prioress has just brought in a younger man to help him with his duties. He is getting on in years and I hate to watch him struggle.'

So. Christopher was now present. Good.

They began walking beside the churchyard. A fourth grave now lay among the others. That was quick. The prioress's expediency, no doubt. He glanced at the priest again. A wiry man but with a handsome face. His cassock was made well from an expensive tailor, it seemed, which made Crispin wonder at such an expense. Perhaps one of the sisters here had made it for him. Or it could be he came from a wealthy family. Either way, he was meticulous with his person, and seemed to enjoy the finer things.

'May I ask you, then,' said Crispin, 'where were you directly before Dame Mildred was murdered yesterday?'

The priest stopped and Crispin and Jack stopped with him. 'And now you suspect me. What makes you so great at this work you do, sir?' He looked Crispin up and down as if buying a horse. 'Do you simply spout any rude thing you can think of? Whatever seems to work at the moment is the one that sticks, eh?'

'I am good at what I do because I have patience, Father Holbrok. I bide my time, I listen, I observe. And when something seems out of place, I hunt it down and jab at it, just as I would take down a hart with a spear. I can be unrelenting, sir.'

Holbrok seemed to pale at that. 'I was with your man, as it happens,' he sputtered, glancing at Jack.

Crispin offered him a smile that barely passed his lips. 'Oh yes. I had forgotten.'

When they reached the church, Holbrok bowed curtly to Crispin, swiveled on his heel, and stomped in the opposite direction.

Jack rested his hands on his hips. 'He didn't like you accusing him.'

'No, he did not. And *I* didn't accuse him. I merely stirred him up to see what emotions might bubble to the surface.'

'"Jab at it . . . as I would take down a hart", indeed,' Jack guffawed. 'You certainly pricked him.'

'We'll see what comes of it.'

'You found out Crouch was a thief.'

'Yes. He was lucky he only lost half an arm.'

Jack shivered. 'That could have been me before I met you,' he said softly, and he drew a grateful cross over himself when they entered the church at the font.

'We were both lucky,' said Crispin, equally quiet, and he drew his own cross with the holy water.

One of the nuns was just extinguishing the candles at the quire seats as they strode up the nave. 'Jack, go check the reliquary. See if there are the same number of relics as there were yesterday.'

Jack audibly swallowed. 'Right, sir.' He seemed to gather himself, and marched through the quire to the raised step of the altar. He got down on one knee, crossed himself again, and raised his head to peer through the door of the reliquary. He leaned closer and seemed to satisfy himself, then glanced over the ghastly painting once more before he returned to his master's side. 'They're all still there, Master Crispin.'

'Tell me, Jack. What do you think about the stolen relics?'

'Well, I suppose each one was stolen to mark the Deadly Sins. As a sort of . . . symbol of each death.'

'That would make sense. Except for one thing.'

They left the shadowed church and came out into the sunshine near the dorter stairs. 'And what's that, sir?'

'The particular items stolen do not signify the sins of the murders. For instance, the stolen items were the girdle for lust, the ring for envy, and the cloak for pride. But the murders represented sloth, greed, and gluttony. Those relics are still there.'

Jack turned his head and stared at the church. 'God blind me, you're right, sir. That's strange, innit?'

'Is it? What are some of the reasons one would have for stealing a relic to begin with?'

Jack bit his lip in thought. 'To . . . venerate them?' he said with doubtful tenor.

'You *could* venerate them, I suppose, but how do you justify murder and theft? Other reasons?'

They passed the flagged stone path and made the turn, following the walls of the dorter to the bakehouse.

'Well . . . to . . . to sell them.'

'And though you can sell a pillow or a wooden bowl or even an empty coin purse, it won't get you as much as a ring, a cloak, and a saint's belt.'

'God's blood. They wanted the money.' He slapped his hand to his thigh. 'So what were the murders, then? A ruse? Tell me it wasn't no ruse.'

Crispin shook his head as they came out of the shadows of the buildings and to the bakehouse. The woman from yesterday was at the gate again.

'Not with this amount of anger associated with them. No, the murder was the thing. Perhaps the theft was an afterthought. There was method to these murders, and great emotion as well. For the relics could have simply been stolen without the murders.

No, there is a specific reason for the murder *and* the thievery. They somehow work together. But what, Jack, does it signify?' He ticked his head. 'It's a puzzle. But it will not remain so.'

'No, sir. Not with the two of us on the trail.'

They were quiet, until Jack asked, 'Are we to find the stolen relics, sir?'

Crispin sighed. 'If they were sold for coin, it isn't likely we will ever retrieve them. Think of how many pawnbrokers there are in London and how many people might purchase such a thing. Especially if the thief never said they were a relic.'

'But wouldn't they be worth more?'

'Yes, but no one wants undue suspicion cast upon them. For an honest buyer would enquire here of St Frideswide, wouldn't they? No, if I were to sell them, and quickly, I would style them as simply an ordinary ring, cloak, and belt.'

'That's a sore thing, sir. To lose such precious relics.'

'As you know, Jack, I do not truck with such objects. They might never have even belonged to this saint. It was some seven hundred years ago. Who could rightly vouch for them?'

'The prioress won't like it.'

'We shall, of course, try to find them. But I shouldn't put out too much effort. Strange that nothing was stolen after this most recent death.'

'Perhaps the murderer hadn't had the time, and didn't expect Dame Petronella to come upon them. I will keep an eye on that reliquary.'

'As you will, Jack.'

It was the first time he felt the need not to worry over a lost relic. And, after all, this church had so many. But even as he tried to dismiss it, he vowed to put his mind to retrieving them. Never mind what he told Jack.

Crispin and Jack stopped at the bakehouse and glanced at the gate. Instead of going around to the laundry, Crispin led the way to the gate instead and to the woman standing there for the second day running. 'Demoiselle, do you still await the apothecary?'

The woman eyed him suspiciously and then glanced at Jack. 'I do, sir.'

'Is she not aware that you wait for her?'

'I . . . I do not know.'

'What is your purpose with her?'

She put a hand to her heart and turned slightly away. 'It is my business alone, good sir.'

'Forgive me.' He bowed. 'I am Crispin Guest. Perhaps you've heard of the Tracker of London, and his apprentice, Jack Tucker.'

Jack bowed.

Her eyes widened and she curtseyed. 'I have. That's you?'

'It is. Why don't you come around the wall through the church instead and *we* will take you to the apothecary.'

She turned to look in the direction of the church. 'Yes. Thank you. I shall.' She hurried off, and Crispin motioned for Jack to follow him back the way they'd come.

They reached the priory door to the church and opened it. When he stepped through, he saw her just coming in. She clutched her hands together and moved cautiously up the nave, curtseying to the cross, and threading her way through the quire to him. 'Thank you, Master Guest and Master Tucker, for this kindness.'

'It is no trouble. And you are . . .?'

'Elena Forthey. My father is a wool-monger.' She set her lips suddenly, as if she'd said too much.

'Well, demoiselle, let us go to the apothecary.' Crispin paused, wondering in which direction to go, when the woman stepped forward to lead the way. 'You have been here before,' he said, following.

'Yes. I was sorry to hear of Dame Audrey. And . . . confused.'

'Why confused?'

She shook her head. 'It's nothing. I'm certain to be flummoxed because of my . . .' She glanced back at him and then shyly at Jack. 'Because.'

'I'm certain Dame Petronella can assist you as well. I understand she worked closely with Dame Audrey.'

Instead of turning at the dorter, she took them past it almost to the chapter house, before veering through an opening to the other side of the dorter and around the necessarium. 'How did she die?'

'They said it was a fever.'

'The ways of the Lord are mysterious.'

'Indeed they are.'

Once past the necessarium, they came to what looked like a private garden, a sanctuary hidden in the depths of the priory. The cloister had its own pleasant garden of flowers and herbs with a central pond. The vegetable garden lay on the other side of the bakehouse.

But the apothecary garden was for a particular course. These were the plants and herbs for the infirmary, to help to heal the sick. The garden was raised in wattle beds and filled with fragrant blossoms of both tall and shorter blooms. He recognized some of the herbs from Isabel's garden: sage, betony, hyssop, chamomile, rue, and many more he did not know.

A nun hoed carefully between the plants, her veil covering her face as she leaned forward.

There also stood a small stone cottage whose door lay open. Crispin could see herbs in bundles drying upside down from the doorway and rafters beyond.

An old table and bench, weathered from time and exposure to snow and rain, sat just outside the cottage, likely used for the apothecary art.

'Dame Petronella?' said Crispin to the nun in the garden.

She startled and snapped her head up, hoe in hand. 'Master Guest.'

He gestured toward the woman. 'This is Elena Forthey. She has been waiting to see you for two days.'

Dame Petronella put a hand to her heart and bowed. 'Forgive me, madam. We have been . . . out of sorts here.'

'I have only just heard that Dame Audrey died. So strange. But . . . she helped me before. I'm certain you can too.'

'Oh? What ails you, madam?'

Elena glanced toward Crispin. He didn't need a second hint. He lifted a hand in farewell. 'We will leave you two. I have work to do.' He turned and took Jack by the arm to lead him away.

TEN

'What's that about, do you suppose?' asked Jack. He looked back as their view of the apothecary garden disappeared behind the outbuildings.

'Women's complaints, no doubt.'

'Oh, aye. That's Isabel right enough. She goes to an apothecary on the Shambles to help her with her morning ague. This last time, she said she was as healthy as a horse and felt no mean stomach as she had done before.'

'You mean with her . . .' Crispin gestured a rounded pregnant belly.

'With her pregnancies, aye. She *is* healthy as a horse but comes the day she gives birth . . . I still worry.'

'As does every man, I'm certain.'

'The Lord has been good to us. The children are hale, and Isabel is too.'

Crispin offered a smile. 'I am glad of it.'

'Just more children for you to fuss over.'

'I do not *fuss* over them.'

'Spoil them, then. I've never seen an unmarried man fuss over children so.'

'Possibly because they are not my responsibility. The moment one cries or wets himself, I can turn him over to his mother.'

'I see. So, when I find you comforting them and wiping their tears and their bums, what is that, then?'

'I've never done any such thing, Tucker.' He turned his face away, but perhaps not in time to conceal his smile.

They got back to the laundry area and Crispin took out his list again. Dame Sibilla was the overseer and Dames Cecille and Margaret worked beside her. He watched them at their tasks, from carrying hot water in buckets, to moving the clothing around in the steamy vats, to slapping them with laundry bats over tables. They all looked so much alike in their black habits that he wondered which nun was which. They all had their sleeves rolled up to the elbow and he noticed how red and raw their hands looked.

The closest nun peered up at him through the steam but did not stop her stirring. Presently, she laid in with her paddle and pulled out dripping wet chemises, which she piled on a table where the next nun slapped them with her flat bat. The other, who had been carrying a bucket, wrung out the shifts and chemises and carefully laid them out flat on the grass to dry. But then, she suddenly craned her neck to cast about the yard. She seemed upset about something and trotted toward a pile of folded clothing.

'May I speak to Dame Sibilla?' he announced.

The short and somewhat wizened older woman at the vat laid aside her paddle and rolled down her sleeves. 'That is me, Master Guest. We met yesterday.'

She made her way over to him and he spoke quietly. 'What do you know of the dead women? What might they have had in common?'

She looked down at her damp shoes. 'We are all sisters here. That is the greatest thing that we have in common.'

'Can you think of any reason that these particular sisters were chosen to die?'

'"Chosen." Ah, I see your meaning. That has a different color to it. And yet, they were all so different. I see no reason in it.'

'Your cell, Dame. It faces the cloister.'

The constant slap, slap of the laundry bat began to irritate him.

'Did you happen to hear any footsteps late into the night, the night that Dame Marion was slain?'

'No. I was asleep all through the second sleep.'

'One thing more. Where were you yesterday before Dame Margaret screamed and Dame Mildred was killed?'

'Washing and wringing out shifts, as you see me doing now.'

'Can the other sisters verify that?'

'Yes, I suppose they can. But they were busy too.'

'Very well then. If you think of anything unusual, you may alert me. Please send one of your workers to me.'

'And so I shall. Blessed Mother, Dame Margaret, what ails you now?'

'Forgive me, Dame, but . . .' She leaned in and whispered, 'There are items missing. Again.'

'Have you consulted your list? You might have counted wrong.'

'No, I am certain . . .' She glared over her shoulder at Crispin.

'Is there a problem, sisters?' he asked mildly.

Dame Sibilla sent young Margaret off with a gesture, and the nervous nun disappeared, still muttering to herself, into the building. 'Just a careless sister. She's miscounted again, no doubt.'

'She thinks items are missing?'

'She *miscounted*,' she said sternly and, without further comment, returned to her vat.

'I don't like the way she's brandishing that paddle,' said Jack.

Crispin turned his back on them and moved away. Jack scuttled to catch up.

'How do we know they're not lying?' said Jack.

'I'm afraid we don't. For the moment. But this business of lost clothing . . .'

He was interrupted by the presence of the next sister with the bat – red-cheeked, wedge-faced, with a perpetual line down the middle of her brow – who bowed and introduced herself as Dame Cecille, the cellarer. She seemed young for so important a task, but Crispin supposed that responsibilities had to be given to those with the best aptitude.

'We are attempting to determine, Dame, where the sisters were when Dame Mildred was murdered. Were you here in the laundry or elsewhere at the time?'

'I was . . . not in the laundry. I believe I was just coming from the cellarium. It was my time to do inventory. I left the laundry and was setting out for my task, when I remembered I needed more ink for my accounting scroll. So I didn't quite make it to the cellarium when I turned around to head toward the dorter.'

'And then what?'

'I heard the screaming and came running to see what the matter was. I made my way first to the laundry, to the source of the noise. But that was just our excitable sister, Dame Margaret.' She shook her head. 'She's just out of her novitiate. Young yet. So I left the laundry when I realized it was nothing important, and went on toward the cellarium once more. And then the other screams happened at the church.'

'I seem to recall you . . .' He closed his eyes and found the pin in the map in his mind. 'At the west entrance.'

'Yes. I'd just rushed in from the cloister door. It was the one closest to the cellarium.'

'Do you have anything to tell me about these deaths, Dame Cecille?'

She shook her head, frowning. 'Nothing, Master Guest. I am at a loss as much as any of our sisters.'

He excused her and turned to Jack thoughtfully. 'I should like to draw a map, Jack. A map of where everyone was positioned when we arrived at the church just after Dame Mildred was murdered. We don't know the whereabouts of some and this should help fix it in our minds.'

'Aye, sir. I can get parchment and ink from home.'

'Do so now. I will meet you at the apothecary garden. I saw a table and bench there.'

Jack bowed and was away in long strides.

Next, Crispin questioned Dame Margaret, the one laying out the shifts to dry. She couldn't be more than sixteen, a woman with a plain face. She seemed intimidated by Crispin, looking up at him then lowering her eyes, time and again.

'Dame Margaret. Yesterday you screamed because of the . . . the ghost?'

Her face suddenly became animated, her bright blue eyes glittering with life. 'Oh, sir! I *did* see it. A gown trailing away just behind the building.'

'How can you be certain it wasn't one of your fellow sisters here?'

'Because it just wasn't.'

'You saw her face?'

'Only in profile, Young, but harsh features. Her eyes might have been green.'

'You saw only a profile but you claim harsh features and green eyes?'

She bit her lip. 'Well . . . I thought so.'

'Was she . . . like a mist? Strange to the eye?'

'No.'

'Then why think she was a ghost? Why not merely another nun here? Or a new nun coming to visit?'

She glanced behind her, veil whipping this way and that. 'I . . . I don't know. It . . . startled me, is all.'

Crispin blew out a breath. 'Dame, do everyone the kindness to assume the nuns you see are all alive. A nun shouldn't be screaming and carrying on so when you are only startled.'

'It's just that . . . I thought it looked like . . . it seemed to look like . . .' She lowered her voice to whisper, 'Dame Audrey.'

He sighed. 'It is not unusual to *think* you see someone recently dead. It is the mind, you see, merely showing you what you *expect* to see. That is, a nun you've spent your days and nights with. And what of the missing garments?'

She shot a frightened look back at Dame Sibilla. 'It's nothing. I miscounted.'

'Are you certain?'

'Yes. I just . . . miscounted.' She gathered her soggy skirts, and returned to her tasks.

'Ghosts,' he muttered as she walked away, her own gown trailing after her.

He took out the list the prioress had given him and counted the names. He was missing a nun somewhere. He hadn't yet talked to a Dame Elizabeth. She was supposed to be assisting Dame Petronella as an apothecary apprentice. But before he headed in that direction, he decided to peruse the dorter from the outside.

He took the path that led to the night stair and the chapter house. Standing on the covered corridor of the night stair, he stood and glared at the locked dorter entry. He supposed he could break in while the nuns were praying their Divine Office. He wouldn't be disturbed then. He tilted his head to measure the angle of the sun. He was certain Sext would be soon. But the notion of breaking in when he had been strictly told not to left him with a feeling of guilt. But then again, he had work to do, and investigating the dorter was part of that work, even though he had to lie to the prioress to do it.

Little Crispin's admonitions not to forswear himself pricked his conscience. How simple it was to be a child, when right and wrong were laid out so purely. It took becoming a man to understand that the shades of nuance were numerous.

He walked past the night stair and around the other side of the dorter; he stood below and looked up to the first-floor windows. Why did so few nuns require a ground floor *and* a first floor in their dorter? Perhaps some were guest rooms? He'd have to ask.

The first floor on the east side overlooked the necessarium and the apothecary garden, with five windows facing them. The building beside the dorter was, presumably, the prioress's lodgings. He went back the way he had come and took the path to the south side of the dorter, where Dame Jemma said she heard footsteps on the path, and the gate to where the animals were kept. Also five windows on that side.

He stepped into the middle of the path and looked down to where the pigs were. It was a fair distance, and he supposed in the middle of the night, if the window were open, someone could hear a gate if there were no other sounds. It would be impossible to hear it now, not with the business and people bustling on the street just outside the priory walls.

He walked on the path and listened to his own feet on the dirt and grass. It didn't make much of a sound. But again, if it were dead quiet at night, one *might* hear the tread. It was possible.

But was it probable?

What was it Dame Emelyn seemed to know but didn't want to mention to Crispin? Something about an angry person? He would have to press her on that.

And Dame Jemma, the only one to have heard these footsteps, seemed to think that the 'sin of our sisters' was killing these nuns. She had told him as much when he ran into her on the night stair when he first arrived, but she had since reversed herself on it, or, at least, shrugged it off as mere gossip.

There was something here, something unusual. And the nature and cruelty of the murders seemed to indicate that the menace came from within rather than from outside forces. But could he be so sure this early in the investigation?

It was his gut, he decided, that told him so. And he had relied on this barometer for many years now.

He wanted to talk to Crouch again, certainly without Father Holbrok around. With such protection, Holbrok could be relying on Crouch to do his bidding. And just what *was* that bidding?

He mustn't leave out the prioress herself. She could move within the priory anywhere she pleased at any time. But what would be her motivation? She was strict. Did these nuns not adhere as strictly to the Rule as she desired? Was it the 'sins of our sisters' after all? But was not every monastery run with strict rules? And what exactly was that sin?

He glanced at the sun again and realized that while he had been speculating his apprentice had likely returned and would be waiting for him at the apothecary garden. He hurried his stride in that direction, going – again – around the dorter and past the necessarium to the garden gate.

The woman who had so anxiously awaited the apothecary was no longer there, and Dame Petronella was again in her garden, this time with a basket and shears.

Jack Tucker sat under the shade of a tree at the table and bench, scrupulously penning something on a piece of parchment. He worked as he had as a child, with tongue between his teeth, and eyes concentrated on his fingers tight on the quill.

Crispin decided to let him work for a time while he talked to Dame Petronella. He stepped up to the raised bed and stood, watching her for a time. She hadn't noticed him and so finally he cleared his throat.

She startled, as she'd done before, and grasped her shears in both hands. The basket's handle stayed in the crook of her arm.

'Forgive me, Dame,' he said with a bow. 'Ah, but what a lovely garden is here.'

'It is not for vainglory, Master Guest,' she said, recovering. She set her basket down and returned to her task of snipping off leaves and flowers. Butterflies and bees hovered around her, but they didn't seem to bother her any more than she bothered them. 'This is a garden with a specific purpose. Everything grown here is to help the body recover from some illness. Are you acquainted with the physician's art, Master Guest?'

'I'm afraid I am not. Only in the most rudimentary of ways.'

'Physicians tell us there are four humors in the body, you see, related to the four elements of air, water, fire, and earth. And the humors are blood, phlegm, yellow bile, and black bile.' She stood very straight as she recited, as if being tested by a tutor. 'As an apothecary, I have learned many of these arts and know how to treat those who come to our infirmary. Blood, you see, is the air and is considered hot and moist, to be dealt with if the body has too much. Bleeding, for instance. If there is too much phlegm in the system, we must treat it for its cold and moist qualities. Yellow bile is hot and dry, such as a fever. While black bile in the body is of the earth and therefore cold and dry.' She picked up her shears again and snipped off a leaf with each pronouncement she made. 'When one is healthy, the humors are in balance. And when they are not, it is up to the skilled individual like a physician – or in this case, apothecary – to determine what the imbalance is and to treat it. We have herbs that will alleviate the overabundance of one humor over another. This, for instance . . .' She reached toward a round globe of a plant and delicately cupped one of its many flowers that looked like daisies. 'This is feverfew. As the name implies, its leaves can soothe the yellow bile in the body.'

Crispin reached out and touched a dusky leafed plant beside it, rubbed it between his fingers and smelled the musky scent of it. 'I recognize sage here. My servant uses it to cook with.'

'True, but sage may also purge the body of venom and pestilence.' She reached out to a tall, purple stalk of flowers and brushed them with her fingers. 'Betony can cure a number of ills. And here hyssop. A hot purgative can be made of this to soothe away chest phlegm. If rubbed on bruises, it can ease the pain and the purpling.' She gestured to each plant and smiled as any parent might extol the virtues of their child. 'This is rue for plague; this chamomile for a sedative; dill for cordials to ease the stomach; cumin for its seeds to use to soothe; boneset for healing wounds . . . oh, so many things, Master Guest.'

He shook his head in wonder. 'I never realized.'

'You must certainly be accomplished in ways I can never conceive of, and so it is the same with any expertise, whether it is with furnace and anvil, or with plants in a garden.'

'You have the right of it, Dame. For they all look more or less the same to me.'

She smiled indulgently. Yes, she was proud of her garden and her expertise.

'Is Dame Elizabeth here? I have yet to speak with her.'

Her smile faded. 'She might be in yon cottage. As my apprentice, she is being schooled in how to prepare the herbs for each physic.'

Crispin gave a little bow again as he excused himself. He walked to the cottage and stuck in his head. The tight little room was darker than the garden in the light of day, and it took a moment for his eyes to adjust, but it was plain there was no one there. The rafters were full of drying herbs, and the table within was crowded with canisters, wooden containers, bowls, several mortars and pestles of different sizes, flat dishes in wood and ceramic, and cooking pots. A busy space, to be sure. It smelled weedy, of the many herbs drying in the rafters.

He left it to go to Jack and he welcomed the cooling shade as he scooted in beside him on the bench. Jack had drawn a plan of the priory and showed Crispin his handiwork. 'Will that do, sir?'

'It will do very well. Now. Let us place everyone in the church as I remember them. Put your corpse there at the altar, Jack.'

Jack drew in a crude stick figure lying on its side, below where he had drawn in an altar against the church wall.

'Now. Dame Petronella had found Dame Mildred, so put her just in front of the body. And Dame Emelyn was just there in the quire approaching.'

Jack dutifully scratched in their names in small letters. Crispin pointed out where the various people had been, and which entrances they were close to. He even got Jack to include Prioress Drueta in her lodgings, where he assumed she had been, and Crouch out in the churchyard, where he had to assume *he* had been.

And with his quill, Jack penned in his own name nearest the west entrance bell tower. He set the quill aside and corked the ink bottle. 'That's everyone, sir.'

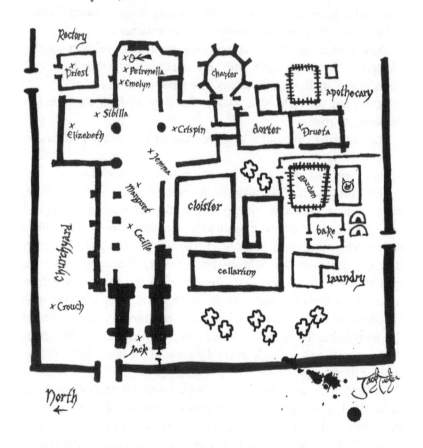

'Not everyone.' He spread out his list beside the map. 'Where is Dame Joan?'

'Oh, aye. Where *is* she?'

'Who is this?' asked Crispin, pointing to a name in Jack's confoundedly small script in the north transept.

'Dame Elizabeth, sir. And Dame Joan is . . .' Jack ran his finger down Crispin's list, '. . . the bakery overseer. She could have stayed behind in the bakehouse.'

'Could have. Crouch never came running. He's got *two* legs.'

'I don't trust him, sir.'

'He's a grouchy fellow, to be sure,' said Crispin, 'but that doesn't necessarily make him a murderer.'

'And him with his one arm, it would be difficult to set them bodies up as they were.'

'Difficult but not impossible.'

'Aye, sir. What's next, then?'

'We must talk to Crouch without Father Holbrok nearby. And, I suppose, I must also question Prioress Drueta.'

Jack made a sound. 'Better you than me, sir.'

'Why Jack,' he said with a devious smile, 'you're just the man.'

'Oh, now, sir . . .'

'Now Jack, you must acquaint yourself with how to question your betters. How will you be an accomplished Tracker if you shy from that?'

'I suppose you're right, sir. But . . .'

'A prayer beforehand wouldn't go amiss, Jack.'

Jack crossed himself. 'What shall I do with this map?'

'I'll keep it for now.' He made sure the ink was dry before he carefully folded and creased with his fingernail each edge and slipped it into his money pouch. He supposed Dame Elizabeth would have to wait. Like Jack, Crispin didn't trust Crouch.

Crispin and Jack parted ways as they traveled together to the night stair. Jack headed south to the prioress's lodgings, while Crispin turned west at the cloister, making his way around the church to the churchyard.

When he turned the corner, he startled slightly at the sight of his son Christopher digging a grave. He had removed his coat, which was folded and placed by the hole, and rolled up the sleeves of his chemise, looking for all the world as any other workman.

If Christopher had looked up, Crispin hadn't noticed, for the boy was rightly focused on his task and did not try to acknowledge Crispin. His son looked strong as he shoveled. He'd grow to be a sturdy man. Crispin was proud and pleased that he was doing the work as he had promised. *It will be good for him. Nothing like labor to appreciate what your servants have done for you.* Yes, he certainly appreciated all Jack did and what his servants on his estate used to do for him, since he had had to do it for himself for the years since his banishment. *Every rich man should*, he decided. It was humbling, that was a certainty.

Where is Crouch? he wondered, getting back to it and searching across the churchyard for the man . . . There! In a shadowed corner near some trees. Crispin strode purposefully toward him when someone banged on the west gate, yanking the chain and clanging the bell.

Crispin waited for a nun to arrive . . . but then felt foolish. There were so few nuns. Fewer in these dangerous days. He could simply answer the gate himself and moved to do so.

He stood at the barred entry and decided he should ask what the agitated man wanted before opening it. For this man might prove to be part of the deadly goings-on at the priory.

'What is your business, sir?'

The man had a scowl when Crispin first saw him, but now that he was staring at Crispin, his face had gone slack and pale. He looked Crispin up and down with an expression of shock.

He was young. Not as young as Jack, but he, too, wore a well-tempered beard close-cropped to his long face. A face that struck Crispin as familiar. He was dressed well, like a man of the court. He could even have been a knight, for his horse – a creature with a fine saddle and decorated reins – stood just an arm's length from him.

'Are you,' he said in a hushed voice, 'are you . . . Crispin Guest?'

'As it happens, yes. What is your business?'

'Why are you here, of all places? Why?'

'I am doing a service for the prioress.'

'But . . . don't you know me, sir? I'm . . . I'm Edward Grafton.'

Crispin's mouth parted. A strange combination of shock, affection, and humiliation twined and swept over him. He grabbed the bars and pressed himself against them. 'Edward . . .' Throwing the latch aside, he flung the gate open. He took a step, but then Edward shot forward and encased him in a long embrace.

'Sir Crispin,' he muttered into Crispin's shoulder, sobbing.

'Steady, Edward. You know I am no longer a knight. You of all people.'

'My God. Oh, Holy Mother!' The man held him still tighter and abruptly clutched his arms and pushed him back. 'Look at you!'

'I am well. Never fear.'

'I feared. I feared so much for you. And I was forbidden to . . . to . . .' He collapsed on Crispin again and held him, weeping.

'Now, now, Edward. Come inside.' Crispin pulled him through the gate and sat him down on a bench under a tree.

'I never thought I'd see you again. I feared you might be . . . dead.'

'Surely you've heard of the Tracker of London.'

He looked up with a wet face and tear-filled eyes. 'No. That can't be you.'

Crispin chuckled. 'I'm very much afraid that it is. That's why I am at this priory. Investigating crimes.'

'I can't believe it. You, in the flesh. My lord . . .'

'These days I am simply "Master Crispin".'

'Master Crispin, sir!' Jack came trotting around the corner and nearly ran into them. He measured the situation and still seemed perplexed as to how to proceed.

'Jack.' Crispin placed his hands on the man's shoulders. 'Jack, this is Edward Grafton. He . . . he was my squire.'

ELEVEN

'Your squire?' Jack paled and gave him a wary nod.

'It's worse than that,' said Edward, rising. 'I am now *Sir* Edward, for these past seventeen years.'

Crispin couldn't help but smile. 'I am truly pleased.'

Edward seemed to have recovered himself – wiping his face – and put forth a more formal air. 'But who is this fellow?'

'This is Jack Tucker. My apprentice.'

'Apprentice? For this "tracking" you do? Extraordinary.'

He didn't reach out his hand to Jack. It was obvious that Edward recognized an inferior. Yet Jack faced him as he would an equal. It was Jack's way these days, and Crispin couldn't fault him. After all, it was *he* who had taught Jack not to yield to superiors. How was he to do his job if he had to cower at every turn?

'Aye, sir. My master has taught me all I know. I still have much to learn and he is a patient tutor.'

'I see. My, my. Our Master Crispin hasn't changed, for he taught me all *I* know. It is only proper that he reach down to uplift others.'

Jack frowned and his eyes narrowed just that much. 'It is not that he "reached down" so much, as you would call it, but that imparting his wisdom to me suggests that he stands by his beliefs that *dignity does not consist in possessing honors, but in deserving them.'*

'Holy Mother, you've taught him Aristotle.' He laughed. 'I don't know why I am surprised.'

Jack's frown became a sneer that just as quickly vanished. 'Master Crispin, I have not meant to interrupt, but I must speak to you . . . in private.'

'Yes, of course. Stay a moment, Edward. I must attend to this.' He grasped Jack's arm and pulled him away from his old squire. 'What is it, Jack? I thought you were talking to the prioress.'

'Your old squire, eh?' It seemed Jack couldn't help but say it. 'And how come we've never heard from his like before now?'

Crispin straightened his coat. 'As you well know, Jack, those who knew me were forbidden to contact me or render me aid.'

'The Duke of Lancaster didn't fear to. The old duke, that is. Nor his son.'

'The old duke was uncle to the king. I can't blame Edward for protecting himself and those he loved.'

'Didn't he love you?'

Crispin studied his apprentice. The man was envious. There was no other way to interpret his scowl, his darting glances back at Edward. Crispin let his expression fall to something more neutral. 'I'm sure he did. He was as loyal as you, Jack.'

Jack snorted at that. It made Crispin glower.

'I'm sure there are many people from my past that you don't know. It is presumptuous of you to assume you know the reasons for their absence in my life.'

Jack stood with chin raised for only a moment more before he lowered his face. 'I'm sorry, sir. It just . . . it makes me furious with these people who knew you, knew what you suffered, and never tried to help you. *I* would have.'

Oh. That was a different color to the matter. His heart warmed. Crispin placed a hand on his arm. 'I know you would have. You'd have risked it all. As you have done for my sake many times. But Edward had a widowed mother to care for. If something had happened to him, I dread to think what would have happened to her. We can't know what is kept in a man's heart.'

'Aye, sir,' he said reluctantly.

'Now. Why are you here instead of being with the prioress?'

Jack's face fell again. 'I tried, sir. I tried to question her. But she reckoned what I was about and refused to talk to anyone but you.'

'Damn the woman,' he muttered. 'Very well. Then find Dame Elizabeth and question her. She's the apothecary's assistant. She wasn't there when we left Dame Petronella, but perhaps she has returned. Or she has other duties. Find her.'

'Aye, sir.' He cast one last wary look toward Edward and hurried off to his task.

When Crispin returned to Edward's side, the former squire chuckled. 'He's a hot-blooded fellow, isn't he?'

'He is as loyal as the day is long, Edward. He would gladly die for me.'

The squire's face paled. Even though Crispin couldn't blame him for keeping away, there was the merest spark of . . . something . . . in the back of his mind that wondered why, after all these years, he hadn't sought out Crispin, hadn't girded himself to at least find out about him and how he fared. Oh, but it was foolish treading that path. As he told Jack, there was no telling what was in a man's heart and what he would have to sacrifice.

He smiled again. 'Tell me of yourself, *Sir* Edward. Have you the time?'

Edward faced Crispin with a gladdened smile. 'Of course I do. But your tale is far more important to me. When you . . . when you left court, what happened?'

Crispin sighed. It didn't pain him to recount it as it had in the beginning. It was almost a lifetime ago now. 'I was alone. Set adrift. I didn't have the first idea what I should do. But I knew I needed shelter and food. I needed employment of some kind. It didn't start out well.' There was pain in Edward's eyes. Regret, too. Crispin dismissed it all with a brush of his hand. 'Some kind strangers succored me, helped me to find my way. They became my good friends, people I wouldn't have noticed at all when I was a lord. And yet, in their charity, they did for me what I failed to do for others. At any rate, I became a scribe for a time. Until I stumbled on this profession.'

'This very interesting profession that all of London talks about. But I somehow never heard that it was you. I never heard your name. Except . . . it makes the most sense. You were always curious about things. About what motivated people to do the things they did. I can't say that it surprises me at all.'

'I suppose that's a compliment.'

'Of course it is, sir! You've always had a marvelously quick mind. It gladdens me that you didn't stay a scribe.'

'It paid better,' he muttered, smoothing the hair at the back of his head.

'And this Tucker fellow of yours. Where did you ever find him?'

For some reason, he didn't want to share that Jack had been a cutpurse and that they had first become acquainted when he had tried to steal Crispin's money pouch. 'He found me,' he said impartially. 'I tutored him, taught him to read and write and languages. He excelled at it all.'

'God's teeth and bones. Of all things.'

'I have discovered in my wanderings about London that a man's worth is not measured by how well-tailored his clothes are, but by the degree of his integrity. The wealthiest of men can be curs, and the lowest can be angels.'

'That doesn't sound much like the London *I* know.'

'It depends on the circles where you keep yourself.'

'I do remember your saying as much when I was but a lad. You don't mean to say it is true?'

'It is very true.'

'Well! I am fascinated by that premise. Perhaps I will explore it.'

'And so. As for you, when I left court, who . . . who . . .' He couldn't quite say it. Who would have taken on the squire of a traitor?

But Edward understood him anyway. 'Master Chaucer took me in for a time. And then a close friend of his trained me. The king himself knighted me.'

'I am grateful for Geoffrey's intervention. He never told me.'

'You . . . you spoke to Sir Geoffrey?'

'Yes. I encountered him a few times.' He didn't offer up the fact that he'd saved Geoffrey's life in the course of his work as a Tracker.

It didn't seem necessary. Though it stung a bit that Geoffrey hadn't mentioned seeing *him*. He was beginning to feel invisible again, as he had in the beginning. 'Nevertheless, I am glad you were so situated. And doing well, I hope.'

'I am one of the king's household knights. And I should have been with the king's army in Ireland but His Majesty preferred I stayed in London.' He raised his eyes to Crispin when he asked quietly, 'Have you heard that the upstart Hereford has returned *illegally* to the realm?'

Crispin bristled. Edward seemed to have hardened himself against Lancaster after the scandal. Perhaps it had been for the best. Being the squire to a traitor surely did not open doors for him as it otherwise might have, had Crispin never got involved in the scandal. Edward had poured his hopes into the king, and how could Crispin blame him? 'I . . . had heard something of the kind.'

'Forgive me. I know how close you had been to Lancaster and his ilk.'

'I helped to raise his *ilk*, as you call it. Henry Lancaster has been fair to me.' The sword hanging from his hip told him so. Henry had given it to Crispin, incised it with the words 'he has the right'.

'I . . . I mean no disrespect Sir . . . M-Master Crispin. You must know that.'

He wiped the frown from his face and offered a gentle smile instead. 'I do, Edward.' He ticked his head. 'I can't quite get over the sight of you. You look like a man.'

He chuckled. 'I *am* a man, sir. Have been for some years.'

'Of course you have been. I sometimes feel suspended in amber while the world changes around me.'

'And I have a wife and children.'

'Do you now? That is good news.

'And you, sir? Are you . . . married to some gentlewoman?'

It was just then that Philippa, dressed as a nun, but looking disturbingly fetching, crossed his path in the distance, speaking to Christopher in a covert manner. The sight of her, as it always seemed to do, froze him to the spot. As she turned, she caught sight of him and a smile passed over her face and her sleepy eyes took him in as she made a slight bow with her head and a wink before proceeding onward to whatever business she intended.

'Master Crispin?'

'What?' Damn. How that woman could distract him! 'Oh. No, I never married. I came close once or twice, but . . . no. I live on the Shambles, you see.'

Edward flinched at that.

'Yes. I didn't feel that . . . Well.' He shrugged. 'It doesn't matter. Jack and his wife live with me as my servants and I enjoy the role of patriarch to their many children.' It was something that always made Crispin smile, for he did dote on those children as if they were his own.

But it didn't seem to have the same effect on Edward. He barely contained his disdain at the prospect. Crispin supposed he could understand his view. After all, if Crispin were still a lord, he couldn't imagine one of his peers being content in a servant's household with that servant's children crawling all over him.

How times had changed.

'It has occurred to me,' said Crispin, 'that I am detaining you from your business here. What was it that had so darkened your brow when you were at the gate?'

Edward huffed an impatient breath. 'Well . . .' He reddened but then casually flipped his hand. 'We are men here, after all. I'm certain in your banishment that you have not remained a monk . . .'

Crispin refrained from glancing toward his son. 'Certainly not.'

'Then I can confess to you that I have a mistress. And before you scoff at me, I well remember that Swynford woman in the Lancaster household.'

'The dowager *duchess*, you mean,' Crispin said stiffly. It had only been seven months since Lancaster's death, and it still rubbed raw a place in his heart.

'Of course,' said Edward, not noticing Crispin's expression. 'I know you never approved of Lancaster and his mistress, but so it happens to men that their eye wanders. Home and hearth will always be there, but a young, pretty thing . . . well. She had got with child. Most women would welcome that, the financial stake of raising a lord's bastard. But not her. Her eye had been to find a husband. I don't suppose I could blame her as I was never going to marry her should something happen to my dear wife. She wasn't of noble blood. I supposed she reckoned that for herself. And so she told me she was coming to this priory to get her potions to rid herself of that pregnancy. Of *my* child. Everyone in the parish knows this about the priory.'

Crispin couldn't speak. He hadn't any idea. 'And she came here?' The image suddenly brushed his mind of the anxious gentlewoman at the gate, waiting for Dame Audrey who would never come. And an idea came to him that he gnawed on.

'I wanted to make very clear to the apothecary how little I think of her witch's brew. And to inform that prioress what I thought of their secret business.'

'I can understand why you are distressed, but this may not be the proper time. There is murder here and I have yet to find the culprit.'

'By the mass, that truly is your reason for being here?'

'As I have said, I am doing a service for the prioress.'

Edward swiveled his head, taking in churchyard, the graves, and looked the other way toward the prioress's lodgings. 'I see. Perhaps they have more on their minds at this time.'

'Yes,' he said distractedly. He had no idea that the priory was in the business of miscarriage. That sounded like a motive for murder to him.

'Now I feel foolish,' Edward went on. 'I tell you, Master Crispin, I think I will leave it for now. Perhaps . . . perhaps we can get some ale somewhere. Talk.'

'You can meet me at my home on the Shambles. It used to be a poulterer's. Anyone would know it. I would be pleased to host you.'

Edward hesitated. 'Perhaps. God keep you, Master Crispin. I know He in His wisdom has done.'

'Farewell, Edward. Don't hesitate to call upon me.'

'I won't.' He seemed suddenly embarrassed again, and quickly pivoted on his heel to march back toward the gate.

Crispin watched him leave with his own misgivings. He knew people could change. God knew *he* had over the years. And no doubt Edward had had his own trials after Crispin's banishment. He had cleaved to Richard, and Crispin was grateful that Richard had succored him, had taken no vengeance on him as he had done to so many.

It was foolish to ponder it now. Now he had his own questions to consider. If Edward was angry that his mistress was forcing a miscarriage, might other men be just as angry? It was a motive, at any rate, something he hadn't had before. It was time to enquire of Prioress Drueta. Because he was beginning to have his doubts that Dame Audrey *had* died of a fever.

TWELVE

Prioress Drueta received him with an unreadable face, throwing a gesture toward a chair for him to take as she stood by the window, looking out. Since she wasn't sitting, Crispin did not either.

'Prioress, why did you send my man away?'

'He was being impudent and asking questions above his station.'

'He is my apprentice and therefore my emissary. I asked him to make enquiries.'

'Not to me.'

'Yes, even to you. Even to the king if it is required. So now, Dame, since you have wasted his time and mine, *I* must ask my questions. Where were you when Dame Mildred was murdered?'

She slowly turned, looking down her nose at him. 'I was in prayer.'

'Surely you heard screams and exclamations?'

'I did not.'

He glanced toward the open windows, and the door that lay ajar. 'And were you in here?'

'Yes.'

'When did you finally awaken to a situation and go to the church?'

'When a nun fetched me.'

She answered each of his queries with a simple and unqualified reply. Somehow, it did not comfort. He rubbed his forehead. 'Lady Prioress, about Dame Audrey . . .'

'But her death has naught to do with these others.'

'Perhaps. But are you certain that it was a fever that killed her?'

'Of course.'

'Who was at her bedside administering to her?'

'That would have been Dame Marion and Dame Katherine.'

Crispin reached into his pouch and retrieved the note that the chaplain had penned for him, then stopped. 'But . . . Prioress, those are the first two murdered nuns.'

'Yes.'

He glared at her, she with her hands tucked into the opposite sleeve and measuring him down the length of her nose.

'Prioress, did it never occur to you that these three deaths might in some way be related?'

She heaved a sigh. 'Of course not, Master Guest. Is that the best you can do?'

She is a holy sister, he reminded himself, even as his hand curled into a fist. He loosened his grip and took a cleansing breath. 'Lady Prioress, are you aware that your apothecary – the late Dame Audrey and her successor Dame Petronella – offer potions that induce miscarriages?'

'Yes.'

'And you have no objection to that?'

'Master Crispin, women have sought and obtained the means to end their pregnancies for centuries. Even the ancients spoke of it. Sometimes in disdainful tones and sometimes in tones of little commentary. Unmarried women who get themselves into such situations often seek to undo the damage. It may be distasteful, but a woman risks her life in childbed, and if she and the babe survive, their circumstances are worse if there is no father. Many of the women who seek our help are the mistresses of men who discard them if they are found to be in such a predicament. This is the way of it, Master Guest.'

'Some men wish to have their bastards, especially in a situation where they are only given female children by their wives.'

The prioress snorted at that. 'Do you not find it strange, Master Guest, that the wives of rich men are able to run an entire household and, indeed, entire estates – castles, even – but somehow their daughters are not credited with the ability to do so if they are not married?'

'A husband gives a woman the wisdom of his counsel.'

'But not by her own merit?'

He cast a thought toward Philippa and had to admit that the woman was full of her own intelligence and guile on the matter. He certainly would have trusted Philippa to run *his* estate at Sheen.

In answer he made a vague gesture and said nothing more on it.

'It still leaves the question of the two nuns who attended Dame Audrey and subsequently died. I know that such things as friendships – though against the Rule – still happen in monasteries. Was this the case with Audrey, Marion, and Katherine?'

'What strange questions you ask.'

'There are strange events afoot here, Prioress.'

She turned her hands palm up. 'I am not close to the nuns here as a confidante. Only as a guide to the narrow path. You'd best ask the other sisters. Dame Petronella, perhaps.'

'I shall. Thank you, Lady Prioress.'

She gave a matriarchal nod of her head and promptly turned away from him to look out of her window.

Finding himself dismissed, he pivoted, left her lodgings, and stood on the gravel path just as Philippa came walking swiftly along. She bowed. 'Master Guest.'

He glanced over his shoulder to make certain no one saw them and spoke low to her. 'How are you faring?'

'It's not as bad as all that. I can see how a woman of means would take her retirement here. Few cares. Lovely gardens. Prayer whenever one wished.'

'Oh? Are you planning on becoming a pensioner?'

She smiled secretly behind the shadow of her veil. 'Well . . . I think I would miss the more *earthy* pleasures.'

'Philippa!' he hissed.

She shook her head. 'Crispin, you are still such a misery.'

He huffed, exasperated. 'I am what I have always been, madam.'

'A misery. And yet, you indulge in your own earthy pleasures. He's out digging in the churchyard now.'

'Philippa!'

'Crispin. You do carry on so. It don't make no matter. I'm certain that Christopher will care for me in my retirement.'

'Of course he will. But why speak of such matters? You are young yet.'

'How sweet of you to say. Even though it isn't true. I'm your age, you know.'

'Madam, was that designed to sting?'

She laughed. 'Not a bit of it.' She put a hand to her mouth and looked about. 'Do nuns make full-throated laughs? I've never seen them do so.'

'I can't imagine them doing so here in this priory under that prioress.'

'Did you just come from the prioress's lodgings?' She glanced at the arched door. 'I should say not. She is rather . . . prim.'

'I daresay you can take her on.'

'Master Guest, the things you say.'

'I can't be talking to you now . . . unless you have anything to report.'

'I don't.'

'I do need a favor of you. Can you get yourself onto the first floor and look out of the windows? See what you can see *and* hear.'

She turned to examine the outside of the dorter and the story above the ground floor. 'Some of those are the nuns' private rooms.'

'Yes, they are.'

She turned back and frowned. 'There is little you won't stoop to.'

'In the course of an enquiry? No.'

'They might be locked.'

'Then here.' He reached into his money pouch and retrieved his pick locks. He took her hand and pressed them into her palm. 'I don't suppose you know how to pick a lock.'

'Don't I, though? Wait here.' She smiled and winked and folded her hand over them as she moved away toward the dorter. She hadn't always been the wife of a wealthy mercer. She had been a scullion in that household and had probably undertaken her fair share of unsavory activities to supplement her income. In another day he might have been scandalized. He'd learned a great deal since.

Crispin looked both ways along the path and tried to project a relaxed attitude as he plucked a leaf from a bush and tore it to little pieces. He wished he hadn't agreed to allow her here, but since she *was* here, he might as well put her to work. At least she had her own cell which she could lock at night.

He heard a casement open above and he twisted round to look up. He saw only her hand push the window open, pause, and close it again. It was repeated until all the west-facing windows along the path had been opened and closed. And then she seemed to disappear.

It took longer than he was comfortable with, but she finally returned and looked again to make certain no one was watching them. 'I went to each cell facing this path and listened. The street was rather noisy but I could still hear you below breaking twigs.'

He glanced down and kicked the pile of broken twigs and torn leaves under the bushes.

'Then I went to the cells facing away from this path and could hear far less.'

'Good, Philippa.'

'When I was in each cell, I looked about the room, under the mattresses and such. I found this in one of them.' She held up a small ring.

He took it and examined it. 'In which cell did you find it?'

'The one yon.' She pointed to the last in the row. 'Under the mattress.'

'It could be the nun's own. Or . . . it could be the relic.'

'St Frideswide? Blind me. I never touched a relic since . . . since . . . the veil . . .'

He locked eyes with her. Her first husband, the false Nicholas Walcote, guising himself as the brother of Clarence, had shown her the relic he possessed, the Mandylion, something of a Veronica's Veil. The veil might have been real, even if the husband had been false. No one ever discovered his true name. Sad, in a way. Nicholas was as forgotten as Crispin, in many ways. Crispin would leave no legacy, no name to leave behind. And this man who had masqueraded as Nicholas Walcote went to a pauper's grave with only a wooden cross to mark that he had existed at all.

'How are we to know?' she asked.

'I shall have to ask the prioress, I suppose.'

'But if it isn't? And it belonged to that nun?'

'Hmm.'

'If it was hers from her former life, then she risked much by keeping it. I shouldn't want to be the one to have exposed her.'

She had such a tender look in her eyes that Crispin surrendered to it. 'Maybe . . . I shall take it to another. Dame Petronella is charged with overseeing the relics.' He glanced again up to the last window. 'Whose cell was that?'

'I believe it is Dame Jemma's.'

'Indeed?' The one who was not in the bakehouse as she said she was. And the one who said that it was the sin of our sisters that murdered those nuns. And the one who heard footsteps that he was beginning to think had not existed.

'I must get back to my duties,' she said. 'I hope that helped you.'

'It did. Thank you, Philippa.'

'You see? You did need a female spy.'

'Go on,' he said with a flick of his head. He almost swatted her behind but refrained.

She smiled, her cheek dimpling, and brusquely turned away. He let loose his held breath. How was it he could love her as much now as when he first realized it some sixteen years ago? *Foolish man*, he admonished himself.

Shaking it off, he realized he needed to talk to Dame Petronella about a ring and a potion.

THIRTEEN

Dame Petronella caught sight of him as he passed through to her garden and thrust her hoe into the ground with a weary sigh. 'Truly, Master Guest. When you and then your man take my time I can get very little done.'

'I apologize, Dame, but we are investigating three murders. Possibly four.'

'Four?'

He gestured toward the shady table and bench. 'Can we not take a moment now, Dame, to talk again?'

Reluctantly, she laid down the hoe, lifted her skirts to step over the herbs and fence, and walked sedately to the bench. She sat and Crispin settled opposite her. 'Dame Petronella, you occupy a cell on the first floor of the dorter?'

'Yes.'

'The one facing west?'

'Yes.'

'On the night of Dame Marion's murder, did you hear anything, anyone walking, and opening the gate to where the pigs are?'

'As I said before, I did not. And in any case, one would have to be awake to have heard a sound, even with the window open, as mine was.'

'I see.' He reached into his pouch and laid the ring on the table between them. 'Is this the ring that was in the reliquary?'

She paled as she stared at it. 'Where did you find that?'

'Is it the relic?'

'No.'

'Then why do you look so concerned?'

'Because . . . because it is Dame Audrey's. I saw her with it before.' She pressed her fingers to her mouth. She looked as if she were going to cry.

'How did she die?'

She closed her eyes for but a moment and laid both hands on the table, fingers rolling over and over one another. 'She died of a fever.'

'You were her apprentice. Did you attend to her?'

Her brow furrowed. 'No. She insisted that I attend to my duties.'

'Was it Dame Marion and Dame Katherine who attended to her?'

Her eyes flicked up to his. 'You clearly know it already.'

'I'm merely confirming it. Why were those particular sisters charged with attending to her?'

She sighed in exasperation but shook her head.

'Was it the "sin of our sisters"?'

She pulled up short. 'Why would you say that?'

'It was something one of the nuns expressed about why those two died. What sort of sin was she referring to?'

'You should probably ask her.' She rose. 'I have much work to do.'

'Sit down.' His tone was sharp and meant to be. He wanted her attention and, by the shocked look to her face, he had got it.

'I'm investigating murder, Dame. If that is not serious enough for you then . . .'

Dame Petronella flattened her expression and sat.

'There is something else I wish to discuss with you.' He glanced over his shoulder and saw that they were alone. 'Tell me, Dame, do you give many potions that cause . . . miscarriage?'

'Many? A relative term. Enough, I suppose. You're not another man who disapproves, are you?'

'I have no opinion one way or the other. I can understand a

woman who needs to . . . to take such a potion. But I wonder, since you brought it up, how many men have come here to accuse Dame Audrey. Angrily.'

'To accuse her?'

'Of taking away their child.'

'Oh, that.' She laid one hand over the other on the table, the fingers nearest the surface moving over the wood. 'There were some. Even the women's mothers.'

'What I mean is, were there any men angry enough to . . . to threaten her?'

She stared at the table a long while. 'I don't know. I wasn't privy to every one of her exchanges.'

'Are you subject to the same vitriol? The man who called Demoiselle Forthey his mistress, for instance.'

He watched the agitation grow on her, in the way she tensed her shoulders, how the hands on the table curled into fists. Had Edward come back after their encounter? 'I . . . I . . .'

The bell rang out, pealing in long, slow rolls. Crispin swore under his breath.

Dame Petronella rose slowly. 'I must attend to the Divine Office.' She didn't look at him as she turned and walked a little more quickly than normal away from him.

Jack met him at the garden. 'Have you got anywhere?' he asked.

'If it weren't for the damn bells . . .'

'I know your meaning, sir. It seems that every time I get close to something, the bells ring.'

'Did you find Dame Elizabeth?'

'Aye, and a frightened little thing she was. She would squeak instead of talk and I couldn't get much out of her.'

'Where was she when Dame Mildred was killed?'

'Here, she said. In yon cottage, chopping herbs, she said. But she's so little, so frail a thing. I can hardly believe she is up to murder and all the arrangement of the bodies.'

'Now Jack, as I have pointed out before, do not be fooled by the look of them. Anyone can act small and frail and be capable of much mischief. Dangerous mischief.'

'Aye, that's the truth of it. I should be less discriminating.'

'Keep an open mind.'

'What of your apothecary?'

He took out the ring again from his pouch and laid it on the table.

'What's that? The relic? How'd you find it?'

'Madam Walcote found it. In one of the cells.'

'Whose?'

'Dame Jemma's.'

'God's blood.'

'But it isn't the relic. It did not even belong to Dame Jemma, who had it secured under her mattress. It belonged to Dame Audrey.'

'What? Are there thieves as well as murderers in this priory?'

'Perhaps. Dame Petronella was shocked that I knew of the so-called "sin of our sisters" being responsible for the murders, the phrase that Dame Jemma used when I asked her about the murders yesterday.'

'"Sin of our sisters"? What can that mean?'

He shook his head, thinking.

Jack pressed his thumbs into his belt. 'Blind me. The more we ask, the more muddled it becomes. So Dame Petronella knows something, as does Dame Jemma. I suppose we should concentrate on them.'

'As soon as this liturgy of the hours is done.'

'What do we do in the meantime?'

The bell at the gate clanged furiously, and both Jack and Crispin glanced at one another. They hurried through the garden, through the night stair, and down the path between cloister and church.

The woman he'd brought to the apothecary, Elena Forthey – and consequently whom he believed was Edward Grafton's mistress – hung on the bell chain, obviously in pain.

They sprinted toward her and tried to open the gate. Jack was quicker, and withdrew his own lockpicks; in no time, he had released the heavy lock and pulled the gate open. She fell into Crispin's arms.

'Demoiselle!'

'I need Dame Petronella . . .' She gasped.

Crispin tried to help her walk, but she could barely hold herself up. He swept her up in his arms and hurried to the apothecary garden. When he turned the corner, he heard a rumble in the little stone cottage. He set Elena carefully on a bench, withdrew his dagger, and crept to the doorway.

Crouch, face contorted with rage, pushed over canisters and kicked at baskets of herbs. He tore down the drying ones from the rafters, and turned to see what other damage he could do when he spied Crispin and stilled. His wild eyes seemed to understand that he was trapped.

'What is your business here, Crouch?' said Crispin. He had not sheathed his dagger.

Someone skidded in the gravel behind him.

'Jack, go fetch Dame Petronella.'

'But . . . they are in prayer.'

'I don't give a damn for that. There is a soul suffering. Tell her Elena Forthey is here.'

Jack released a loud breath. 'I will do my best, sir. Have, er, you secured this situation?'

Crispin's fingers readjusted on the hilt of his dagger. 'It's secured, Jack.'

He heard the man retreat before he settled in the doorway. 'Now, Crouch. What is the reason for your wrath?'

'Get out of my way.'

Crouch feinted one way, and then jerked in the other. But Crispin was not fooled. The caretaker had no other way out save the window, but he doubted that the old man could make that move over the narrow counter filled with jars up to the small sill . . . especially with one arm.

'Sit down.' He motioned with his dagger to a stool Crouch had cast over.

'You can't order me—'

Crispin pointed the blade at his face. 'Sit. Down.'

Crouch muttered several oaths, leaned over, and set the stool right. Slowly, he lowered onto it.

Crispin flicked a glance to the mess. 'What are you doing here?'

'None of your affair.'

'Everything is my affair. Have you forgotten the graves you've dug?'

He scowled and turned away.

'What have you against the apothecary?'

He turned his head toward Crispin and spat as he said, 'She's a witch is what she is. All those who meddle in them herbs and such.'

'You little understand the healer's art, Crouch. She's no more of a witch than I am. Or you are.'

'I say she is. I seen the women come in. I seen them with bellies bulging with babes and she gives them a potion and they are gone. That's witchcraft, that is.'

'Again, Crouch. You don't understand the sciences. Leave it to those who know.'

'She's more than a witch. There's evil in her, in all who do this work.'

'And why would you say that?'

He squirmed on his stool as if he had spoken too much. 'Never you mind.'

'Crouch, if I take this to the prioress, you will surely lose your situation. You had better explain yourself to me.'

'You can't do naught. Father Holbrok—'

'He can't protect you against the prioress, Crouch. Even you must know that.'

But by the look on his face, he knew no such thing. 'He'll protect me.'

'Why? Are you doing this destruction on his say-so? Tell me the truth!'

'I won't say naught.' He rose. 'And you can't stop me.' He raised his chin and walked forward until he was almost right up against Crispin. And Crispin, looking at his knife, then at the man's half arm, knew that he would do nothing to him. He scowled and sheathed his dagger, and the one-armed man pushed past him.

He was ready to follow him when he remembered Elena Forthey. He rushed to her side again and took her hand. She appeared to be in great distress.

'Is there something I can do for you, demoiselle?'

'I must wait for Dame Petronella. Her potion . . .' She cried out and clutched at her middle. 'So much pain.'

'She's coming.' He looked back toward the church. *She had better be coming.*

She squeezed his hand hard, gripping it with unnatural strength. He bit down on his own shout of pain.

Thankfully, Jack trotted around the corner with Dame Petronella in tow. 'Mistress Forthey!'

'Blessed Holy Mother,' cried Elena. 'The pain is unbearable.'

Dame Petronella knelt beside her and lifted her skirts. They were spattered with blood. She turned to Jack and Crispin. 'Help me get her to the infirmary.'

Crispin took her shoulders and Jack took her feet, and they carried her as quickly as they could, following Dame Petronella to the dorter. She unlocked the door and they entered. Apparently, the infirmary took up the ground floor, except for a few extra cells for guests and other nuns. The nun directed them to lay Elena on a cot by the window while she went to an ambry, opened the cupboard, and took out a pile of folded sheets.

'Master Tucker, unfold and lay these sheets beneath her one at a time. Master Guest, return to the apothecary cottage and retrieve for me a blue jar near the windowsill . . .'

'Dame, I am afraid that much damage was just done to the cottage by Edgar Crouch.'

'What? That devil! Well, see if you can find it, Master Guest, and hurry back.'

Crispin ran. He couldn't abide a sickbed, and a woman's sickbed when it had to do with birthing was the worst, in his estimation. The woman was obviously miscarrying, but he didn't think that a potion was supposed to cause so much distress.

He got to the cottage, cursed Crouch loudly and at great length, and stepped over the broken crockery to get to the window. He found the blue jar – still intact – and ran like the Devil was after him back to the infirmary. Out of breath, he handed it over.

'Now, gentlemen, I ask that you leave. Delicate matters are ahead.'

Gratefully, they left together, but Crispin heard her say, 'Mistress Forthey, it is the potion doing its work. The creature is miscarrying but I am afraid the pain can't be helped . . .'

Jack was shaking his head. 'This is what I always feared for Isabel,' he panted.

'Isabel is strong,' said Crispin without thinking. He was trying to listen at the window.

'This one took a potion.'

'It's different for an unmarried woman. Though . . . she . . . she is the mistress of my old squire.'

'Eh? I thought a woman would want her lover's babe, especially if he were a lord. Like . . . like the Dowager Duchess of Lancaster.'

'Lady Katherine's situation was different. Important men of the court . . . well. Their mistresses hold esteemed positions. As you climb down each rung of the ladder, the, er, less esteemed it is. He admitted to me that he wouldn't take her for a wife even if he were free to do so.'

'I see. That's hard on the lady, isn't it? Especially if she wanted to find a husband.'

'Yes. You are lucky to be married. And faithful.'

'Never doubt it. She'd flail me alive.'

Crispin smiled grimly. 'It's not in your nature to be unfaithful.'

Jack thumbed back to the window and to the wailing heard behind the shutter. 'Do you suppose she'll be all right?'

'Dame Petronella seems to know what she is doing. How did *you* fare when you came to fetch her?'

'That Prioress Drueta. She was in a spitting rage at me. But when I insisted, telling her that a life was at stake and surely our Lord wouldn't want a soul to die, well, that changed her tune. But I'm certain you will be hearing how your apprentice did not respect the Divine Office.'

'Don't worry, Jack. I will defend you.' He looked back at the window and then toward the rectory behind the church. 'Stay here in case Dame Petronella needs you. I have something to do.'

'Where are you going?' he squeaked. Jack didn't like women's complaints any more than Crispin did.

'I'm going to talk to that priest. I'm sure he sent Crouch to wreak havoc on the apothecary cottage and I want to know why.'

'I'll . . . I'll be here, then,' he said weakly. Crispin felt bad for the man, but not bad enough to stay in his place.

FOURTEEN

Crispin found the rectory and heard talking within the structure that was no bigger than a cottage. He approached the open window and let the wall shield him as he listened to Crouch complaining about him with lies aplenty. *I never touched you, you carbuncle.* Now he wished he had. He had other choice phrases whirling in his head, until the man left, stomping away, calling out for someone named Tobias . . . and it only took a moment more for Crispin to realize that this was the name Christopher had chosen for himself. Named after Crispin's *horse*! He suppressed a chuckle.

He moved around to the door and, without knocking, pushed it open.

Holbrok whirled. 'How dare you come in unannounced!'

'How dare I? How dare you send that wretched fellow to ruin the apothecary's cottage. Why was he doing so? Or . . . was he searching for something?'

Holbrok sputtered before he managed, 'He wasn't . . . I didn't . . . it wasn't . . . Get out of here, Guest!'

'Three denials. Three lies.' He shook his head. 'That's a great deal of confessing to do, Father. One wonders what else there is to confess. Murder, perhaps?'

His mouth dropped open with a gasp. 'You dare accuse *me* . . .'

'I suppose I am in the business of daring.' He looked down at his dagger. 'I drew my dagger on Crouch but I must confess that I was loath to use it on a crippled man. However, I seem to have no impediment when considering using it on you.' He drew it. 'Or would you prefer my fists?' He dropped the dagger back into the sheath and clenched his hands. 'Yes, I think I prefer the latter method to get what I want from you.'

He took a step toward Holbrok who took two away. 'What are you talking about? Do you mean to do me harm? What sort of man are you?'

'The kind who is impatient with murderers.' He took another step toward him until Holbrok found himself trapped against a wall. 'Now. It seems to me you have two choices: tell me all or take a beating.' He allowed a smile to reconfigure his face as he rubbed the knuckles from one hand in the palm of his other. 'I think I'd prefer the latter. Just one punch, at least.' As he drew back his arm, Holbrok threw his open hands forward.

'Stop, Master Guest! In the name of Jesus Christ, stop!'

Crispin didn't lower his arm and neither did he stop his posturing. 'Well?'

Holbrok wiped the sweat from his face. 'I . . . er . . . I did send him. Not to destroy. But . . . as you said . . . to search.'

'For what? This perhaps?' He lowered one hand to reach into his pouch to withdraw the ring.

Holbrok passed his glance over it without recognition. 'No. For
. . . something else.'

'*What?*' Crispin pronounced through gritted teeth.

The priest seemed to surrender something. His body wilted and
it was only the wall that appeared to hold him upright. 'Coins. A
cache of coins.'

'You wished to *rob* the apothecary?'

Holbrok's eyes suddenly lit with fire. '*Rob?* Rob *her*? It was *she*
who robbed *me*!' The fire did not last and he crumpled again, running
a hand through his hair. 'She robbed me,' he muttered, defeated.

'I find it hard to believe that Dame Petronella—'

'No, not *her*. The other. Dame Audrey.'

'She stole from you?'

'She . . . *extorted* me.'

Crispin lowered his hands at last, stuffing away the ring. 'Dame
Audrey extorted you for money? And, er, how was she able to do
so?'

'Master Guest, is it not enough that she did?'

'Forgive me for stating the obvious, Father, but Dame Audrey is
dead and cannot corroborate your tale.'

'Why would I admit such a humiliating thing if it were not true?'

'To hide another truth, perhaps. For instance, I am having my
doubts that Dame Audrey died of a fever.'

It took but a heartbeat for Holbrok's face to open in understanding.
'You're accusing me of *killing* her? Blessed Virgin.' He crossed
himself desperately.

'You see my predicament, Father Holbrok. How am I to discern
the truth?'

'I am a holy priest. I made vows. I was anointed by my bishop.'

'Then tell me why Dame Audrey extorted you.'

His eyes sank into despair and he moved slowly away. His hand
groped for a chair and found it. Pulling himself forward he sank
into the seat. 'There is no avoiding it, is there? No reprieve for my
final humiliation?'

'Consider me your confessor, Father. That unless it is absolutely
necessary, it will go no farther than me.'

'But will it be necessary?' he mused, head back, eyes scanning
the rafters.

Crispin slouched against a table and crossed his arms over his chest. He let the man stew as the priest tried to decide how best to tell Crispin his secret. Crispin tried not to speculate, for he had met all manner of clerics, both saints and sinners . . . and the sinners had a wide variety of sins they were guilty of.

'It . . . it started innocently enough,' Holbrok began in a subdued tone. 'I passed her every day. It is difficult in such a small priory not to come across the same nuns over and over. Perhaps she went out of her way to encounter me. I don't know. I never asked.'

Crispin adjusted his seat. 'Dame Audrey?'

Holbrok shook his head. 'No. Another. I was flattered, naturally, at the attention, and then disturbed because such things must not be. But she was . . . endearing. Charming. Pretty.'

Crispin rolled his eyes. Foolish. Foolish of the priest to fall for such a simple test of his mettle.

'You had an affair with her.'

The priest looked up. 'An affair? The word is inadequate for the feelings on the matter. It was . . . almost . . . holy. I know that something so pure, so gentle would never occur to a man like you—'

Crispin snorted at that.

'But I never wanted to break my vows of chastity,' he went on. 'And I know *she* did not. At least, I thought as much. I *had* thought . . .' He dropped his face into his hands and began to weep.

Crispin sighed, waiting for his crying to subside.

Holbrok lifted his face and wiped the wet away from his cheeks. 'It wasn't long after it started that Dame Audrey came to me and told me she knew. "I know what you are getting up to, *Father*," she said in that sly way of hers. "And I want payment to keep silent on it." Well, Master Guest, I couldn't have that. I couldn't have her speaking to the prioress or it would go straight to the bishop. Then I'd be sent to some distant place, to some hole of a monastery on some windswept plain. No, I couldn't abide that. Even in obedience. Though . . . I suppose, I wasn't keeping any of my vows very well.'

'Where did you get the money?'

'From my own stipend. And – I dread to say it – but from the alms box as well.'

'Dear, dear. Vows indeed.'

'There's no need to rub my nose in it, Guest. I know my sins.'

'And so. How long did this go on? It doesn't seem that she would have stopped at one chance at extortion.'

'You have the right of it. She did not. Every week she came back to me. I begged her. I threatened her. But she was relentless.'

'Why did she want the money?'

'There was a rumor amongst the sisters. Dame Audrey wasn't happy with her place as a holy sister. It was said she had never wanted it. There was a man she loved, so they said. But she was forced by her family to lead this life. It is not a life for everyone, Master Guest. There are harsh penalties for disobeying. And a woman may need the fulfillment of children and a husband to care for. A woman who becomes a nun must fully understand the sacrifice. It is never a good idea to force anyone to this life.' He scowled, no doubt thinking of Dame Audrey.

'So she thought to gather enough funds to escape?'

He shrugged. 'She had tried before when she was first brought here and was dragged back. She wasn't happy, but outwardly, since that time, she seemed to conform to the life here. She did her task as apothecary with industry and intelligence. No one would have known on the surface what lurked beneath.'

'Then how did *you* discover it?'

'Her closest friends, sisters here. It isn't supposed to be thus. Friendships like that are not encouraged in a monastery. Much mischief can come from it and, indeed, mischief did come of it. Her friends were discouraged by punishments from the prioress, but they persisted.'

'How do you know this?'

Holbrok sighed. 'Because my . . . my paramour was one such close friend to Dame Audrey. Before our affair ended, she confessed to me that . . . that . . . she had only seduced me for the money for Audrey.'

Crispin's brows shot upward. He had sympathy for the man for only a moment until he remembered that the priest wasn't supposed to indulge himself with a lover in the first place. How did a celibate consider his manhood? And how did a man breaking that vow of celibacy consider it afterward?

Crispin shrugged. 'I don't know what to say to that.'

'No. There is nothing to say. It was only what I deserved. It was the Lord's punishment for my deception. I acknowledge it.'

'Who was your lover?'

He winced at the word and lowered his head again. 'Dame Marion.'

'One of the murdered nuns?'

'Yes.'

Crispin pushed away from the table. 'You do realize, Father Holbrok, that you have given yourself motive for two of the murders.'

He huffed a harsh breath that could have been a laugh. 'One murder at least, Master Guest. For Dame Audrey died of a fever.'

'Is that a confession?'

Holbrok shook his head. 'No. I did not kill Marion, especially in that way.' He shivered. 'Those murders were horrific. Angry, sinful things.'

'Were *you* not angry . . . and sinful, Father?'

'I understand how you might think that, Master Guest. But I was not capable of it.'

'Was Crouch? If you ordered him, I have no doubt that he would have had the capability.'

He frowned. 'No. I never ordered him.'

'But he is in the palm of your hand. If you merely suggested it—'

'No! I never spoke to him of my anger or my sin. And I *never* would have sent him to do such devil's work.'

'There is only your word on it. A man who had already forsworn his religious vows. And you did send him to the apothecary cottage . . .'

Holbrok pushed himself from his chair and walked to the window, opening the shutter wider to inhale the warm, damp air. 'I know you think that. But it was not me. Nor Crouch. Yes, he dotes on me for the care I have given him, but he would not act on any such thing. Dame Mildred's death . . . What was the reason for that? She had naught to do with Dame Audrey. She was not her friend.'

'Who was the other friend?'

'Dame Katherine.'

'The first two murdered nuns.'

Holbrok shook his head. 'I know what it looks like.'

'It certainly does.'

Still looking out through the window, Holbrok took a shaky hand and plucked a flower from the vine growing on the outside of the cottage's wall. 'What will you do?' he asked softly.

It seemed so utterly decided. There was Father Holbrok served to him on a platter. And yet . . . the situation did not stir Crispin as it might have. When he was certain, he pounced on a thing. But for this, he was *not* certain. Somehow, the logic of it eluded him. Why keep killing and killing and in such a way as to cause attention to be put upon him? This killing for revenge would have been swift and secret. He might have even stashed Marion away where no one would find her. He could have thrown her to the pigs and she would have been devoured. But she was positioned only *near* the sty, not in it.

And what of Dame Audrey and her fever?

'I . . . will do nothing, for the moment.' The words fell from Crispin's mouth before he had time to think about it. Holbrok was surprised, but not as surprised as Crispin was. He let out a breath. 'No more of this wrecking of the apothecary. Consider the money to be gone.'

'Yes, Master Guest.'

'And behave yourself and keep your vows. Good God, man. You've been put here to test yourself and you've failed. See if you can pass the next test that comes at you.'

'You are courteous and generous, Master Guest.'

'I am nothing of the kind. I am angry. Angry that this thing has happened here. Angry that these deaths are so little mourned. And I am angry at you for being such a damned fool.'

Holbrok lowered his head. 'No more than I am with myself, Master Guest.'

Without another word, Crispin hurried out of the rectory. He stopped when he noticed Edgar Crouch standing several yards away in a flower bed, hoe in his one hand. Crispin pointed a stern finger at him. 'No more mischief from you, Crouch, or you'll be out on your ear.'

Crouch only sneered and went back to his hoeing. Had he heard what they had talked about? He hadn't been close enough to hear Holbrok's soft confession, surely. Unless he had been under the window and hurried away in time. Crispin wondered.

It had been brewing in his mind during Holbrok's confession. Now Crispin could see no alternative to it. He came back to the dorter where he found Jack pacing. 'Come, Jack. We need to find Christopher.'

Jack looked grateful for the reprieve.

Crispin glanced back to the dorter they were leaving behind. 'How is Demoiselle Forthey?'

'It sounded as if she was doing better. Dame Petronella explained to her that the potion was forcing a miscarriage which was much like a birth, hence the pain. There was . . . there was blood . . .'

Crispin shivered. 'You need not explain more, Jack.'

'Why are we looking for Christopher?'

But when they turned the corner, there he was, repairing a bit of fence. If Crispin hadn't known better, he might have thought the boy was enjoying himself.

Crispin remembered at the last minute to use his false name. 'Tobias!' Christopher looked up and Jack laughed and quickly covered it with his hand.

'Yes, Master Crispin?'

'Tobias.' He came in close and smiled. 'Remind me why you named yourself after my horse?'

Jack laughed again and tried to stifle it.

Christopher glared at Jack. 'It was the first name I thought of. I've never had to do this before.'

'Don't worry,' said Crispin, elbowing Jack hard. 'It doesn't matter. I will need you for a little task tonight, after Matins. Meet us in the churchyard after the nuns have retired for the second time to the dorter. And bring a spade.'

'Why, sir?'

Crispin took in Jack as he leaned closer. 'Because tonight, we need to dig up a body.'

FIFTEEN

The priory lay quiet under a staggering veil of stars above. Crispin and Jack entered through the lychgate and directly into the churchyard. There was only a sliver of moon but the stars, unmarred by clouds, lit the area enough for Jack and Crispin to see everything.

Jack carried a spade leaning over his shoulder and they looked around for Christopher. Crispin crept up to the church and looked through one of the glass-paned windows. Candles lit the quire and he could see the sisters still at their Divine Office, when they suddenly rose. One by one, they trailed out. A line of candles drifted as if by sorcery through the church to the night stair. He rounded the other side of the church, barred by a wall, and lifted himself up just enough to see over it. Yes, there they went, a line of seemingly floating candles against their black habits, striding through the night stair. One peeled away and headed toward the prioress's lodgings – and must have been Prioress Drueta. Soon enough, even the candles disappeared as they moved into the dorter, each one in their own cells on the first floor. One by one, the lights were snuffed out as the nuns retired for their second sleep.

Crispin hopped down from the wall, searched in the windows for any more candles or movement, and was satisfied that all had retired.

He returned to Jack to await Christopher.

Presently, someone with a lantern in one hand, a spade in the other – just a dark figure without distinguishing details, except for the walk that looked much like Crispin's – appeared in the gloom. He lifted the lantern and smiled. 'I learn the strangest things from you, Crispin; stealing bodies.'

'We aren't stealing a body. We are merely going to examine it.'

'Er . . .' Jack's eyes were wide, his mouth slack. 'Why, sir, do we have to do such a dreadful thing?' he whispered. Crispin realized Jack was probably recounting their time in St Modwen's churchyard when they dug up a body there.

'Because I am becoming more and more convinced that Dame Audrey was murdered.'

'But . . . she's been dead more than a sennight. What do you hope to discover?'

'I'll never know unless I look.' He turned toward Christopher, whose expression was similar to Jack's. 'Are you all right?'

All his mirth was gone. 'I . . . I never knew to what extent you would go to solve a crime, is all.'

There was enough light for Crispin to see Jack shaking his head, but the two of them set to, digging into Dame Audrey's grave.

Crispin stood guard, occasionally checking their surrounds to make certain no one was watching. He even went so far as to Crouch's hut, but nothing appeared to be stirring within, no candles were lit, no movement could be heard.

'Crispin,' whispered Christopher when Crispin returned. He continued digging in and shoveling the dirt aside. 'I wondered what your thoughts were about the rumors.'

'Rumors of what?' he whispered back, ears pricked for sounds in the distance. Had he heard rumors about Dame Audrey too?

'Rumors about Henry Lancaster.'

Crispin's blood ran cold. He had blessedly forgotten about Henry through his enquiries, but now it crashed in again on his consciousness. He breathed, long and slow. 'I . . . don't know all the details.'

'But surely you must have a thought on it. I mean, it sounds as if he's marching to London with an army. And he's captured the king. Do you suppose—'

'I . . . don't like to speculate without all the facts, Christopher. Now . . . you must be silent.'

Before he turned away from the two of them, knee-deep in a grave, he noticed Jack elbow Christopher hard. They exchanged a silent argument that Jack appeared to have won.

Of course Christopher would want to know. Everyone wanted to know what Crispin thought. Crispin and Jack had gone to the Boar's Tusk after leaving Christopher, waiting for nightfall with a little ale and some food, and there was barely a man in the place that did not stop by their table to ask Crispin's opinion about what was going to happen or what *should* happen. And Crispin managed to avoid making any declarations one way or the other. For, in all truth, he did not know what was going to happen. In all the precious few details he had heard, Henry had an army and had already captured Richard. There is only one reason to capture a king: to take his crown for yourself.

As far as he knew, Henry hadn't any ambitions in that regard. But times were different. Richard had infuriated the nobles when he illegally took Henry's lands and inheritance, with a fabricated charge to banish him for life. The warrior that Henry was now would never stand for such a thing. Didn't Richard know that? Didn't Richard realize how much more popular Henry was than him? His pride and arrogance stopped him from seeing the facts, as well as his favorites propping him up with praise and distorting the truth of the matter.

God's blood! He didn't want to think of what Henry might do. The last thing he wanted was civil war. But none of these fools, gleefully discussing this scenario or that one, ever took into account the toll it would wreak on London, the lives lost. More than anyone else in those taverns, Crispin *had* waged war in cities and knew what an army could lay to waste; had done it many a time as one of the leading lords of those armies.

But – and his heart lurched at the thought – if Henry could manage to be made king, crowned duly and proper at Westminster, well. Then life could be secure for once in London. Oh, how he prayed for that to be. A proper Plantagenet on the throne again. That *would* be something.

Still, he knew better than to get his hopes up.

He pricked his ears when he thought he heard a tread nearby. He motioned for Jack and Christopher to halt what they were doing and they all listened hard.

There *was* a tread. And another. Silently, he went to investigate. The sounds of footsteps seemed to be from beyond the priory's walls. He hurried to the gate beside the church and remembered that he'd given his lockpicks to Philippa.

There was nothing for it. He jumped at the wall, dug his fingers into the stone caps at the top, and hauled himself over. He dropped a little awkwardly to the ground on the other side, threw himself against the shadowed wall, and waited.

A rustle, and the treads again. There was someone walking but he couldn't yet see anyone . . . Wait. There. The stars illuminated a figure by the cellarium. He crept closer to watch whoever it might be.

They stood silently, unmoving, a cloak covering all their body. Until they moved. They seemed to be stalking toward the dorter. A flash of steel in the moonlight and Crispin recognized a dagger. When the breeze picked up the edge of the cloak and cast it up, he noticed one arm missing.

Crispin rushed forward and leapt. He brought down the struggling Crouch and pinned him to the ground. 'What mischief are you up to, Crouch? A little murder?'

He hissed in quiet tones, 'Get off me, Guest!'

'I think not, you churl.' He wrenched the dagger from Crouch's hand and took it, holding it to his throat. 'Confess! You need not suffer the humiliation under the prioress's eye, nor Father Holbrok.'

'I done naught! Now get off me!' He wrenched his knee up into

Crispin's gut, whooshing the air out of his lungs. Crispin fell to the side and Crouch leapt to his feet. He grabbed the knife that Crispin had dropped and took off with it. Crispin rolled and stood unsteadily. 'Crouch!' he whispered into the darkness. He staggered forward but didn't see any point in pursuing him. He was long gone.

When Crispin turned, he spied someone mincing tentatively near the dorter. Crouch? No, definitely not. The figure kept starting and stopping, as if listening. He could make out their silhouette now. Clearly a nun, or someone wearing a nun's habit, he corrected. He knew he couldn't make assumptions.

He watched the figure as it made its way along the path. Watched it stop, straighten, and look around.

Out of the shadows, another figure flew at the first one and they both went down in a grunting struggle of flailing legs and soft cries.

But when he heard the sound of Philippa's distressed call, he launched himself from the shadows of the wall and pelted toward the struggling figures.

SIXTEEN

His oncoming footsteps aroused the attacker. The shadowed face turned and, in a heartbeat, the person leapt up and fled into the darkness. Crispin skidded, paused, wondering whether to go after the fleeing figure or to help Philippa, when it was decided for him with her gasp.

Philippa seemed to struggle to breathe, and he knew he could not leave her. 'Philippa,' he whispered, dropping to his knees beside her.

He saw her eyes in the starlight, wild and desperate, until they softened upon recognition. 'Oh, Crispin!' She threw herself into his arms and he held her, sinking his face into her shoulder. He stayed that way for a long, satisfying moment, until she pulled back enough to find his face with her hands, and closed her mouth on his in a desperate kiss.

He held her tighter, sinking into the ecstasy of kissing her. All his senses came alive; the rough woolen of her gown, the warm scent of *her*, alive; the feel of her warm body, soft and pliant; the sound of her soft moans as he continued to kiss her, taking his fill when he had ached for it for so long.

Finally, reluctantly, he pulled back and scoured her face, as much of it as he could see in the dim starlight. 'Are you all right?'

'I am now.' Her lips glistened under the stars. He could not help himself and he drew close to taste them again.

'Philippa,' he whispered to her mouth. 'How I burn for you. How will I ever go on without this between us?'

'It is foolish of me to succumb to you now.'

'And foolish of me to make you.' He took one last gentle peck before he softly pushed her back. 'What are you doing out here, Philippa? You should be safe in your bed.' He helped her to her feet.

She brushed down her gown and put a hand to her throat, clearing it softly. 'I heard someone walking out here and I came down to investigate.'

'As you can see, that was unwise.'

'But *I* was following *them*. How'd they get behind me, I'd like to know?'

'Did you see them?'

'Just a gown. I think . . . I think it was a woman. A rather strong one.' She cleared her throat again and touched her neck once more. Crispin pushed her hands away to look. Yes, there was some bruising there. But his hand lingered at the soft skin. His gaze met hers before he dropped his hand away.

'I'd let you touch me,' she said, almost too soft to hear. Yet he heard it.

'You mustn't. I am a very weak man.'

'And I am a weakening woman.'

'I find that hard to believe. Can you . . .' He took a breath. 'Can you describe the assailant further?'

Philippa flicked her gaze away to consider. 'As tall as me, thinner, bony hands, strong.' She shook her head. 'No smells that I can remember. No sounds. But Crispin. I *was* following her. And she suddenly slipped away into the darkness and deliberately got in behind to ensnare *me*.'

'Are you certain it was the same person and not an accomplice? For instance, did you detect, by any chance, if the assailant . . . had only one hand?'

She glared at him, appalled. 'What in God's name . . .' But then she stopped to think. 'In all truth, I cannot say for certain.'

'That is disquieting. But it settles one thing. This is the end of your work here.'

'Crispin!'

'You promised to obey me in this. It's too dangerous. In the morning you must leave. I'd much prefer you leave now.'

She frowned. 'I thought I could be of help.'

'You have been. You investigated the cells and found that ring . . .'

'And I've heard some talk.'

A shutter opened above them and someone stood at the window. 'Is someone there?' they asked.

Crispin put his arm around her and the two of them bent at the waist to scurry along the shadow of the wall to the gate.

'Philippa, do you have my lockpicks?'

She dug into her décolletage and pulled them out.

Crispin stilled. 'I am suddenly envious of those lockpicks,' he muttered.

She quirked a smile.

He set to and easily got through the lock. He opened the gate carefully, trying not to make any noise.

They hurried to the graveyard.

'Mother!' Christopher rasped.

'Hush now, my son.'

'Christopher, you must get your mother home. Now.'

'Why?' He motioned toward the half-uncovered grave.

'What, by the mass, are you doing, Christopher?' Philippa asked, wide-eyed.

Crispin stepped in front of her. 'You and Jack will have to hurry to fill it in. I want you to escort her home.'

Philippa shook her head. 'But Crispin, there are things I need to tell you—'

'God's blood!' he growled. 'Fill in the grave, you two, and then we'll take you to my lodgings. We'll talk there.'

'We're not to uncover no body?' asked Jack, an anxious pall on his face.

'Crispin!' cried Philippa, aghast.

'Not tonight. Hurry up.' He looked about, keeping his ears pricked for the nun from the dorter who had heard them. 'Keep an eye out for Crouch. I was nearly ambushed by him this evening.'

Jack looked up, mouth agape. He swiveled to stare at the darkened cottage.

But no one came nigh, and the grave was quickly covered. Jack made certain it looked as close to how it appeared before they disturbed it, and finally nodded to Crispin. 'Will that do, sir?'

'It will have to. Let us go.'

The four of them made haste out of the graveyard and down the silent streets to the Shambles.

Isabel had awakened with the commotion of their entering the lodgings, and scurried about, rousing the fire in the hearth and providing everyone with a cup of warmed wine.

Christopher knelt by his mother and held her hand. 'I failed. I failed to protect you.' There was a tremor in his voice and Crispin dropped a hand to the boy's shoulder.

'You did not take into account your mother's tendency to get *herself* into trouble.'

He rose and faced Crispin. 'You saved her. You saved her life.' Before Crispin could reply, his arms were suddenly full of Christopher's embrace. 'I shall never forget it,' the boy whispered to him.

Crispin's glance fell on Philippa's and she had the grace to lower hers first.

Patting Christopher as he gently extricated himself, Crispin nodded to them all. 'We are all safe and sound. That is what is important. And now, Philippa, there was something you were going to tell me?'

She set her cup aside. 'There is talk amongst the nuns of Dame Audrey having close friendships with Marion and Katherine, the two dead girls. I thought that something could be made of that.'

'Yes, we have heard of these rumors.' Crispin crossed his arms, and tapped his lip with a finger.

'Some of the nuns seem to me to have been quite envious of their close relationship. It was talked of with belittling, but I know jealousy when I see it.'

'It is the monastic rule that there be no close relationships,' said Crispin. 'But being forced to follow a certain set of rules can make some individuals crave the breaking of them all the more, and some individuals adhere to them more strictly, with the self-righteousness of the truly envious. Did the prioress seem to know of this relationship?'

'Oh, aye,' she said, nodding. 'And she did her best to discourage it.'

'Sounds like motive for murder to me,' said Jack.

Crispin raised a brow. 'I rather think Father Holbrok had a better motive.' And he quickly related the tale.

Jack whistled. 'Blind me. You can't trust no one, can you?' He shook his head and crossed himself. 'The prioress is a strict rule-follower. She wasn't impressed with me doing my job to question her. There could be fire buried under all them woolens.'

'Which reminds me,' said Philippa, rising and spreading out her skirts, 'this is my shift. Have you a cloak I can borrow, Madam Tucker? I can't go about London in my shift, even for the sake of the notorious Tracker.'

Before Isabel could answer, Crispin said, 'You can borrow my cloak, Philippa.'

She smiled. 'Then I will take it with much thanks. Come, Christopher. We must let these good people get to bed.'

'Will you . . . shall I escort you . . .'

'I can protect my mother from the Watch, Crispin,' said Christopher, taking Crispin's cloak from the peg by the door and draping it over his mother's shoulders.

'Erm . . . if I may have a moment with your mother first,' said Crispin.

Christopher nodded as Crispin opened the door. He and Philippa stepped out into a shaded recess on the street. Crispin had made sure the door was closed behind him.

Now that he had her alone, he didn't quite know what to say. He took her hands in his and bowed his head. 'Philippa . . .'

'I know, Crispin. We will not speak of it again. But blind me! We seem to keep doing things and not speaking about them.'

'We have to not do them in the first place.' He felt miserable. He didn't want to let her go. He wanted to lift her into his arms and march her up to his bedchamber. But that would be the very height of foolishness. He cleared his throat. 'That wasn't all I wanted to say. Quite the opposite.' He had promised Clarence that they had not sinned against him. But he was weakening. He had yearned for this woman for so long . . . He forced his breathing to a slower pace. 'We should keep our meetings brief.'

Her face looked miserable too. 'Yes,' she conceded. 'Brief.'

He was being drawn into her eyes again, and before he realized it, he had enclosed her in his arms and was kissing her once more.

He savored it for as long as he could before they both broke away. Then he only held her, eyes closed. Some things were not meant to be, he decided. He held her for many more moments, somehow sensing this would be the last time.

Finally, he drew back, touched her chin to lift her face, and bestowed a last, gentle kiss. His hand trailed down her arm until he clutched her hand, and then only their fingers touched before they fell away.

He opened the door. 'Christopher, you must take her now. I shall see you tomorrow night to get back to the grave-digging.'

Isabel shivered in the doorway. 'Do you have to, Master Crispin? That's not a fit thing for a Christian to be doing.'

'Neither is murder, Isabel. I'm afraid it is necessary. You must return to the priory tomorrow morning, Christopher, as if all is well. I will tell the prioress of your mother's untimely departure. And keep an eye out for Crouch. I fear he is dangerous.'

'Is he our murderer?' the boy asked.

'He might be. Don't be alone with him. As a matter of fact, if you do see him, send for me.'

Christopher nodded his good nights, and ushered his mother down the lane.

Crispin hoped she would look back . . . but she didn't.

'Still?' said Jack. 'We've still got to dig her up?'

Crispin closed the night away behind the door, closed Philippa away. 'Yes. Get a good night's sleep. We'll be up late again.'

Crispin did not relish telling the prioress about the doings last night. He told himself a sin of omission was still a sin, but he'd rather tell the prioress what he found out about Dame Audrey *after* her exhumation.

The prioress wasn't free to speak to him until well after Terce, but he awaited her in her sparse lodgings and, when she arrived, she greeted him with a frown.

'I see we are absent your false nun this morning,' she said without ceremony.

'She was attacked last night.'

He watched the prioress's face for reaction, and couldn't decide whether he was disappointed or not at her complacent expression.

'Is she well?' was all she asked.

'She is. But I spirited her away last night to her home. Her son still works here as a laborer to keep an eye on other things. Crouch is my chief suspect at the moment. Has anyone seen him today?'

'I don't know. You'd best ask—'

'The other nuns. Yes, I surmised that.' Crispin folded his hands before him. 'Is there anything you care to add to the proceedings?'

'Such as?'

'Do you know who attacked her? Which two people might be working together to kill in your priory, Lady Prioress?'

There was only the slight narrowing of her eyes. 'I thought you said Crouch . . .'

'I suspect him, yes. But there might be others last night who attacked Madam Walcote. Someone was lying in wait. It could have been Crouch alone . . . but I suspect not.'

'I see. There was the merest of accusations in your statement, Master Guest.'

Crispin said nothing, only waited.

'If I knew the answer to that, I would scarce have needed to hire you . . . which is adding up to at least one shilling six pence.'

'She was attacked, Lady Prioress. If I had not been there, she might have been killed. And since she is a dear friend of mine, I would not have taken kindly to that.'

'Then it seems you had better hurry along your investigations, Master Guest.'

There was no surrender in her eyes, no betrayal of anything in the upward tilt of her chin. Crispin recognized a wall when he saw one. He didn't even bother bowing to her as he left.

There was little to do but wait for nightfall.

They went to the Boar's Tusk for a bit of food and refreshment. It didn't take long for the usual patrons to step up to Crispin – when they usually knew enough to leave him on his own – to ask his thoughts on Henry Lancaster.

'My master has naught more to say,' said Jack, hand on his dagger. 'Leave the man to eat in peace.'

Reluctantly, they edged away and sat in their places but keeping an eye on him.

He didn't want to think about Henry and what might be transpiring. Why, oh why had Prince Edward of Woodstock died? He would have been a proper king, instead of leaving the country in the hands of his ten-year-old son, prone to the wishes of favorites and flatterers.

Well . . . they'd all know anon, when Henry finally made it to London.

He'd barely lifted his cup of ale to his lips when another shadow fell across his table. He was about to admonish the miscreant, but when he looked up, it was the face of his former squire.

'Master Crispin,' he said with a bow, and spared Jack a glance. 'May I join you?'

'Of course, Edward. Please. Jack, fetch another cup from Gilbert.'

'Aye, sir,' he seemed to say grudgingly. He rose, keeping his eye on Edward all the way to the back of the tavern.

'I don't think he likes me,' said his squire.

'Oh, it's just that Jack is jealous of his place with me. He's been my servant for fifteen years . . . since he was eleven years old. He's naturally protective of me.'

'What has he to fear from me? I don't need to squire for anyone anymore.'

Crispin said nothing. He drank, and rested his arms on the table. 'Perhaps he wonders – as do I – why you are seeking me out now, after all these years.'

'It was mere happenstance that we met again. And . . . well. I've wanted to know that you've been alive and well.'

'Surely whilst at court you had ample opportunity to hear of my tidings.'

Edward lowered his face. 'It's funny. Even after all these years and all my achievements, I still feared to ask about you.' He rubbed the back of his neck as he chuckled uncomfortably. 'And you were scarce spoke of at court these last twenty years. But I did think about you, prayed for you.'

Even after all Crispin had done *for* Richard recently, he supposed it was to be expected that no one spoke of him. 'That makes no matter,' he said, drinking again.

Jack returned and placed the cup sharply before Edward, paused, and grabbed the jug to pour in some ale. He slid back to his stool to sit beside Crispin, who wanted so much to reassure the man. But he reckoned Jack had to learn to deal with his feelings on his own, or he never would do.

'This business of tracking. I have since asked about it and you seem to have a barrel-full of tales. You're like a legend, Master Guest. A ghost. To have accomplished so much, to have solved so many crimes, making the sheriffs look like fools, seems to be an unnatural feat.'

'The latter was never my intention. But, in many cases, it was unavoidable.'

Edward laughed. He raised his cup to Crispin and drank. He leaned on the table toward Jack. 'Do you know, Tucker, that your master is exactly the same as he was when I waited on him? The same jests and pranks. And by God, he looks the same too.'

'I find that hard to believe,' said Crispin.

'Well . . .' Edward looked at him with a tilt to his head. 'Perhaps a little underfed. And a bit grayer.'

'Master Crispin looks just fine!' Jack growled, sitting straighter. He was taller than Edward Grafton, and it seemed to Crispin that Jack might have felt a certain satisfaction about that.

'I meant no offense, Tucker. He is still the great man he always was in my eyes.'

Crispin felt his cheeks warm. 'There's no need for all that. I suppose I should be glad that no one speaks of me in the halls of the king.'

Edward edged closer. 'And what *of* the king?' he said quietly. 'The rumors I hear . . .'

Jack nearly jumped from his seat. 'Master Crispin don't want to talk about all that!'

'Jack,' said Crispin mildly, urging him back to his stool. His apprentice slowly sat. 'Sir Edward has a reason to know. He is a knight in the king's household. But I am afraid I know as little as the messengers that come to town. I do not know.'

'You were close to Henry Hereford once.'

'He doesn't send me private missives. I am still dangerous to know. And I am in the dark, Edward.'

'I see.' He took up his cup and drank a long draught. He licked his lips and slid his gaze toward Jack. 'Master Tucker, will you do me the service of leaving us for a time? I wish to speak with your master in private.'

Jack stared desperately at Crispin. But there was nothing Crispin could do to appease the man. 'Jack, for only a few moments. Why don't you see to the door? Make sure all is well.'

'Make sure all is well?' He pointedly glared at Edward. 'Aye. I'll . . . I'll make certain "all is well".'

He pushed himself from his seat, took up his cup, downed it, and slammed it back to the table. Stomping toward the door, Crispin watched him with a frown.

Edward chuckled softly. 'I can't say I blame the man. I'm certain I was that protective of you once.'

'I remember as much.'

Edward slid the jug across the table and refilled his cup and then filled Crispin's. 'I . . . I wanted to talk to you of Elena Forthey. I . . . understand that you . . . know of her.'

'She is well. Recovering.'

'Recovering? From what?'

'From . . . what you were so angry about.'

'Oh. That.' He waved his hand. 'I suppose that is now past.'

'It was my impression that she was very ill from the potion.'

Edward's eyes burned with anger for only a moment and then cleared. He shrugged, though it was a mere gesture. He took up his cup. 'I suppose it's only what she deserves.'

'You have a wife, Edward.'

'I don't recall you being particularly celibate.'

'I wasn't married.'

'You were betrothed.'

'To a murderer as it turns out.'

Edward paused with his cup halfway to his mouth and slowly set it down. 'I had heard that.'

'You see? You *have* heard about me, then.'

He had the grace to look abashed. 'Yes. And yet . . . it doesn't give you leave to remind me of my wife.'

'You asked about Elena. I reckoned the subject was completely open to discussion.'

He frowned, clutching his cup. 'It isn't.'

'Then what do you want from me? Absolution. You're in the

wrong church.' He gestured to the low-beamed ceiling of the tavern.

'No. I just wanted to know what happened.'

'She aborted. And now you are free to carry on with others.'

'You don't approve.'

Crispin stared into the foliate swirls of foam on the top of his ale. 'It's not my business.' He drank.

'No, it isn't.'

'Then don't ask leading questions.'

'You're a lot sourer than you used to be. Not that you weren't stiff and clipped in those days.'

'I am who I am.'

'Rather a bit entrenched on that moral high ground . . . for a traitor.'

Crispin stopped and slowly raised his eyes.

Edward gasped. 'I . . . I didn't mean to say that. I apologize.'

Crispin's brows drew down and he stared again into his cup before he drank it, foam and all. 'No need to apologize. You're a knight. A lord. Your opinion is freer than mine. If you wish to think of me as a traitor, then that is your prerogative.'

'But I never meant to say—'

'*Our characters are a result of our conduct.* You saw me at my worst, so of course it is foremost in your mind. You speak the truth though you loathe to.' He shrugged, though he didn't feel it. 'I was a traitor in deed and in actuality. And I have paid for it a thousand times. It might have been kinder to simply execute me. Though . . . the manner of the execution would certainly have been worse.'

'I never wanted that to happen to you!' he rasped.

'No? Even after *you* were treated so cruelly for being my associate? You must have felt your life was over too. But . . . I am pleased that you survived it and prevailed. I hold no ill will toward you for thinking of me as a traitor, for it is the truth.'

Edward's eyes were full of tears though he did not shed them. He wiped them instead.

'We've strayed from the subject. It was about your mistress.'

Once wiped, Edward's eyes seemed to forget the emotion of moments ago. 'I just wanted to know if she'd gone through with it.'

'Demoiselle Forthey has bid you farewell, I think. Leave her be, Edward.'

'The woman disobeyed me, and after all the money I'd spent on her.'

'Let me put it this way.' He set his cup aside and squared with Edward. 'I would be displeased if I discovered that someone had hurt Demoiselle Forthey, either in rumor or in her person. Do you understand me?'

Shocked into immobility for only a moment, Edward's eyes narrowed and he leaned back in his chair. 'Are you threatening me?'

Crispin smiled the way he used to; the way he did to those who hoped to best him. 'Yes.'

Edward kicked the chair back and jerked to his feet. 'I am a knight of the court, Master Guest. And a lord. Don't threaten me.'

'Sit down, Edward.'

'You will not threaten me.'

'If you don't sit down,' he said in low tones, 'I will show you I am in the same fighting fettle as I always was, and I will humiliate you in this room full of people. Now either sit down . . . or get out.'

Edward slammed his cup to the table, pivoted, and stalked to the door.

Crispin sighed. It seemed his lot to cultivate underlings with tempers.

Jack hurried back to the table, staring now and again toward the door. 'What did you say to him, sir?'

'The truth. Some men won't embrace it.' Would Edward Grafton have turned out like that if they had stayed together? he wondered. Instead, he glanced at his apprentice and gestured toward the jug and the stool that Jack had left. 'There is still ale in the jug, Tucker, and your seat grows cold. Stay awhile.'

'But sir . . .'

'Don't worry about him. Life moves along. And for the record, I am glad *you* are my apprentice. I don't think you would ever change as he has.'

'Never, sir!'

Yet so, too, did Edward think once, he mused. He drank his ale in silence.

Much later, Crispin and Jack were back in the graveyard, back under the velvet sky with its pinpricks of stars, waiting for Christopher to arrive. Crouch was still missing. Perhaps he lay hidden in London somewhere. He had asked Father Holbrok earlier, but the man was stubbornly silent on the subject.

Christopher finally slipped through the darkness of the lychgate. When he reached them, he handed Crispin his cloak. 'My mother thanks you,' he said. Since the night had a bit of a chill, Crispin was grateful to don it. And, with a sniff of the wool, he realized it smelled like her. That was damnable. But he could not help but press the edge of it to his nose and inhale.

Christopher commenced digging again with Jack. There was no conversation to spill into the night. It was like a recurring dream, doing the same thing again to little avail. But Crispin shook the notion loose. There was a reason to see what had happened to Dame Audrey. It would be dreadful opening her coffin after a week of death and decay. But there might be something to indicate that she died from other than what the prioress said. Oh yes, he certainly could have asked the prioress for permission, but Crispin would much rather ask for forgiveness.

Lulled by the steady movement of spades in dirt, Crispin reckoned he might have dozed off until awakened by Jack's hissed, 'Sir!'

Jack tapped his spade on a hard surface again within the grave. Crispin hurried over and lifted the lantern.

'The coffin,' said Christopher, whey-faced.

Crispin grabbed the coils of ropes they'd brought and lowered one end into the grave. Christopher worked, cutting in below the coffin, and fed the rope through. When they had both rope ends draped on either side of the grave, they climbed out and took up position on either side.

'We could have used one more person for this,' said Jack, juggling two ropes.

'We should have asked my mother,' said Christopher.

'Out of the question,' grunted Crispin.

'How heavy are corpses anyway?' said Christopher, wiping the sweat from his brow with his sleeve and leaving a streak of dirt there in its place.

They managed to bring up the coffin with difficulty, and secured it next to the open grave. Crispin knelt beside it, pulled out his knife, and worked on prying open the lid, which turned out to be easier than he thought.

He pulled off the coffin's lid and set it aside.

'Sir,' said Jack, grimacing as he looked inside at the body wrapped in linen. 'How are you going to examine a corpse that's been dead a sennight and more?'

'I will look for obvious wounds, I suppose.'

They all seemed to merely stand there, the weak lantern throwing pale light on the corpse that seemed to be tied with ropes.

'Why do you suppose she was buried like that, sir?' asked Jack. 'All tied up as she is.'

'Perhaps it is the custom at this priory. Though I only recall such a burial technique from those buried at sea. Trussed up.' He stood, looking it over. 'Jack. Is there anything you notice about this corpse? Anything different?'

He shrugged. 'I don't know, Master Crispin. All I know is that I'd like this done and over with.'

Christopher peered close, bending over. 'I've never seen a corpse fresh from the ground. How . . . how decomposed is it likely to be? I mean . . . will there be . . . fluids? Worms?'

'Yes,' said Crispin. 'But Jack, you haven't answered my question.'

'I don't know, sir,' he said impatiently.

'You should be observing, Apprentice Tucker. Think, man. Think about it. We've just dug up a week-old corpse.'

'How well I know it!' He looked at the dirt and mud he was caked in and, no doubt for his expression, assumed some of that was not just mud. But his grimace fell away and he stared at the linen-wrapped body, flaring his nostrils. 'Begging your pardon, Master Crispin, but shouldn't she . . . well . . . stink?'

Crispin glanced at Christopher's widened eyes and saw him flare his nostrils too. 'That's right. Crispin . . . why does she not . . . smell? Is this a sign of holiness?'

'She *was* a holy sister,' said Jack.

'I don't think holiness had anything to do with it.' He crouched and reached into the coffin. Jack made a sound of distress as Crispin grabbed the linen draped over the body's face and tore the damp material away.

Jack and Christopher drew back with a gasp.

'Blessed *Jesu* and all His saints! What *is* that, Crispin?' said Christopher.

The face was covered with . . . well. Hay, he supposed. Why would such a thing . . .?

Crispin used both hands and tore through the hay, certain – praying at this juncture – that he would *not* find a face, decomposed or otherwise. He continued to tear apart the 'corpse', but all it appeared to be was hay and rocks tied with linen in the shape of a body.

Crispin sat back, dusting off his hands. 'There is no corpse,' he said. 'And I'll wager . . . there never was.'

SEVENTEEN

'Someone stole it?' cried Christopher before Jack shushed him. 'Master Crispin means that there never was no corpse,' whispered Jack. 'That's right, isn't it, Master Crispin?'

'Yes, Jack, you are correct. I don't believe there was ever a corpse in the first place.'

'But you thought she was murdered. Then . . . where is she?' asked Christopher, still staring at the strange apparition. 'Did they bury her somewhere else?'

'You don't understand,' said Crispin. 'Dame Audrey . . . is *not* dead.'

'But . . . Crispin . . .' said Christopher.

'Is Elena Forthey still in the infirmary?'

'As far as I know,' said Jack.

'You two bury this again. I'm going to talk to her.'

Christopher jerked forward. 'Wait, Crispin! You can't leave us here with all this without explanation.'

'Christopher, that's exactly what I am after. An explanation. If I don't alarm Elena Forthey and awaken the whole priory, I'll be back directly.'

Crispin hurried away, dusting his hands off on his cote-hardie, trying to relieve himself of grave dirt. His eyes traveled up that wall and he thanked God that he'd got his lockpicks back from Philippa.

He picked the lock even faster this time, and pushed the gate open slowly, wincing with its hinges' soft whine. He closed it carefully so it wouldn't slam shut with a breeze, and crept back toward the dorter through the shadows.

Elena Forthey had been under the infirmary's window before. Might she still be there?

The night was mild. He reached the dorter and searched over its plastered surface at all the shutters above and below. Perhaps the window wasn't latched . . . He pulled the shutter open and hauled himself up to the sill. His eyes adjusted and he saw that she was there below him. Grabbing hold of the sill, he pulled himself the rest of the way and climbed nimbly to the other side. Approaching her cot, he whispered to her, 'Demoiselle. Demoiselle Forthey!'

She opened her eyes, focused them on Crispin, and opened her mouth to scream. He clamped a hand over her mouth. 'It's Crispin Guest. For God's sake, do not scream.'

Her breath gusted over his fingers. Her eyes calmed and Crispin slowly pulled his hand away. 'Forgive me.'

'Master Guest,' she gasped. 'What are you doing here?' She rose on her elbows, looking about. 'At this hour?'

'Er . . . how are you faring? You seemed in great pain when you arrived yesterday.'

'I . . . I was. But . . . Dame Petronella ministered to me and I am much better. I will be leaving in the morn.'

'Oh. That's good. I am glad.'

'Yes. So am I. Is . . . that what you came in the dark of night to ask me?'

'Well . . . no.' And now who was being hasty? He admonished Jack frequently that he jumped too quickly to act. 'The fact of the matter is I need to ask you a question.'

'It couldn't wait till morning?'

Could it? He thought of the straw dummy packed into Dame Audrey's coffin and shook his head. 'No, it cannot. Demoiselle, you told me when I first met you that Dame Audrey being dead wasn't possible. Why?'

She stared at him for several heartbeats. 'A strange question.'

Crispin shrugged, feeling a bit foolish. 'And yet an important one. Why did you think it was impossible?'

'Because I saw her. I thought I did. In town.'

'Here in London?'

'Yes. She wasn't dressed as a nun but I saw her. I'm sure of it. Except . . . that you said she'd been dead more than a sennight.'

'Nevertheless, can you be absolutely certain you saw her?'

'But . . . if she was dead . . .'

'If you had not known, would you swear it was her?'

'Yes. Or her sister, if she'd had one.'

'And when was this that you saw her?'

'No more than a few days ago. Five days, maybe.'

'And where did you see her?'

She thought a moment. 'Near Old Dean, I think. Not too far from the priory.'

'Thank you, demoiselle. That is all I wanted to know.'

'Wait, Master Guest.'

Crispin turned at the window. She looked very pale but it might have only been the starlight.

'Is it true that . . . that Edward Grafton was once your squire?'

He shuffled his feet, thinking of his recent encounter with Edward. 'Yes. It is true.'

'He came to the priory yesterday. He knew why I was here. He was terribly upset. I daresay, you must have surmised why I came here to the apothecary.'

He nodded. 'I have.'

'Edward doesn't love me. I know he has another mistress. He could easily have abandoned me. I didn't feel I had a choice.'

'I make no judgments, demoiselle.'

'But you knew him. Knew him well, though it was long ago. Should I . . . should I have trusted him?'

Crispin frowned. What could he tell this woman? Should he lie? No. Lying was not his way. 'When I knew him so long ago, I could trust him. With my very life. But . . . time changes a man. He was vilified unfairly because of me. That can change a man too. I do not know Edward Grafton today. He could be the same man I knew. Or he might not be.'

'I see *you* are loyal. Even after all that has happened to you, you will not malign him. You are a strange man. I know you carried me here to save my life. I thank you for that.'

He bowed. 'If . . . if he proves troublesome to you, demoiselle, please contact me and I will see to it that it stops.'

She looked down at the blankets that she smoothed absently with her hand. 'I think . . . I wish it had been you in his stead. You would have been an honorable man.'

He said nothing to that. Bowing again, he finally turned to the window, climbed up it, and slipped out.

Walking carefully across the gravel path, he got to the wall again and quietly opened the gate. He closed it just as cautiously behind him, and locked it, before trotting back to the graveyard.

Jack and Christopher were just smoothing out the mound of dirt when he arrived. 'And so, gentlemen, we have much to discuss. Christopher, why don't you come to my lodgings and have a cup of wine?'

Christopher glanced back toward Crouch's dark cottage and jerked his head with a nod.

Together, the three skirted the Watch and made it to the Shambles unmolested.

Christopher stared into the fire. They still had need to be quiet, lest they awaken Isabel or any of the children. 'So this Dame Audrey was never dead,' he said, barely above a whisper.

'No,' said Crispin, nodding his thanks to Jack as he filled Crispin's cup again.

'Then this fever was concocted,' Christopher went on. 'And the two sisters who cared for her . . .'

'Likely helped her in her scheme. They were all friends, weren't they, those three. Dame Audrey had planned carefully. She first had Marion seduce poor Father Holbrok, and then Audrey extorted him for money. She stole some of the more expensive relics to sell. It was clear she planned to escape the priory and this time had help. She devised this business of a fever and her accomplices helped her to appear dead, create the false corpse, and bury it.'

Christopher drank a little wine and turned his face toward Crispin. 'But then they were murdered.'

'Aye,' said Jack, the plot dawning on his face. 'And Dame Audrey killed them to keep the secret.'

'Yes, I believe so. In that most foul of ways.'

'But why in that way, sir? Using them deadly sins?'

'Vindictiveness? A deep cruelty? Who can say?'

'Still, if she was free of the priory,' Jack offered, 'why did she return to kill Dame Mildred?'

'That's a good question. Was she yet another accomplice?'

Jack shook his head with a frown. 'That's an awful lot of people to keep a secret.'

'It is. I'll have to think on it.'

'Then why did she attack my mother?' Christopher clenched his hand and scowled. 'Or . . . God's blood! Was that Crouch or not?'

'When I think of the mechanics of it, I have eliminated Crouch from the equation. But, as it happened, your mother was in the wrong place at the wrong time. Though, now I wonder: are there two doing these murders? Madam Walcote said she had been following someone, and either they were stealthy enough to run around the building to come up behind her in order to attack, or there was a second there waiting to ambush her.'

'Then there *were* more accomplices,' said Jack. 'And Crouch? How does he fit into it? I don't see Dame Audrey befriending him.'

'No, because he was certainly not enamored of her.'

'But Crispin,' said Christopher, 'why wouldn't the accomplice, or any others that there might be, say something to the prioress? They must be terrified that they will be next.'

Crispin sat back, his wine cup drooping in his hand. 'Perhaps they have something to gain.'

'That's awful!' said Jack a bit too loudly. He shushed himself. 'I mean,' he began, much more quietly, as he cocked an eye upstairs, 'they were all willing to participate in so many murders for gain? What sort of priory is that?'

'We have much to think about.' Crispin rose, listening to his bones crack and pop as he stretched. 'It is late. We must all go to our beds. Christopher, you can stay here, if you wish. We don't have much in the way of bedding, but a fur or two before the fire might be comfortable.'

'Thank you. I will stay.'

'Then I will say good night.'

Jack saw to Christopher's needs as Crispin trudged up the stairs and found his room cool. It was a relief from the heat and humidity of the day. He had thought he was tired enough to simply sleep, but there were too many thoughts spinning in his mind: of Dame Audrey and her audacious scheme; always of Philippa; and worry over what Henry was doing.

But at some point, he must have dropped off, for the next thing he knew there was sunlight basking the room through the open shutters and Jack was stoking the fire in his chamber.

He sat up and rubbed the sleep from his eyes.

'Good morn, sir,' said Jack, handing him some warmed wine.

'Thank you, Jack.'

'I was thinking about Dame Mildred last night, sir.'

'Were you?'

'Aye. And I don't think she was part of Dame Audrey's conspiracy.'

He blew on the wine before he drank. 'And why not?'

'I don't know, sir. It was so long after the others. If she were part of the conspiracy, she might have reckoned what was going on and told someone to save herself long ago.'

Crispin nodded, drinking the last of the wine and handing Jack the cup. 'That makes sense.'

Jack poured hot water from a kettle to a basin and set it next to Crispin's razor, which he picked up and stropped against a leather strap. 'So it was a whole sennight and more later. What would make Dame Audrey return to dispatch Dame Mildred? Did Dame Mildred come upon her whilst she was stealing something? We didn't see any evidence of that. And nothing more was missing from the reliquary. Dame Audrey got the relics she came for before she left.'

'I never checked the alms box.'

'But I did. Naught was amiss.' Jack made room for Crispin to sit in his chair by the fire. He soaped up his master's face and neck.

'Good work, Jack.'

'Thank you, sir. Now.' He carefully slid the razor up the soapy neck and flicked the residue into the fire that spat its reply. 'If not to steal, what was she about? Maybe she was interrupted and had intended to steal. Remember when Dame Margaret screamed and nearly brought the rafters down? She said she saw a ghost. The ghost of a nun. She must have seen Dame Audrey still wearing her habit.'

Crispin waited for the blade at his cheek to do its work before he replied, 'She said as much. That she thought it was Dame Audrey. And that would account for her going about the priory undetected. Just another nun in a sea of nuns.'

'Aye. It's a bit . . . unnerving, isn't it?'

'Very. Hurry it, Jack. We must get back there.'

Jack did his shaving slowly and carefully, pushing at the tip of Crispin's nose with his finger to control the direction he wanted him to tilt his head. 'Then why do you suppose Dame Audrey killed Dame Mildred and was present to attack Madam Walcote? What more does she want?'

'Now *that* is a good question. She was free. She wasn't dead, her accomplices made certain that everyone thought she was, and she had money from Father Holbrok. In all appearances she could have gone anywhere she wanted to. So I suppose that the big question is why. Why did she come back? Why possibly expose herself in order to murder again? And if Philippa had not seen her, she most assuredly would have killed another of the nuns. But was she alone?'

'We'll have to ask about her history. If she still has family, perhaps I should go and talk to them.'

'That's good thinking, Jack. The first thing to do is go to the prioress and have it out with her.'

'Better you than me. And it's best it *is* you this time,' he said before he applied a hot cloth to Crispin's face.

EIGHTEEN

Crispin and Jack stood outside the prioress's lodgings, waiting for her to allow them in.

'What do you think she'll say, sir?'

'I haven't the least idea. I'm curious to see if she will lie.'

Jack turned to him with opened mouth when a nun, Dame Emelyn, appeared at the door to escort them inside.

But before she could, Crispin pulled her aside. She didn't much like that, if her expression was anything to go by.

'What is this, Master Guest?'

'When I first questioned you, Dame, I had the sense that you wanted to tell me something about the murders.'

She let out an exasperated breath. 'It was foolishness. It is nothing.'

'I beg that you allow me to decide that, Dame.'

She clutched her hands together, eyes flitting here and there in the corridor. 'The thing of it is . . . the murders came from such anger. It . . . it made me think . . . of Dame Audrey. But as you see, it can't be her.'

'Because she's dead.'

'Yes.'

Crispin rubbed his newly shaved chin. 'Have you seen the priory ghost of late, Dame?'

'The ghost? Why would you ask such a thing?'

'I merely wondered.'

'Well . . . *I've* never seen it before. But . . . but . . . it couldn't have been that.'

'You *did* see it? And was it a nun? Even a nun you would have recognized?'

Her eyes widened. 'It was. I . . . I did see it. It looked like Dame Audrey.' She whispered the last.

Crispin exchanged a brief look with Jack. 'Very well, Dame. You may take me to the prioress now.'

In silence, they walked under an arched doorway and to a small room the prioress used as an office. It had a prie-dieu in one corner under a window, a stand for a prayer book, a chandler full of unlit candles, a few chairs by the hearth, and a table behind which she had situated herself with what looked like accounting scrolls. There was nothing else. Nothing of any personal nature. No cat, no dog, no tapestry or painted mural. Only a solitary crucifix on the wall nearest the prie-dieu.

Dame Emelyn, eyeing Crispin, left them, closing the door after her.

Prioress Drueta worked at her scrolls for some time, never looking up from them until she had dotted the last 'i'. With a careworn sigh, she finally lifted her face and skewered them both with a glare.

'Have you found our murderer, Master Guest?' She set the quill aside and covered her pot of ink. 'For if you have not, you should also be looking for a grave robber. One of the graves in our church-yard has been disturbed.'

'I have come to talk to you about that very thing, Lady Prioress.'

She folded her ink-stained hands one over the other and settled in.

'It was I who disturbed the grave of Dame Audrey,' Crispin told her.

Her wrath was swift. She jolted up from her chair and postured over the desk. 'Master Guest! Such desecration! And you never bothered to seek permission? Never asked me, never asked the bishop . . .'

'I could have waited, I suppose, but I feared that the answer might have been "no", and I couldn't have that.'

With mouth agape she sank back into her chair. 'The audacity. The utter lack of decorum.'

'That is what you are paying for, my lady. Now. Do you wish to hear my conclusion or not?'

She seemed to consider it. Would she have the gall to send him on his way without hearing what he had to say? It was entirely possible. Of course, Crispin would never let it lie and *someone* would have to dig deeper. Possibly the Bishop of London, Robert Braybrooke. Not that he was particularly enamored of Crispin . . .

'Madam?' he urged.

She frowned and steadied her gaze on him. 'Very well, Master Guest. As you say, this is what I am paying for.'

'I ordered her disinterred because I had become certain she was the first victim of this murderer. But upon opening the coffin, we discovered that the body was a dummy, made of straw and rocks. There was no body of Dame Audrey at all.'

Her frown vanished and in its place was a look of shock. 'No. That's impossible. We buried her. I was there.'

'But you did not prepare the body for burial, Lady Prioress. And that was when the switch was made. Dame Audrey's accomplices – Dame Marion and Dame Katherine, both her close and trusted friends – helped her with this deceit. Once buried, no one would know. And once Dame Marion and Dame Katherine were murdered, there would be no one left who knew the truth.'

'They were murdered for that?'

'Unquestionably.'

'But then . . .'

He waited for the gears to turn, for her to come to the same conclusion.

'But then, that would mean that Dame Audrey was . . . was . . .'

'The killer, yes.'

'Holy Mother Mary,' she muttered, holding a trembling hand to her lips. Was it a performance? Crispin watched her carefully. His instincts were that it was not. But he'd been wrong before.

'We believe that Dame Audrey – after obtaining extortion money from Father Holbrok and stealing the relics . . . and selling them . . .' the prioress made a sound of surprise, '. . . and having acquired enough funds to flee this place,' Crispin went on, 'and, having shared her tale with her closest friends here, they all devised her escape by forging her death. Once effectively "dead", she was free to go about her business. But she couldn't leave those loose ends. So she had to kill both of them. Why she chose so alarming a manner of their death . . . well. Only the lady can answer that.'

'Still . . . why kill poor Dame Mildred?'

'And why try to kill Madam Walcote the other night?'

The prioress nodded.

'Can you tell us about the time Dame Audrey escaped before and in what manner she found herself at this priory to begin with?'

The prioress couldn't seem to keep her seat but restlessly paced behind her chair. 'I am very troubled by these tidings, Master Guest. Very troubled.' She moved back and forth, back and forth, rubbing her hands together. She said nothing for a long time until she stopped before her prie-dieu. She touched the top spindle that braced the prayer-book rest and rubbed her fingers on it – as she must have done many a time, for that particular spindle was not only polished to a sheen, but its stain was nearly rubbed away.

'Audrey had not wanted to come here,' she said, her voice now mastered to the clipped and even tone she had employed since Crispin had met her some days ago. 'She was brought by her parents eight years past. She was in love with a boy they did not approve of. It was intimated that she and the boy had acted . . . improperly. Their fear – and rightly so – was that they would never now find a suitable husband for her, and so it was decided to use her dowry to force her to become a sister. She resisted. Strongly. And escaped almost immediately.'

'What happened?'

'She was discovered in London by friends of the priory and brought back. She was punished; locked away on scant rations of bread and water.'

'To teach her the love of Christ,' said Crispin, face neutral.

Prioress Drueta narrowed her eyes. 'You are cynical, Master

Guest. I know you. You, who seem to be entrusted with relic after relic but is skeptical of them. It seems you can't accept a message when it is given to you full in the face.'

That seemed to pierce him true. For indeed, he was not inclined to believe in the power of the many relics that had crossed his path. Too many greedy men stood in the way of them or to gain from them that he couldn't imagine they could remain holy through the sins of others. Still, in his pouch that he kept at his side lay a thorn from the Crown of Thorns. He well remembered the strange vigor he acquired when he had pricked his finger on it. He feared to experiment a second time.

'Surely one should come to holy orders with the love of God in their hearts, not have it forced down their throats.'

'I have served as a holy sister for well over forty years, Master Guest, and I have seen it all. I have seen willfulness turn to respect and yes, to the love of God. Audrey was a willful *girl* when she came to these gates. Selfish, obstinate, malicious. She changed after a time. I have seen this change often, Master Guest. A girl who becomes a woman in a monastery learns temperance, the meaning of work, the self-satisfaction in the helping of others. And she had a talent for the herbs. She took to it, and the solitary nature of her artistry of the apothecary. I do not know whether she herself was with child when she came to St Frideswide, but she learned her art with herbs quickly and perhaps made her own potions to rid herself of that pregnancy. Soon, she excelled in that and was known throughout London for the help she gave to other desperate women. The apothecary fees don't amount to the same we receive from our baking and laundry, but they are substantial enough on their own.'

'I would have thought that she would have gladly borne her lover's child.'

'She would not have been allowed to keep it here. This is a monastery. There is no room for children.'

Nor heart. 'But as you say,' he said aloud, 'she was here eight years. What would have caused her to suddenly kill those who had been close to her?'

She looked up at the crucifix as she must have done each day of her long years here. 'I don't know.'

'Perhaps I need to talk to the other nuns here about that.'

'Yes, perhaps you should. Though it is true that I tried hard to discourage her friendships, she had a way about her that seemed to call out to others, like a pied piper. They were attracted to her. After many punishments to stop the practice, I had to give up. For she would persist in these attachments. Now I see that it is I who will be punished for allowing it, for allowing those dreadful deaths.'

Crispin flicked a glance at Jack.

'Master Guest,' she continued, 'you say that Dame Audrey extorted money from Father Holbrok. Under what circumstances did this happen?'

'Ah. Well . . .'

'You are reluctant to say.' She strode purposely to her door, opened it, and called out to any assistant nearby. It was Emelyn again. 'Go fetch Father Holbrok.'

'My Lady Prioress . . .' said Crispin.

'You brought it up, Master Guest. I must see it through.'

He made a feeble shrug and stepped back to stand beside Jack. 'Prioress Drueta, my man here wishes to speak to Dame Audrey's family. Are they in London?'

'The Hildeways. Yes. Talk to my chaplain, Dame Emelyn, when she returns. She will find their address for you.'

They waited as they were, standing stoically, while the prioress had returned to the nervous rubbing of the spindle on her prie-dieu.

It wasn't long until Father Holbrok appeared in the doorway, Dame Emelyn hovering behind him. But one glance at Crispin drew all the color from his face.

Jack moved then, skirting the priest who had not moved. 'Dame Emelyn,' he said, disappearing through the doorway with her.

'Come in, Father Holbrok,' said Drueta. She strode to her chair behind the table and sat with the regality of a queen. 'Master Guest has told me an interesting tale.'

Holbrok shot him a nasty look.

'I hope you can elaborate.'

She offered nothing, like any good prosecutor, Crispin thought. *Let the man hang himself.*

But the priest didn't appear to be prepared to allow it, and postured insolently, one foot forward. 'To what are you referring, Lady Prioress?'

'Dame Audrey extorted you for funds. What sin was she privy to that allowed her to hold it over your head?'

Crispin raised his brows. She was obviously not going to hold anything back. Even *he* felt uncomfortable for the man.

Holbrok nodded and looked like a man who was relieved to be caught. 'Very well. You seem to understand it all. I . . . it was all so innocent at first . . .'

'I am not a patient woman, Father.'

He changed the position of his feet. 'I had a love affair with Dame Marion.'

The prioress never changed expression. 'I see.'

'Oh, but there was more to it than that. It was a sham. It was all a sham. Her whispered words, her expressions of love. All of it.'

'Your attempts to provoke sympathy are for naught, Father. Explain.'

'It was a sham because Dame Audrey put her up to it . . . just so she could have a reason to extort me. Isn't that clever? Isn't that disgusting?'

'It does not excuse your own sin, Father. You went into it with your eyes open. I trust you will confess it at the next opportunity.'

Crispin's glance jumped from one to the other, like a game of tennis, wondering which opponent would waver first. Of course, it was no contest. The prioress seemed to dominate the priest. He was already a thin figure of a man, and his character seemed just as slight.

'Of course, Lady Prioress,' he said stiffly.

'You could have stopped this, sir. You should have told me and the proper disciplines could have taken place and prevented the murders to come.'

'Yes, Lady Prioress.'

She shook her head. 'We live in the very priory dedicated to the Seven Deadly Sins. Lust is among the worst, for it can involve the innocence of another. Not that Dame Marion was innocent, as it turned out. And by indulging Dame Audrey's greed . . . well.'

'Yes, Lady Prioress.' He spoke between clenched teeth.

'There will be much to discuss in Chapter today,' she said, tapping her lips with her fingers, and staring into a far corner of the room.

'No doubt. Are you done with me, Lady Prioress?'

'In more ways than one, Father Holbrok. I will, of course, have to write to the bishop.'

'Of course, Lady Prioress.' He gave Crispin a scathing look before he pivoted and strode out of the room.

'Most troubling,' she said, moving those tapping fingers to her table. 'You will naturally need to find Dame Audrey in the city.'

'She does keep returning to this monastery to do her damage. Since I haven't reckoned why she is doing so, I fear I will still need to haunt St Frideswide.'

'Haunt. Interesting choice of words. Have you heard of our ghost, Master Guest?'

'I have, Lady Prioress.'

'I never believed in such fancies. Our Lord would not see fit to let a soul wander so. But it was a convenient fiction for Dame Audrey, was it not?'

'You are very quick, Lady Prioress.'

'I am sixty-five years old, young man. Did you reckon that?'

'I could not have guessed.' Even now, when he scrutinized her face, he could not detect the lines that might give away her age.

'Sixty-five years old, and I have seen sin play over and over again. Sin never seems to change, Master Guest. The world never seems to grow less sinful. Why do you suppose that is?'

'It is not God's will?'

'But it is God's will that we *not* sin.' She focused her sharp eyes on him. 'You will remain to continue your investigation.'

'It must be done, lady, to stop a killer.'

'Two shillings for your fee,' she mused, seeming to tabulate it on her fingers.

And counting, thought Crispin.

NINETEEN

Crispin sat in the back of the nuns' Chapter meeting, invited to do so by the prioress. He had requested to talk to all the nuns at once. It seemed foolish to continue to talk to them separately. He had wasted much time.

After the prioress read a chapter of the Rule of the house, she closed the book on its stand before her, and looked out to her charges. 'Today, we will not discuss our grievances with one another or ourselves. I have asked Master Guest to speak to all of us at once regarding the murders here at St Frideswide. Master Guest informs me that the killer – hard as it might be to believe – is our own Dame Audrey. She did not have a fever, and, with the help of her accomplices, Dame Marion and Dame Katherine, perpetrated a falsehood on us all. Her death was faked. There is no body in her coffin.'

The nuns gasped. One – Crispin thought it might be Dame Elizabeth – cried out.

Prioress Drueta waited for the others to quiet again. 'It is true. There has been much sin bubbling under our noses. Our own Father Holbrok was not immune and sinned with Dame Marion at the urging of Dame Audrey in order for her scheme to take shape, for she extorted him for money in order to escape. And, I am loath to say, that it was also she who stole our most precious relics of St Frideswide. If any of you have any shred of news, any bit of information that could be useful to Master Guest, I urge you to share it now.'

Crispin moved forward to stand on the dais beside the prioress's chair. He scanned their stark faces.

He noticed Dame Petronella slowly raising her hand. 'Is there something you wish to say, Dame Petronella?'

She rose from her seat. 'It is merely a question, Master Guest. You have encountered people who kill through your business of tracking, have you not?'

'I have.'

'Is there . . . something they have in common, I wonder? Some sin that lives in them that makes them take a life?'

He slowly shook his head. 'I don't think there is any one thing that compels all of them, except a singular need. A need to be right, to be their own master, to protect themselves, for greed. And, of course, there are those who have been driven mad by their own compulsions.'

'Was she mad, Master Guest?'

'In truth, I do not know.'

'In your experience,' she went on, 'have there been many women on this course?'

'Just as many women as men, Dame, I am sad to say.'

The nuns murmured.

'How peculiar. That a woman could be so . . . designing.'

'The same woes bedevil them as they do men. This is not the first *religieuse* I have encountered who murdered.'

She threw a hand to her mouth and whispered, 'I can't understand it,' between her fingers. She lowered again to her seat.

'I must have from all of you any information, no matter how slight, that concerns Dame Audrey. Did she speak of friends outside the monastery? Did she speak of places she favored or dreamed of going to? And what of her young man from so long ago? Any information could be the key to my discovering her whereabouts.'

The nuns sat mute in their seats, staring up at him with hollowed eyes.

Until one began to stand. Dame Joan. 'I . . . I remember her speaking of the young man she was forced to leave behind.' She dropped her eyes when she said the word 'forced'. She seemed not to want to be under the scrutiny of the prioress when uttering it. 'Not long before she fell ill, she got word that he had died.'

'Oh?' said Crispin. 'How did she react?'

'It seemed that all the years of training here had fallen away. She was very upset.'

'I remember that,' said Sibilla, standing. 'Oh, she was in a frightful mood. Violent. She threw things, wouldn't do her chores.'

Cecille stood next. 'But I don't recall anyone ever asking her what was wrong.'

'We all did,' said Dame Jemma accusingly, jumping to her feet. 'You never cared for her and so didn't bother. But others did.'

The rest of the nuns got to their feet, arguing with one another, voices rising in echoes in the small space.

Prioress Drueta stomped her foot until order was restored. She motioned for all of them to sit. 'You're a disgrace, all of you.' They lowered their heads, some bringing prayerful hands to their chins. 'Why was I not informed of this?'

Silence, until . . .

'You just would have punished her.' It was Dame Jemma. She rose defiantly. 'We all knew you didn't like her. Truth be told, *I* didn't like her. She was willful and cruel.'

'I neither like nor dislike any of my charges here . . .'

'That's a lie,' said Dame Jemma, raising her face. The others gasped. 'You always disliked her, and treated her harshly.'

'A disobedient nun must be treated with a firm hand, otherwise chaos would reign as it seems to be doing now. You are out of order, Dame Jemma.'

'I am not. This is Chapter. We are supposed to point out faults in our fellow sisters. Even when it is our prioress. That is in the Rule.'

The nuns sitting on either side of her hissed their warnings. One even tugged at her gown to make her sit. She slapped that hand away. 'When he died, she went mad, plain and simple. Perhaps we should have seen this coming.'

Crispin stepped forward, trying to bring the proceedings back under his control. 'And when was this, Dame Jemma? When did she get word?'

'It was over a month ago. After a sennight she calmed down completely. It was as if God had reached down to console her. But now I know that was a lie as well. It is plain she began to plot from that day forward. And now you say Father Holbrok was also part of it? That is also not surprising. He had a leer about him whenever he encountered one of the sisters on his own. I saw it. From afar. I knew that one day he'd be trouble.'

'Dame Jemma!' shouted the prioress. 'Clearly you should have come directly to me with any grievance of this kind.'

'Clearly I did not feel anything would come of it had you known.'

Prioress Drueta drew back. She seemed to have thought her priory was orderly and that all the nuns were practicing their holy orders with satisfaction. The cracks were beginning to show.

Perhaps it was time to lay the truth bare. He reached into his pouch, took out the ring, and held it up. 'Dame Jemma. This ring was found under your mattress. But others have said it was Dame Audrey's. Why did you steal it?'

More gasps. Dame Jemma paled. 'It was not Dame Audrey's,' she said, voice low and even.

Dame Petronella stood. 'That's not true. I saw Dame Audrey with it many a time.'

'Sit down, you witch with your potions,' said Dame Jemma with a sneer. 'You were her apprentice. Little wonder you believed everything she told you. It wasn't her ring. It was mine. She stole it from me, and I could never find a moment to steal it back. It was only when she was dead . . . or appeared so.'

Dame Petronella's mouth flapped but no sound came out.

The prioress strode to the edge of the dais. 'Dame Jemma, if it is true that the ring is yours, you well knew you had to surrender it. A nun must have no possessions from the world she left behind.'

'It was my mother's ring. The only thing left of her. I will not surrender it.'

'Dame Jemma!'

She strode forward and moved with such speed that even Crispin was unprepared for her to snatch it from his hand. She enclosed it in her fist. 'It's mine.'

The prioress faded back to her chair and stumbled into it.

'Dame Audrey was a foul creature who never should have come here and never should have stayed. Did you know that she kept some of the fees from her apothecary work? We all knew it.'

'That is not so!' cried Dame Petronella.

'And again, Dame,' said Dame Jemma, 'you know nothing. Who among us did not know this?'

Many nuns lowered their faces from guilt.

'She never surrendered all of it as she should have done. Many of us wouldn't have minded seeing her flogged. But almost as many kept their own council because they feared you would punish her too much. And now we reap what *you* have sown, Lady Prioress.'

'You condemn Dame Audrey but with the same breath you defend her, Dame,' said Crispin. 'First, you say you fear the prioress would punish her too much, and next you say Dame Audrey was a thief and didn't belong. Which is it?'

'One doesn't rule out the other,' she said, raising her chin haughtily. 'No, she should never have been allowed to stay, but once here, kindness would have helped her. Little wonder she cleaved to friends. I was once her friend until her true nature was revealed and she stole from me. Her friendships were false, as we see from these murders. Every one of her utterances turned out to be a lie.'

A scream pierced the tense atmosphere.

Everyone looked up. Who could it possibly be? Dame Petronella looked at the shadowed seat beside her and cried out, 'Where is Dame Elizabeth?'

'But she was here!' said someone else.

'She was,' said Dame Petronella, confused.

'Never mind that!' cried Crispin. He leapt from the dais and threw open the doors of the chapter house. He ran out to the path to the apothecary garden and skidded on the gravel as he came to a stop. 'Dame Elizabeth!' he called. No one was in the garden. He rushed to look within the stone shed. Nothing.

He tore from the garden and down the path to the cloister. By now the nuns were running about, going in all directions. He saw some peer into the church, some go to the refectory, and some to the laundry and bakehouse.

'Master Guest!' someone shrieked.

He turned in that direction and moved at a trot. Dame Jemma appeared around the corner of the church. 'Master Guest, you must come. I found her. By the rectory.'

She didn't wait for him and ran back around the corner, but he soon caught up to her. All he could hear was his blood rushing in his ears and the thudding of his own feet. For he could see someone on the grass ahead of him, and the priest was kneeling beside her, praying.

Crispin reached her, breath heaving in and out of his chest. She had been strangled with what looked like a man's braies and part of her bodice and shift had been torn away, though the priest must have lain it back over her for propriety's sake.

The other nuns came running and stopped behind Crispin, every one of them crossing themselves.

'Lust,' someone whispered. Another Deadly Sin.

TWENTY

'How is she gaining entrance undetected?' asked Crispin of anyone. 'Does she have a key to the gates?'

'There are no keys missing,' said Dame Emelyn, her lip trembling, looking down at her own set of keys. She tried not to look at the body.

He supposed she could scale the wall as he had. She was younger and more agile. Still, she knew the schedule. She could have come in through the church to the night stair, whose door would remain open when the Divine Office was being prayed.

He hoped Jack was enquiring of Dame Audrey's family and could bring back useful information.

He waited until the priest was done with his prayers and moved in. 'Father Holbrok, did you see anyone?'

'No, Master Guest. I saw no one.'

Kneeling by her side, Crispin carefully removed the braies from around her neck, looking them over. They were well-made with tiny stitches, and they were clean. 'Dame Sibilla,' he said aloud. He didn't bother turning when he heard the nun's shuffling step. Holding the braies up while still looking at the body, he asked, 'Are these from your laundry?'

They were taken from his hand and examined. 'Why . . . yes. This is our mark, here.'

He examined Dame Elizabeth's neck. *Jesu*, she was still warm. It was plain that the braies were used after to stage the incident, for there were finger bruises on her neck and this looked to him to be the agency of her demise rather than the braies. 'Interesting,' he muttered.

The dress and shift were torn to expose her bosom, but appropriately the priest had covered her for decency. Yes, it was designed to follow the pattern of the sins. Lust. Was it coincidence that it happened outside the priest's lodgings, or was it intentional?

He stood and looked at the grass and dirt path, but it had been trodden all over by the nuns who had gathered. So much for that.

He checked her hands to see if anything was there – skin, hair – and finally stood. 'There is no more for me to discover here. You can take her away.'

The nuns gathered her up and gently conveyed her to the infirmary. All but Dame Petronella, who seemed staked to the spot.

Crispin approached her. 'There is little more for you to do, Dame.'

Her face was stiff, her gaze far away.

'My apothecary mistress and my apprentice,' she whispered.

'Dame Petronella, none of this is your fault. It has nothing to do with you. Listen to your prioress and don't go about on your own. Why is it that Dame Elizabeth left her place in Chapter?'

'The prioress's words upset her. She must have left when everything was in an uproar. Because she did come with me to Chapter.'

'I saw her,' he confirmed. 'The nuns here . . . do not seem to like their prioress.'

'It is unseemly to criticize her.'

'But, as another sister said, is it not the time, in Chapter, to make such feelings known?'

'Only for the betterment of the entire house. These were personal grievances aired when they should not have been.'

'Are *you* enamored of the prioress?'

She glared at him. 'That is not for me to express to the entire body of the monastery. For there is little to be done in any case in obedience. We made that vow.' She shook her head. 'So few here seem to observe that.' She girded herself again and looked back at Crispin. 'With your leave, I will join my sisters.'

'Be careful, Dame.'

She nodded to him and then hurried away, her skirts and veil flapping in the breeze.

He turned and was surprised to see Father Holbrok standing by. 'They were having Chapter,' he said dully. 'Why was she not in attendance?'

'It was a . . . most unusual Chapter, Father. Your name came up.'

He stiffened and pulled at his gown to adjust it. 'My days are numbered here. It is over.'

'You paint an innocent portrait of yourself, Father. The celibate fighting devils to remain in your vows, but succumbing to a vixen in nun's clothing. Yet the other nuns seemed to characterize you with – how did they put it? "He had a leer about him whenever he encountered one of the sisters on his own." What do you say to that?'

'Clearly my facial expression was misinterpreted.'

'Oh, clearly.'

'Your manner, sir, leaves much to be desired.'

'So I have been told, many a time. But it is not *my* manner in question. You claim to know nothing of this plot Dame Audrey had schemed?'

He scowled. 'I was innocent in that, Master Guest.'

'Never fear, Father Holbrok. Your worries will soon be over. You will be relocated, as you say. Perhaps with monks next time.'

Crispin walked away as the man's hands clenched into fists.

Before he could decide what to do next, the same boy who had fetched him to the priory in the first place stood suddenly before him. 'Lad. Are you, by chance, looking for me?'

'Aye, my lord. The sheriffs are seeking you out and bid that you come to the embankment at Old Dean.'

'You wouldn't happen to know why, lad?'

'Because of murder.'

The boy seemed to relish the saying of it.

'Very well.'

The boy didn't leave as expected and stared up at Crispin, licking his lips.

'Oh.' Crispin reached into his money pouch and offered a farthing.

'Thank you, my lord. Bless you, sir.' And he was off running.

Crispin soon found himself outside St Frideswide and on the streets of London. He took a refreshing breath of air. Surely it was an illusion that the air was close and sickly within the walls of the priory. It was the same air, but somehow felt more renewing *outside* the walls rather than *within*.

He had closed on Old Dean Street and stopped to survey the sight of people running toward the Thames.

The sheriffs were there on their horses, and their men stood by surrounding the sodden corpse.

Crispin approached the sheriffs and bowed. John Wade, in his brilliantly colored houppelande, acknowledged him first. His hair was the color of wheat, though his beard and mustache were slightly darker. He had a shovel-like nose that he pointed toward Crispin. He elbowed the other sheriff, John Warner, a squat man, older than Wade, who had dark coloring and piggy eyes.

Wade leaned an arm on his saddle pommel. 'I was told by our predecessors that whenever there was a body found, there Crispin Guest would be. But it was I who called you this time. It seemed a little bird told us that you were in a priory searching for a murderer of nuns. And here we have another. I wonder why you did not come to us with this information. Should we not go to the priory to investigate?'

Who could have told? Crispin admonished himself. *Anyone* could have told. Any of the nuns gossiping to the women who came to the gate to buy bread. To any others who came to the church. Any tradesman who did business with the priory. He was surprised he hadn't heard from the sheriffs before now.

Crispin studied the dead woman in her black nun's weeds, *sans* veil. 'Ordinarily, my lord, that would be so. But the prioress has indicated to me in no uncertain terms that these are ecclesiastical matters. Not matters for the Crown, and I, being a layman, could not naysay her.'

'Well, it certainly looks to be a matter for the Crown now.'

'Perhaps. This woman may have nothing to do with my investigations at all.'

'By the mass, Guest. How many nuns do you think are murdered every day?'

Crispin supposed he had a point. 'May I?' He gestured toward the nun.

Wade made a mocking bow to him.

Crispin knelt beside the body. Her eyes were a pale green, paler by the milkiness of the eyes after days in the Thames. He supposed it could have been Dame Audrey. He was now as eager as the sheriffs to discover if it were true. Could he be that lucky? And then he admonished himself. He tried not to be as callous as the sheriffs. He encountered too many bodies for his liking, and each one seemed to harden him. It was on the battlefield where he had learned to inure himself and, at the same time, pity the loss of brave men. And this fragile corpse was still someone's child. Her loss should be mourned whether she was a whore or a nun. It wasn't about luck or finding an end to this tragedy.

And yet, he hoped.

He looked the body over, trying to breathe out of his mouth for the stink. He examined her head over its wimple and decided to peel the wimple away. He heard Warner gasp. He didn't suppose either of the sheriffs had ever touched a corpse before.

Once he drew away the wimple from her head and neck, it was plain that she had been strangled. The bruising marks of fingers were still evident on her throat. And he couldn't help but conjure in his mind poor little Dame Elizabeth with the same bruising.

'Was it an accident, Master Guest?' asked Wade, never dismounting from his horse.

'No, Lord Sheriff. It was murder.'

The crowd gasped.

'Truly, Master Guest. Must you be so dramatic? How in Heavens can you tell?'

'Observation, my lord. On her neck is distinct bruising from strangulation.'

Warner moved his horse closer. 'How can you be sure? Perhaps it was from decomposition.'

'I have seen a fair few corpses, my lord.'

Wade waved his hand and looked over the heads of the crowd. 'Warner, if Guest says it's murder, I can't naysay him. In truth, he *has* seen more corpses than either of us.'

'Thank God for that,' said Warner, crossing himself.

They waited in relative silence. Those in the crowd only made sounds when those in the back wanted to shift forward to view the body.

For his part, Crispin surreptitiously scanned the many people pushing forth to watch. Might the murderer be in the crowd, observing his handiwork?

How were they to identify her?

A cart squeaked as it stopped at the top of the embankment. There was his answer. 'May I prevail upon your men to convey the body to the priory? Since the cart is already here . . .'

'Very well,' said Wade. 'But look here, Guest. I'm not certain we shouldn't be investigating . . .'

'Do as you wish, of course, my lord, but I am nearly done with my own enquiry.'

'Oh?' Wade hesitated. His mind worked, and Crispin could well tell that he was reckoning how much trouble it would be – the writs, the enquiries, the coroner – and decided that it was Crispin's problem after all. 'Very well. Make haste in your investigations, Guest. I should like to at least be told of the final outcome.'

Crispin bowed while sighing in relief. 'Of course, Sheriff Wade.' He watched them turn their mounts. Wade said off-handedly to one of his men, 'Disperse these people,' before his horse clopped up over the verge and gained the thoroughfare. Neither sheriff looked back.

Crispin climbed up the embankment and trotted to follow the cart. 'Where are we going to, sir?' asked one of the men, holding the bridle of the beast pulling the wain.

'St Frideswide Priory, just up to Thames Street.'

The man nodded and walked on, letting the horse lead at its own pace.

They met a perplexed Jack waiting at the gate. Crispin hopped off the cart and let the sheriff's men ring the bell to await the porter.

'Master Crispin, what is all this?'

'First, tell me what you discovered.'

He shook his head and blew out a breath. 'Not much. The Hildeways were happy to be well rid of her. They had not visited her in all the years since they sent her to the priory. That's a sad state of affairs.'

'Then you didn't think they were lying to protect her whereabouts?'

'No, sir. They were fairly harsh in their judgment about her.'

'Did they know anything of her erstwhile lover?'

'Too much, sir. And they didn't approve of him at all. How will we ever find her?'

'Well, I suspect that yon she lies.'

Jack's eyes widened.

'Found in the Thames. The sheriffs called me.'

'Are you sure it's her?'

'Who else could it be? But I will let the sisters here identify her. She is in a nun's habit. She's been in the water for at least a day. Maybe more. As well as strangled. And, by the way, there's been *another* murder. Dame Elizabeth.'

'God's blood!' Then Jack slapped his hand over his mouth at his loud oath. By then Dame Emelyn had come to the gate and stared at the corpse open-mouthed.

'Dame Emelyn,' said Crispin, rushing forward. 'Can you identify—'

'That's Dame Audrey. What is she doing drowned?'

'It's a long and complicated tale, I fear. If you will allow these men to convey her inside . . .'

Dame Emelyn was clearly shaken, but she opened the gate wider for their cart and directed them toward the infirmary.

The cart's wheels squeaked as it rolled forth.

Crispin and Jack stayed behind and watched as the cart settled by the dorter.

'If she's been dead for a few days,' Jack whispered, 'then who killed Dame Elizabeth? The ghost?'

Crispin talked quietly out of the side of his mouth, making certain the sheriff's man did not hear him. 'It's an interesting puzzle.'

'You don't mean to tell me Dame Audrey wasn't the murderer at all?'

'No. Yet . . . she has marks on her throat just like that of Dame Elizabeth.'

'Blind me.'

'Yes. We'll need to look again at that excellent map you drew to ask where the other nuns were just after Dame Mildred was killed.'

'Dame Audrey had an accomplice?'

'No. I think she had a rival.'

TWENTY-ONE

Crispin believed Prioress Drueta was as stoic and precise as anyone he had ever met, but was definitely beginning to show signs of cracking. The body of one of her own who was thought dead and buried, then was revealed to be alive, and now dead . . . again . . . was, perhaps, too much for even her sensibilities.

She stood by her office window, face covered by her hands. She drew in a deep breath and dropped her arms to her sides. Suddenly, she looked older than she had when he first met her. Sleepless nights. Warring nuns. Murder. Who could stand up to that?

'I find myself at a loss, Master Guest. I . . . I simply do not know how to proceed.'

'I fear there are two courses running side by side, Lady Prioress.' Crispin kept his voice low and steady. Managing the situation was foremost in his mind. 'There may be outside forces with their own agenda. I find it telling that two nuns associated with the apothecary are dead.'

She slowly turned her head. 'Eh? What's that, Master Guest?'

'I merely wonder, Lady Prioress, if there is not more to this. Your priory supplies abortive potions to desperate women. Might there be men who object to this?'

Her eyes seemed cloudy, barely aware of his voice. 'And why should they?'

'Aristotle himself marked a line between what was fitting and unfitting. He believed that before the quickening, the unborn had vegetable or animal souls. But after, they were human.'

'And what does Aristotle have to do with it?'

'There are some men – men who were, perhaps, responsible for the pregnancy of women who came to this priory for aid – who object to their women ending their pregnancies. Women who might be bearing sons.'

'Saint Hildegard of Bingen herself suggested tansy to restore the menstrual discharge in her *De Simplicis Medicinae*, written two hundred years ago. And we all well knew what had interfered with it. Oh yes, Master Guest. I have read much of the apothecary art. Not only for its fascinating information, but for its usefulness.'

'That doesn't change the fact that these disgruntled men may wish for their revenge.'

She stared hard at him. It went on so long he began to feel a certain discomfort with the stagnation of her eyes, their slow blinking.

'I . . . I seem to recall last year. There was some mischief. A man broke into the priory and destroyed the apothecary garden. He was angry for the reasons you cite.' She shook her head in the remembering. 'He did much damage. We were able to obtain cuttings from other priories' gardens. If we had not those plants and herbs, we would not have been able to help those who had fallen ill within these walls. He was forced by the bishop to pay restitution.'

'And what is his name, my lady?'

'He is dead. He died not too long after he paid his restitution. He can do no more harm. But, if you think this is an area worth researching, then please do so immediately, Master Guest. We cannot have more murders here.'

'Yes, my lady. In that case, I fear for Dame Petronella. I suggest she be guarded.'

'By whom? We don't truly know who is responsible. If an outside person, we might be able to protect her, but what if it were not? If it were someone from within and we assigned a guard, what if *they* turned out to be a murderer?'

'Quite so. In that case, I should suggest our laborer, Master Walcote. Or should I say, Tobias, since that is the name he has given?'

She nodded. 'Yes. That is wise. He can do his labor near the apothecary garden. And await her outside the church after the Divine Office. Can your man be stealthy?'

'I will see that he is.' Crispin glanced once at Jack, bowed to the prioress, and took his leave.

He didn't see many nuns about. No doubt, they were preparing Dame Audrey – for the second time – for her burial. When Crispin led Jack to the churchyard, Christopher was disinterring Dame Audrey's grave – for the *third* time.

Christopher looked up as Crispin approached. He used his spade to climb out of the grave, brushing himself off, and approached Crispin, remembering at the last minute to bow to him.

Crispin smiled grimly. 'Tobias, there is a task the prioress has set for you. You must finish here, of course, but as quick as you might, you must guard Dame Petronella.'

'Er . . . which one is she, Master Guest?'

'The older, tall, thin one. The apothecary.'

'Oh. Right then.'

'Good man. Hurry you, now.'

Christopher gave Crispin a significant look that meant he had more questions, but he returned to digging the grave and raising the coffin out of it. Perhaps the prioress meant to reuse the coffin. Well, since it had contained no body, it seemed the thriftiest choice.

Walking away, Crispin and Jack found some shade under a tree. 'Where do you suppose Crouch is, sir?'

'If he had any brains in his head, he'd be far from here. But truly, where else has he to go? Holbrok might be hiding him.'

Jack frowned. 'I don't think the priest's charity stretches that far. After all, he's got himself to worry about now.'

'Best to keep an eye skinned for him, Jack.' Removing the map from his pouch, Crispin handed it over. 'And when you can, take this and question the nuns who are not on this map. And here. Take this list of names the prioress gave me. Compare them and do your enquiries.'

'What are you going to do?'

'I have to find a knight and question him.'

'Not Grafton?'

'He was angry, Jack. Angry enough to do Demoiselle Forthey harm. He might have got it into his head to . . . to do a little murder. And if not him, perhaps he knows of another.'

'But . . . sir. He's your squire.'

'He was, Jack. Long ago. He's a different man now.'

Jack lowered his face. 'I'm sorry, sir, if I made it difficult for you. I'm just . . . I confess that I was jealous of him. Of his years with you.'

Smiling warmly, Crispin laid his hand on Jack's shoulder. 'I've had far more years with you. Good years, Tucker. Years I would not trade for a more comfortable life. Does that surprise you? Those years were the making of me. I hope you can say the same.'

'Oh, yes, sir! I didn't mean to cause you vexation. You shouldn't have to cope with more betrayal. Maybe I should find Sir Edward myself and enquire of him.'

With a gentle clout to Jack's shoulder, Crispin shook his head. 'No. This is a task best left to me. You interview the nuns. And take care, Jack. Make sure Christopher knows his mission. And keep an eye out for Crouch.'

'Aye, sir. I think I may have the easier part. God be with you, sir.'

'And you.'

He watched Jack walk away, staring down at his parchment map. He breathed, thinking. Jack was right about having the easier part. Not only must he question his former squire, but he must do so at court. And that was a place – while the turmoil in the Midlands was going on – that a traitor to Richard would not be welcomed.

You keep trying to look before you leap, Crispin . . . but you leap anyway. He chuckled mirthlessly . . . and set out for Westminster.

He loitered by the Great Gate to Westminster Palace. There seemed to be more guards than usual, likely due to the tidings from the Midlands. Crispin wondered how he was to slip his way in when he saw Abbot William de Colchester of Westminster Abbey ride by on his horse with another monk as retainer.

Crispin hurried to keep step with him. 'My Lord Abbot!'

Abbot William snapped his head around and slowed his horse. The retainer halted his mount a few moments after. 'Crispin. What are you doing here?'

'My Lord, it is rather urgent I get into the palace. There is a knight I need to talk to. Sir Edward Grafton, one of King Richard's household knights.'

Abbot William, knowing Crispin well, looked about the large courtyard he was about to enter into. 'Do you wish me to fetch him?'

'Well . . . I don't know how wise it is to have me walk freely within the gates.'

'No, that wouldn't be wise at all. Especially these days. Should I have him meet you here, then?'

'If it would be convenient, Lord Abbot.'

He studied Crispin steadily with his pale blue eyes, his gauntleted hand wrapped tight around the reins. 'I don't suppose I could ask you—'

'It does concern murder, my lord.'

'As I suspected. But . . . what if the fellow will not come to meet you?'

Crispin heaved a sigh. 'It is true. He might not . . .'

Abbot William considered. 'Crispin,' he began. 'I . . . need I tell you that I am King Richard's man, that I must support my king.'

'It has never interfered with our relationship before, my lord.'

'Yes, but now is a precarious situation.'

'You don't wish to be seen with me.' Crispin conceded it. 'Never fear, my lord.' He bowed and turned to walk away, trying to think of another way round the problem.

'Crispin! You are a bedeviling fellow.' He shook his head, muttered a prayer – or was it an oath? – and then glanced at the monk accompanying him. 'Brother Roland, I wonder if you would be so kind as to lend Master Guest your cassock and cowl.'

The young man looked up at his abbot with some surprise. 'My lord?'

'It won't be for very long, will it, Crispin?'

Crispin raised his face to both men. 'No, Abbot William. Very briefly. Only until I can track him down and talk. I will return it forthwith, Brother Roland, with much thanks. And I shall give you my cote-hardie to vouchsafe for my return.' He began unbuttoning the coat.

The monk didn't look happy when he dismounted and untied his rope belt, glancing at his abbot all the while. They exchanged clothes in the shade of some trees just off the main road. The monk was of slighter build, but Crispin managed to keep the cassock closed with the rope belt, and then pulled the cowl up over his head.

The monk, with his tonsure shining in the sun and Crispin's scarlet cote-hardie hanging loose about his narrow shoulders, looked forlorn.

Abbot William offered Crispin his retainer's horse. 'Brother Roland, you may wait here. And God's blessings upon you for your generous help.'

Brother Roland bowed, having no other recourse. He hugged himself in the coat, and muttered a prayer.

Crispin rode just slightly behind the abbot, keeping his face down as they entered through the gate and into the wide courtyard. Some retainers trotted up to take their horses. Abbot William strode up to the steps of Westminster Hall and entered through the open doors with Crispin hurrying behind. The abbot was older but he had not lost his robust gait and manner.

Crispin hadn't been to court in some years, and found himself looking up into the refurbished interior of Westminster Hall. The posts had all been removed and, instead, the roof was upheld by hammerbeams. It was a sight to behold as the elegant roof reached up, up, without anything seeming to support it.

Abbot William reached the far door and turned to Crispin. 'I'm certain our trails lead in opposite directions, Master Guest. Where will you go now?'

'In search. I do not know where he might be. I suppose I shall ask.'

'Very well. God be with you, Crispin . . . in whatever future we find ourselves.' He made the sign of the cross over him. When Crispin had been younger and in his exile, he had rejected such pretences, believing he didn't deserve them. But that was another day. He gladly took all the blessings he could nowadays.

And it seemed that angels were shining down blessings upon him when he turned away from the abbot and spied Bill Wodecock, one of the king's stewards of the palace. A barrel of a man, round but firm, the only evidence of his aging was a head of nearly white hair. He was blustering as usual to a group of servants, gesticulating and growling. When the servants were able to bow and hurry off, Crispin stepped in. He signed the cross over a surprised Wodecock. 'Blessings on you, Master Wodecock.'

Wodecock glared into the hood, bowed, and turned away . . . until he jolted to a halt and looked back.

'What's the matter, Wodecock? Don't you recognize an old friend?'

Stomping back toward Crispin and standing toe to toe with him, Wodecock peered into the shadow of the hood. Crispin grinned.

'God's teeth! Good Christ, Guest.'

'Not so loud, master.'

'Get out. I'll have no nonsense from you or I'll call the guard.'

'You must know the only reason I'd be here is to investigate a murder.'

'So you always say, Guest, and yet there is always trouble in your wake.'

'I can't refute that. But you won't stand in the way of the king's justice, would you?'

Wodecock's lips pouted into a scowl. 'You are a vexation, aren't you?'

'I am only doing the task God has set for me.'

'That's a new one.' He scratched his ample behind. 'What do you want then?'

'To speak to one of the king's knights, Edward Grafton.'

He stared at Crispin for a long time, and Crispin watched all the changes of thought within the man's eyes: that Crispin should be such an upstart as to ask favors of him; that Crispin should want to vex one of the household knights; that this knight used to be Crispin's own squire . . .

'Well . . . I'll . . . I'll see what I can do. Go to the chapel and await him there. If he will come. At least you can do your penance for impersonating a monk.'

'With the permission of the Abbot of Westminster Abbey.'

'You do have friends in strange places, do you not?'

'I count my blessings every day, Master Wodecock.'

As he watched the little man stride away, his smile faded. How would Edward welcome Crispin? Would he even talk to him? Ignore him? Would he strike out? The man's life lay on a different path now, far different than Crispin's would have been. How would he take their conversation? Especially because Crispin had to – for all intents and purposes – accuse him of murder.

But *was* that so? He had threatened his own mistress. That was one matter. But entering a priory to do harm, and in the way it was done? Was he capable of such deceit in so calculating a way? Poor Dame Elizabeth was killed in the same way the others were killed. And how could he have known about that? Perhaps he went to question Elizabeth about Dame Audrey, killed her, and then sought Dame Audrey in the city . . . But no. That timeline was wrong. Elizabeth was killed well *after* Dame Audrey was . . .

Was Crispin becoming muddled? God's blood, he wasn't *that* old!

No, it was still a legitimate enquiry. Prioress Drueta had said that there was mischief aimed at the apothecary as recently as last year. It wasn't unreasonable that another man would have done more mischief if he were unsatisfied with the priory's meddling in what he might consider private affairs.

Yet, it did not explain the manner of Dame Elizabeth's death, representing lust. And Dame Audrey's death. Clearly, she had killed the first three nuns to hide her own deceit. But her own death was not linked to any of the Deadly Sins. Someone angry with her sought her out in the city – knowing she was still alive – and murdered her. But then . . . why would Dame Elizabeth be killed in the manner of the Deadly Sins if Dame Audrey were already dead? He couldn't help but feel Dame Audrey's death was in answer to her work as an apothecary.

How had they known she'd be in the city?

He made his way to St Stephen's Chapel, these and more thoughts churning in his mind, one tumbling over the other. He stopped as he entered the chapel, and all thoughts of murder stopped with his steps.

The last time Crispin had been in the chapel was at the horrific time of the late queen's death, when she lay resting there in her coffin, and a distraught Richard would not leave her side. That was when the king had confessed that he had never hated Crispin, that he had loved him, and had never wanted him to die. Not then. Not when he was a little boy. But the years had hardened Richard, especially when he had realized what that treason had meant.

And now there was more treason afoot. What the devil was Henry doing? If he were caught by the king's army . . . He dreaded to think it. A fate that Crispin himself would have suffered, had not Henry's father intervened. But no. The rumor was that it was *Henry* who had captured *Richard* . . . Strange, strange times.

He glanced up to the painted vaulted ceilings, the watching loft where a canon of St Stephen's College walked slowly past, and the various statues and chandlers lit up with candles. He dipped his hand into the font and crossed himself, and then strode across the nave's floor, pacing back and forth, his thoughts racing.

Would Edward come? In another day he would have. Crispin would have counted on it absolutely. Just as he counted on Jack's loyalty absolutely. But as he had told Jack, Edward Grafton was now a different man.

He knew he paced for half an hour at least, for he heard the chimes of the Tower Clock. When he turned toward the door for the hundredth time, expecting no one there, he was surprised to see Edward take a cautious step within, searching about.

Crispin girded himself and slowly approached. 'Bless you, my son.'

Edward shot him a look, eyes wide. 'Master Crispin!' he hissed.

Crispin pushed back his hood just a little before replacing it. 'It is me. I apologize for this ruse, but I am still not allowed into court . . . as you have so recently reminded me.'

His cheeks burnished to a dark red. 'I told you I was sorry for saying that.'

'But are you? I fear this conversation will not change your mind on the matter.'

He gestured for Crispin to go to a far and shadowed corner beside a stone saint. 'Good Christ. You truly do not give up, do you?'

'Not while there is breath within me.'

'Then what do you want?' By the flicking of his gaze here and there, Crispin was made aware that Edward was mindful of the circumstances.

'I want to ask where you were today? Before Sext.'

'Why?'

'Do you stall? Or can't you tell me?'

Edward frowned. 'I was here. At court, performing my duties.'

'Can anyone vouchsafe for that?'

'You speak in riddles, sir. Spit it out.'

'Very well. Another nun at the priory was murdered.'

Crispin waited for whatever expression might bloom on Edward's face. Astonishment first appeared, converting quickly to fury.

'Damn you!' he rasped. 'Do you have the gall to accuse me?'

'It is the second apothecary associate to have died from misadventure, Sir Edward. Not long after you expressed your anger at such people that could take your babe away from you.'

'How dare you?'

'Yes, how dare I. I, who solves crimes in the name of the king. And where is my authority to do so? The king himself asked me that once. And I answered that God has granted me permission to do His work. To find murderers and send them to eternity at the feet of the One who will judge us all.'

'Do I have it right? That you are accusing me of murder?'

'You threatened harm to your former mistress.'

Edward took a step closer. 'But you *are* accusing me of murder?'

'Where were you?'

He stared for a moment longer before throwing back his head and laughing.

Other courtiers in the chapel looked back with indignant expressions.

Edward spoke in a quieter tone after recovering. 'Do you know what I always liked about you, Master Crispin? It was your audacity. Such things you said and did. I thought I would never have such nerve. But you did try to instill it in me, to take chances, to stand my ground.' The smile disappeared. 'And look where it's got you.'

'Indeed. Look where it's got me. True, I have no estates, no title. But I have found the comforts of family, and experienced loyalty around me such as I could never have imagined. I think that is worth much.'

Edward's face was painted with disbelief. 'You would prefer to have these comforts from a *servant* rather than your title? Than your family name?'

'I still have my family name, Edward.'

'But it is covered with shame.'

It still stung, but he brushed it aside. 'And yet, the name "Tracker" seems to have with it its own notoriety and admiration. That will last long after I am gone, perhaps even superseding the other. But only time will tell . . . and I will be dead in any case.'

Edward got in close. 'Look here, Master Crispin, I would see no harm come to you. But if you persist in this manner, I cannot see that it will do you any good. And the life you say you now cherish will be . . . endangered.'

'Endangered? By whom? You?'

The man fitted his thumbs in his belt and stood with chest thrown forward. 'You're accusing me of common murder. I consider that slanderous.'

Looking down at his nails, Crispin asked once more, 'Can you tell me where you were before Sext?'

'Damn you! I was here. I have many witnesses as part of the king's household.'

'Well then. I'm certain they will all be reliable and impartial.'

Edward drew his sword with a roar. Others in the chapel turned their heads in alarm. One young page even ran from the place.

Stretching out his arms, Crispin postured. 'I am unarmed, Edward.'

He scowled. 'Then I have but to raise my voice to bring the guards down upon you.'

'Would you?' He took a step closer, even as Edward took a step back. He wondered about the page and if he was running to do that very thing. 'Can you betray me so easily?' He shook his head in disappointment. 'You certainly aren't the boy I raised, Edward.'

The scowl turned to a pained frown. 'And you are no longer the man who raised me.'

That dart hit true. Crispin took an involuntary step back.

Edward's face moved from one emotion to the next: anger, regret, pride, guilt. In the end, he sheathed his sword with a snap, turned on his heel, and walked away.

TWENTY-TWO

Brother Roland looked relieved to catch sight of Crispin as he came around the corner.

'Much thanks for the kind loan of your cassock, Brother.'

Roland couldn't seem to unbutton the cote-hardie fast enough. 'I hope you accomplished what you desired, Master Guest.'

'If only I had.' As he punched his hand into the sleeve of his cote-hardie, Crispin watched, amazed, at how fast the monk donned his cassock and cowl.

'I am sorry to hear that.'

'Mine is not the easiest of tasks.'

Roland adjusted his rope belt and straightened his cassock. 'Nor mine.'

'Indeed.' Crispin patted his arm, asked him to give his regards to the abbot, and made his way back toward London with much to think about.

He had no doubt that Edward was telling the truth. There were surely bountiful witnesses who saw him. And even if he had encountered Dame Audrey on the streets, how would he have known what she looked like? Crispin was getting in his own way again, allowing his emotions to trip him up, despite his better judgment. Perhaps it was seeing Edward again after all these years . . . and witnessing the change in him, a change he didn't like.

It's not his fault, he kept telling himself. Of course, Edward would have begun to regret what happened to him. And to blame Crispin, the man responsible for his own years of disgrace. Hadn't Crispin blamed himself and made his own Hell of drunkenness and moodiness all those years ago?

But if not Edward, then who else resented Dame Audrey?

He pulled up short. It was staring him in the face.

When he returned to St Frideswide, he went immediately in search of Dame Petronella. He found her when he spied Christopher, who was diligently guarding her and trying to look as if he weren't, busying himself pretending to fix the garden gate.

'Tobias,' Crispin muttered in greeting. Dame Petronella heard him and looked up from her work inside the stone cottage's doorway.

'Master Guest,' she said. 'I somehow didn't expect to see you.'

'Oh? Why is that?'

'Hope.'

Crispin offered a lopsided grin. 'I'm not that bad, am I?'

'It is not your person, sir, that offends. But what you represent.'

'Offends? And here I am, Dame, doing my best to protect you.'

'Protect me? Why should you?'

'I don't wish to alarm you, but two of your apothecary associates were murdered. It could be that there is someone displeased with the kind of potions you sell.'

She snorted. 'Preposterous!'

'And yet, your own prioress mentioned that last year someone was so displeased that he tore out your garden.'

Her eyes widened a fraction before they turned back to her work of chopping herbs. 'My understanding of the situation was that a certain man was more upset with Dame Audrey's doings than with her apothecary skills.'

'Oh? The prioress did not seem aware of that.'

Dame Petronella wiped her hands down her apron with an exasperated sigh. 'Of course she wouldn't be. The prioress treated Dame Audrey harshly, but at the same time . . . I think she admired her.'

'Admired?'

'Dame Audrey was disobedient, and there is little that vexes the prioress more than that particular sin. But at the same time, Audrey was audacious. Compelling. They often had long conversations. And I daresay, when she returned from such talks, Audrey was . . . well . . . smug is the only word I should use to define her feelings on the matter. As if she had done the persuading.'

'There seem to be high feelings regarding Dame Audrey amongst the nuns here.'

'That is true, Master Guest. You either loved her or despised her . . . or despised yourself for loving her.'

'And you, Dame. How did you perceive her?'

She went back to carefully chopping her herbs. 'I learned a great deal from her. But I was able to separate the wisdom of her knowledge from the person.'

'Did *you* despise her? Or did you despise yourself?'

Her chopping slowed as she thought but then resumed its rhythm. 'I was not interested in making friends or enemies of her. I was here simply to do my chosen task, Master Guest.'

'Are you . . . sorry she is gone?'

The chopping stopped. 'She was a holy sister,' she said carefully. 'I grieve at the loss to our priory and at the loss of a life.' The chopping resumed.

Crispin bowed and turned away. He got close to Christopher and leaned in. 'Your task is done, Young Tobias. The lady needs no more protection.'

'Oh? Have you caught the murderer then?'

'I'm about to. Follow me, but not too closely.'

They passed through the garden gate and around the dorter, across the night stair passageway, and entered the church at the south transept. They moved through the crossing to the north transept and out the door. Crispin stood on the step and surveyed the rectory, where the priest walked slowly through his garden, face raised to the sun.

'Stay in the shadows, Christopher,' Crispin whispered over his shoulder, and stepped forward.

He matched Holbrok's gait as he approached. The man had not yet seen him. Would Crispin need his dagger? he wondered. For now, he left it sheathed.

'Father Holbrok!'

The priest turned sharply, as if apprehensive of such a call. He seemed even more on the edge when he spied Crispin. 'Master Guest.'

Crispin said nothing. He only met the man and looked about at his garden. Crispin had not been to the rectory before. It was a modest house, though bigger and grander than Crouch's, with an arched entrance and trefoiled arched windows with glass in them.

'A pleasant garden for meditation, eh, Holbrok?'

'Yes,' was all he said.

'Any word from Crouch?'

'No. I fear what might have happened to him.'

'Don't worry. He'll be back. In time. In the meantime, I've been wondering something, Father. You were the first to find Dame Elizabeth.'

'What of it?'

'Well . . . you said you saw no one. She was still warm when I reached her. It had only just happened. Strange that you would not have seen or heard anyone.'

Holbrok cleared his throat. His cheeks were in high color, though the rest of his face was starched pale. 'God forgive me, but . . . I must confess now. I *did* see someone.'

'Oh? Who then?'

'I didn't want to say. I didn't want to believe it.' Still he stalled.

'Who, Father?'

'That . . . that young man. That worker, Tobias. He . . . he was standing over her, tearing her clothes, and when I approached, he looked up and ran away.'

'Indeed. And why not tell me earlier?'

'He's a young man. It had to be some sort of an accident.'

Crispin pinched his bottom lip and made a slow circuit around the priest. 'And so, you took it upon yourself to make a swift judgment about a young man, a man you did not know, a man whom you assumed murdered a nun and tore her clothes in a disgraceful manner, assuming he would – what? Repent? Suddenly recover from his madness? And then you didn't see fit to tell me or the sheriffs or, indeed, even the prioress?'

'Well . . . when you say it like that—'

'Like what, Father? Logically? Clearly?'

'I saw him kill her. He must have killed the others too.'

'Interesting conjecture.'

'Is that all you have to say?' Holbrok sputtered. 'You're supposed to be this celebrated Tracker. Why aren't you going after him? He . . . he's a murderer.'

'And yet, you wanted only a moment ago to protect him. What has changed your mind on the matter?'

Holbrok fumbled with his rosary, fingers skipping hastily over each bead. 'I came to the realization that I couldn't keep the information inside anymore. He must not be allowed to kill again.'

Crispin gazed at him mildly. It seemed to agitate the man, the longer he said nothing.

'Well? Is this how the Tracker of London conducts himself? I told you straightaway that I was witness to a murder. Isn't it your task to apprehend him?'

'Indeed, Father Holbrok, it is. So, allow me to get this firmly in my mind. You said you were a witness to Dame Elizabeth's murder, and you saw Tobias do this heinous thing.'

'Yes! Why are you hesitating?'

Glancing toward Christopher in the shadows of the north transept doorway, Crispin beckoned to him. Christopher stepped into the light and Holbrok gasped.

'There he is, Guest. Get him!'

Christopher stopped, standing some distance away. The sneer he wore must have been in disgust at the priest.

'Tell me this, Father Holbrok. How could this young man have committed the other murders? He arrived well after those crimes were committed.'

There was only a heartbeat of a pause before Holbrok took a breath. 'He could have climbed the walls, committed them in secret, and somehow ingratiated himself to the prioress.'

'All to commit even more murders? Father Holbrok, there is one thing more about young Tobias here that you may not be aware of.'

Holbrok's self-satisfied expression was beginning to irk him. 'And what is that, Master Guest?'

'He happens to be in disguise. Young Tobias here is in fact Christopher Walcote, the son of the wealthy mercer Clarence Walcote.'

Holbrok laughed. 'How do you know this? Did *he* tell you? See how he deceives! I saw him, Master Guest. Will you take the word of a . . . a lying boy over that of a priest?'

'In this instance, yes. Because it was *I* who personally asked him to be here.' Never had Crispin felt as satisfied as when he saw the man's spirits suddenly fall. He stepped closer to Holbrok and dropped his voice. 'You're in a bit of trouble, aren't you, Holbrok?'

He looked from Crispin to Christopher and back again. His face suddenly broke out into a sweat and he seemed tensed to lunge, to fight . . . then all the fight seemed to leak out of him.

'All right,' he said shakily, clutching at his rosary all the harder. The wooden beads clacked together like bones. 'All right. You have the better of me, Guest. It *was* me. I did kill her, but it was a mistake, an accident.'

Anger rising, Crispin leaned over him. 'How is it you can throttle someone to death, Holbrok, by accident?'

'She wouldn't tell me. I knew she knew. She must have been part of this extortion scheme.'

'She wouldn't tell you what?'

'Where Dame Audrey was. I knew she must know!'

'How did you know she wasn't dead as everyone at this priory assumed?'

'Something was strange about her burial. And someone kept disturbing her grave. It changed incrementally for two days. She was sly. I knew there was something . . .'

'And why did you want to know where she was?'

'So I could . . .' He stopped, licked his lips, pulled back. 'So I could talk to her. Reason with her.'

'So you could kill her, you mean.'

'No! Only . . . only to talk to her.'

Crispin studied his face. It was blotchy from sweat, emotion, and newly forming tears. But wait. The timeline was wrong again. Dame Audrey was already dead by the time he killed Dame Elizabeth. Did he know? But there were the same bruising marks on Dame Audrey as there had been on Elizabeth . . .

'Did you kill the others?'

'No!'

'You can only be hanged once, Holbrok. Confess, and make yourself worthy in the eyes of the Lord.'

'But I didn't!' The tears came freely now. He wasn't such a handsome man after all, Crispin mused.

Then those deaths were still on Dame Audrey. But who killed *her*? For he found himself believing the foolish priest's scenario. He was so befuddled and blind with rage that he killed poor little Elizabeth who, all in all, knew nothing of Dame Audrey's extortion scheme until she heard it in Chapter. And he could well see how, in his state, Holbrok had gone too far. He had to make it look like the other murders, tearing her gown, making it appear like another Deadly Sin.

'Did you attack the visiting nun, Dame Philippa?'

'I don't know what you are talking about.'

He believed him. 'You're pathetic, Holbrok. You've sinned in every way possible. Christopher, kindly take this wretched man to the sheriffs. Are you going to be trouble, Holbrok, or do I beat you into submission first?'

He wept, he prayed, he called out for mercy from God, but in the end, he nodded and walked meekly to an astonished Christopher.

'Take him to Newgate.' He trusted that Christopher could do it. He saw that his son *wanted* to, and he was filled with pride . . . and trepidation. But no. Christopher grabbed the man's arm none too gently, and with his other hand he drew his dagger. There would be no trouble from Holbrok. And even if he tried to escape, Londoners would soon stop him.

A figure came running at Crispin, and before he could react one way or the other, someone had leapt upon him, and they both fell to the ground with a fist beating at Crispin's face.

He heard the thud of footsteps approach and he wanted to shout at Christopher not to help him but to get Holbrok away, when he heard the voice of his apprentice.

'Get off him, Crouch, or I'll stab you true!'

Crispin hauled back and slammed his fist into Crouch's face. It felled him, and Crispin was able to roll to his feet. He adjusted his cote-hardie, and glared down at him before he pressed his boot to the man's chest.

'You'll stay down until your precious sinning priest is well away.' He nodded to Christopher, who yanked at Holbrok and, with head down, walked with Christopher out through the gate in the wall.

'Don't take him!' shouted Crouch. 'It's not his fault! It's these horrible nuns and their secrets and their vile, vile sins.'

Crispin took two steps and grabbed Crouch by his coat and yanked him to his feet. 'You annoy me, Crouch,' he said, mere inches from the man's nose. 'Your brief absence annoys me, your fist annoys me, your sniveling after that wretched priest annoys me, and your . . .' He winced. 'Your *breath* annoys me. You waste your time weeping over that murderer.'

'He murdered nobody.'

He shook the man. 'Wake up, Crouch. Merely because he was kind to you doesn't mean he's been an angel. Oh no. Far from it.'

'You're lying!'

'He confessed it himself. He confessed to killing Dame Elizabeth.'

Even Jack gasped.

'He . . . he . . .'

Crispin shook Crouch loose. The man stumbled to right himself. 'He confessed it. He's a murderer. Now what of you? Did you seek out Dame Audrey in the city and kill her?' But even as Crispin said it, he recalled the marks of *two* hands on Dame Audrey's neck.

'I never . . .'

'What of the nuns here? Did you have reason to kill them? At least be as brave as your pet priest.'

He raised his chin even though his body trembled. 'I didn't. I never killt nobody.'

Jack seemed to be trying to catch Crispin's attention and, by the look in his eye, Crispin acquiesced.

'Get out of here, Crouch. Pray. Do your tasks gladly. And forget about Father Holbrok.'

The man sucked in a sob and ran off in a strange loping gait.

Jack watched him disappear before turning back to Crispin. 'You've been busy. Where's he been?'

'Nearby, I'm certain. And Edward Grafton is not guilty of murder. But Father Holbrok is . . . of the murder of Dame Elizabeth.'

'God blind me with a poker,' Jack breathed.

'I am convinced that Dame Audrey killed the others.'

'Even Dame Mildred?'

'Perhaps. Though it seemed unnecessary. But the bigger question is: who killed Dame Audrey?'

'I might have an idea there, Master Crispin.'

TWENTY-THREE

They settled under a tree on a bench between the cellarium and the priory wall.

'I just got done tracking down them nuns we didn't have on our map.' Jack took the parchment from his money pouch, unfolded it carefully, and laid it flat on his thigh. 'These are missing from what we saw with our own eyes: Dame Joan, the prioress, Crouch, and the priest. Now it could have been Father Holbrok as he admitted his killing of Dame Elizabeth . . .'

'But I already threatened him on that score. He can only be hanged once.'

'Is that how you put it?' He chuckled and shook his head. 'Aye, it's true. And he didn't budge? Well then, we'll have to assume it wasn't him.'

'Then I have two big questions. Who killed Dame Mildred and who killed Dame Audrey? I thought that Audrey had returned to kill Mildred . . . but why?'

'And if she didn't . . .' Jack sat back. 'We either have two or three killers.'

'We most assuredly have three. Father Holbrok, Dame Audrey herself, and the one who murdered her. Is it a case of a person we do not know, someone in London?'

'God's blood! If that is so, then how are we ever to find someone in London who disliked her enough?'

'We do what we always do Jack. We investigate.'

'Hold, Master Crispin. You haven't heard what else I learned from Dame Joan.'

Crispin was halfway to his feet before he sat again. 'Well?'

'I asked her why she was absent from the church when nearly everyone else was at the scene of Dame Mildred's murder. Do you know what she told me?'

'She was fetching flour.'

'No, sir. She said that someone had to see to the ovens.'

Even now he could smell the aroma of baking bread. 'Is that all? She could not leave them for even a few moments?'

'That's what I asked her. And she said that she didn't like to leave them on account of what someone put in them. In the fire, at any rate.'

'Oh? And what was that?'

Jack reached into his scrip and pulled out a piece of black cloth. 'She said it was a part of a veil. A nun's veil. And I asked her why anyone would do such a thing. And she said that it might be because there was blood on it and they didn't wish to leave it at the laundry, for any one of the laundresses would know whose veil it was.'

Crispin moved his fingers over the dry and frail piece of cloth. Most of it was singed away, but as he looked closely at one edge, he could just see a bit of a rusty color. He showed it to Jack.

'Blind me,' he said under his breath. 'Just so.'

'Jack, did you get any sense that she was lying? That she purposely provided this "evidence" to you in order to save her own skin?'

'If she did, she was a master of deception, for I did not. She was concerned because she had seen someone who didn't belong by the ovens. But it was late in the afternoon and she could not tell who it was. Damn these nuns' habits. They are difficult to distinguish one from the other.'

'Only if they are of the same figure. Most are not. They are either tall, short, or fat. Those you can well tell from the others. For instance, I can spot Dame Petronella from far off, even from the back. But Dame Joan from Dame Jemma would be difficult.'

'Aye, because they are of similar build.'

'Dame Audrey's figure was similar to most of the others; medium height and neither fat nor thin.'

'Could it have been her who burned that?' he said, gesturing to the veil in Crispin's hands.

'I don't think so. Why would she have cause to do that here when it would have been far safer when she left? Jack, I don't think it was anyone outside this cloister. There are too many high feelings within, and it had been eight years since she was brought to this priory. Even her own parents didn't care to have anything to do with her.'

'That's very sad.'

He glanced at Jack and his worried expression. 'That would never be you, Tucker. Your children are well loved and know it. They will not know how to be deceitful in the ways we have seen so many times in others.'

'I pray that you are right, sir.'

'I am. Were there any other missing nuns?'

'Well . . . the prioress, sir.'

'Dare I hope that you managed to talk to her?'

'I did, sir. And she was most changed from the last time I tried to enquire of her. More subdued. She answered my questions, and she didn't even complain that she had already answered when *you* asked her. But I'll tell you this. Dame Joan went looking to talk to her about two days ago, and she could not be found.'

'Perhaps in the necessarium?'

'No, sir. For I asked that as well. But though she looked high and low, she could not be found. Dame Joan said she just gave up and thought no more of it until she saw her later at None.'

'She was missing from when to None?'

'I asked that, sir, trying to be thorough as you've taught me, and Dame Joan said that it was not long after they celebrated Sext, then had their midday meal, that she went looking for the prioress, but she was not on the grounds.'

'A few days ago?'

'The day Dame Mildred was killed.'

Crispin gazed steadily at Jack. He rose, wiping down his cotehardie. 'I will talk to her. She must be told what I know.'

*   *   *

With heavy steps he followed the colonnade around the cloister garden, along the path that followed the south transept of the church, and to the path before the west side of the dorter, until he reached the connected lodgings of the prioress. He stepped up onto the granite porch and knocked.

Presently, Dame Emelyn, the prioress's chaplain arrived, eyes trying not to meet his, as she humbly allowed him in. He waited in the portico while she went to the prioress to see if she would receive him. It took but a moment for her to return. Dame Emelyn was going to escort him but he raised a hand. 'I know the way, Dame.' She bowed to him and left for her own duties, while Crispin walked along the narrow corridor to the prioress's room, knocked, and entered when told to.

It was as if she hadn't moved from the last time he had encountered her, for she was still standing, hand on the knob of her prie-dieu, and looking out of the window. With the light as it was streaming in through the glass, there was enough highlight and shadow cast upon her face to reveal the wrinkles and lines. Were there more than before?

He stood as close to the table between them as he could, and couldn't help but glance down at the scrolls and parchments lying there. Accountings, documents. A will. He tried to see whose but he could not tell unless he moved the parchments atop it.

'Lady Prioress,' he said softly.

'Have you come to tell me you have concluded your investigations, Master Guest?'

'I . . . I believe I have, Lady Prioress.'

'Well then. Recount it to me.'

'Much of it you already know. Dame Audrey had discovered that her lover of years ago had recently died, and this changed her course. I believe *you* told her that. She then began her scheme, exploiting the weaknesses of your Father Holbrok as well as stealing the relics, meaning to sell them. She then escaped by feigning her illness and with the help of her close friends, falsifying her death perhaps by the use of her herbal skills in simulating shallow breathing. Her nuns and accomplices hid her body, allowing her to recuperate, whilst they created the dummy made of straw, rocks, and a shroud, tying it up to simulate the shape of a woman. It was laid to rest in a coffin and buried. For all anyone knew in this priory – except for her accomplices – she was dead and gone. Perhaps she had always intended to secure the secrecy of her plan by killing her accomplices and in that dreadful way.'

Crispin watched the prioress, but she did not move, nor twitch a lash as she continued her solid gaze out of the window.

'She was mad with grief, no doubt. Or . . . simply mad all this time. I am uncertain if she had returned to kill Dame Mildred or not, but that is for later. Dame Elizabeth met her untimely end almost by accident. Your Father Holbrok was certain that she knew where Dame Audrey was, and he so desperately wanted to know. I am convinced he meant to do Dame Audrey harm . . . because, you see, he didn't yet know that she was already dead. He got too rough with poor little Elizabeth and, before he knew it, he had throttled her to death.'

The prioress closed her eyes at that. Briefly, until she opened them again; dry, contemplative of the trees and birds without.

'He tore her gown to look as if it were the same killer. I don't know where he got the braies. I'm assuming he had just stolen them from the laundry for his own use and had them handy. I take it he had stolen a few items in the short period he had been here, for Dame Margaret hadn't miscounted the missing laundry. It *was* missing. You see, I noticed that his clothing was better than it should be for such a poor priory.'

He tugged on his cote-hardie to straighten it but, truly, it was to take a much-needed pause. The prioress still hadn't moved.

'He confessed it all to me, and what he left out, I surmised. He has since been taken away to the sheriffs.' Still no reaction. 'That has left the mystery of who killed Dame Audrey. She, too, had bruise marks on her neck, as Dame Elizabeth did. At first, I suspected Crouch, as he would happily do the bidding of the priest, but Elizabeth and Audrey both had the marks of *two* hands on their throats. And though Crouch was a thief, it is a very far stretch from thievery to murder. Crouch is a devout man. I think even he would have paused to do murder for Father Holbrok.

'And then I thought perhaps it was a disgruntled man who had congress with the women who sought to end their pregnancies. Because two of the women killed had links with the apothecary: Dame Elizabeth and Dame Audrey. But that too proved to be a dead end. It seems, instead, that this was about discipline . . . or perhaps the lack thereof. And, paradoxically, of Dame Audrey's pied piper tendencies.'

The prioress took a deep breath. Crispin waited, but that seemed to be all. He continued. 'Lady Prioress . . . Dame Drueta. Do you have anything to add?'

She nodded, more to herself than to him, and finally turned. In her hand was a small knife. It was not for eating or even for defense, but something like for cutting parchment. Yet, even though the blade was short, it was still sharp. Crispin eyed it before raising his gaze to her face.

'You see, you must understand. Discipline *must* be maintained.'

'I truly do understand, Lady Prioress. Shall I take that knife from you?'

'No. I haven't decided yet what to do with it.'

He tensed, ready to leap across the table if need be.

'You are a very clever man, Master Guest. Quite, quite clever. I thought, you see, that Dame Audrey and I had come to an understanding. That she understood her place now in the priory. And so I felt that it was safe to confide in her that her erstwhile lover from years ago had died. She accepted that news with aplomb. And I must confess that I sinned in my pride that I had tamed her, accustomed her to her life here; that she had allowed God into her heart and mind.' She swallowed hard. Crispin realized that this was a grave confession for such a one as Prioress Drueta, not only to admit the sin of pride, but to admit to having been duped.

'I did not realize,' she went on, 'how it had crushed her spirit. It revealed the lie of her life. For she had accepted nothing. I knew nothing of her scheme. I was saddened like the others, for I felt it was my fault that she had got this fever, that she was vulnerable and wished herself dead. My fault.'

She glanced down at the knife, watched it gleam in the sun.

'And then the murders began. It seemed like God's retribution for my failures. You heard the nuns. They never saw my discipline as needful, but as cruelty for the individual. It was never that. It was their souls. And time after time, it *did* help them. Or . . . have I deceived myself in that too?'

Crispin kept his eye on the knife. 'I have seen many abbots, abbesses, and prioresses do their utmost in this regard. They have all taken their charges seriously, their actions tempered by

God's direction. Lady Prioress. Surely . . . surely your prayers on the matter . . .'

'Of course. I prayed. I begged for guidance. I even wrote to the bishop when I questioned what I should do, and he agreed with me. The letters there . . .' She gestured with her knife toward the table with the papers on it. 'And, strangely, though there could be no connection, I suddenly thought that it had to do with Dame Audrey. Always Audrey. How she plagued me with her rashness, her anger, *and* her merriment. It seemed at odds and yet – it was easy to accept it all in this one unusual person. I could not sleep. I walked my floors in the dark. And one night, I heard something. I saw out of the window a figure in a nun's habit striding across the path, just there.' She pointed out of the window. 'At first, I thought it might be our ghost. But I wasn't afraid. Because I recognized that walk. It was clearly Dame Audrey. And I thought, "Of course she would return as a spirit." Of course she would stay to vex us. And perhaps she had frightened off our more historical ghost. She returned almost every night and I waited for her in the dark so that she wouldn't see me. And the more I watched, the more I began to realize that . . . she was no ghost, no phantom of my imagination. But miraculously, it was her, alive. And so, you see, when the murders began, I did think it was her.'

'Why did you not tell me this?'

She cocked her head to one side, the veil moving with her. 'That I suspected a ghost? I suppose I *wanted* to see her, even in this strange guise. But . . . I couldn't let her continue to kill. It was she who killed Dame Mildred. I am certain of it. Why, I don't know. I think it was because she was the first to walk into the church where Dame Audrey lay in wait.'

'Why did she murder at all?'

'She was angry at us. She was angry that we had kept her here, away from her lover. And when he died, she must have snapped. I . . . I found her veil on the path. It was covered in blood. I took it to the bakery ovens and burned it.'

'You were seen.'

'Was I?'

'But not identified. Prioress, what made you decide you'd had enough?'

'It was when she attacked your friend. I followed Dame Audrey that night when she was on her prowl. I wanted to stop any mischief she might be planning to cause. I kept well away from her. I didn't know your false nun was following *me*.'

'And Dame Audrey got in behind her.'

'I should have stopped her. I heard the commotion. And then I heard . . . you. And I knew all was well.'

Good Christ. All of this could have been spared. All the murders.
'And then what did you do?'

'The next day, after the midday meal, I left the priory to find her. I knew where she would be. She had told me much over the years. I thought she was unburdening herself. But I think perhaps she was laughing at us, at our little lives in this little priory. There was a place near Old Dean that she had favored. A tavern. She found lodgings there, still wearing her habit. I confronted her in an alley. I had no weapons . . . but these hands.' She looked down at them, and at the one still holding the knife. 'And I . . . I lashed out. I must have been mad for those long moments. I crushed her throat, stopped the laughter, stopped the lies, the charm she exuded.' She took a deep breath. 'I could have left her there, I suppose. But I wanted her gone. I wanted her in the Thames where she would be swept out to sea. Where all her sins could finally be washed away. That was more fitting. So I hefted her up, pretended she was drunk, and dragged her to the street. God was with me even in my sin, for He had kept the streets empty of people and I was able to get her down the embankment. I tied rocks to her girdle, and I rolled her into the river where she sank. But there are no secrets from the Lord. And though I tried to make myself believe He was with me, He made the death known so that all matters of sin would come to light, as they must.'

'I am sorry it has come to this, Lady Prioress.'

'So am I, Master Guest. Fear not. You will be paid your due. I have left those instructions.' She looked at him serenely but with a forlorn shadow in her eyes, and suddenly raised the knife and stabbed it into her throat through the wimple. Blood spurted forth and sprayed her table and all the parchments upon it.

Crispin gasped, slid across the table, and grabbed her, taking her down to the floor. But he knew a wound like that – cutting the artery as she had – would be mortal.

He shouted for the chaplain out of instinct, and she came running but, as he suspected, there was nothing to be done.

TWENTY-FOUR

B ishop Braybrooke sat in his office, shaking his head. Crispin – cote-hardie spattered with the prioress's blood, and a dazed Jack standing by his side – had just finished telling his tale for the *fourth* time. First, he had told it to Jack, then to the sheriffs, and then to the coroner, who – wondering if this were an ecclesi-astical matter rather than a Crown affair – ordered him to go to the bishop immediately to tell *him*.

'It can scarce be believed,' said the bishop. His eyes seemed haunted by what Crispin had told him, and Crispin vaguely wondered if *his* eyes looked similar after all *he* had seen.

'Such events . . . have been known to happen,' said Crispin softly, remembering those instances when he had been just as help-less to stop them.

Braybrooke looked up at him then, appraising him with brown eyes in the kindest manner they had ever gazed upon Crispin. Then his glance moved to Jack. He must have been wondering if this was the same boy who had escorted Crispin for all these years. 'Is your man trustworthy?' he asked.

Surprised by the question, Crispin couldn't help but turn his head toward Jack. 'Yes, Your Excellency. He is my apprentice, Jack Tucker. There is no man more reliable in all of England. He's been with me these last fifteen years.'

Jack lowered his face. His cheeks seemed almost as red as his hair.

'Very well. I feel I must tell you this because . . . well. Because you sacrificed all for the sake of Lancaster and I have it on good authority that you are still a Lancaster man.'

Crispin never stopped to think if he'd be in the fire for saying so. It simply came out. 'On my oath, my lord.'

The bishop picked a letter from the layers of parchment on the table before him, grasped it between his ink-stained fingers, and raised it up. 'The Duke of Lancaster is coming to London.'

The title startled him. But of course the bishop meant *Henry*, not

John; not Crispin's mentor, who had been dead now for these past eight months. Henry was now Duke of Lancaster, a title he held along with those of Earl of Derby, Earl of Northampton and Hereford, and Duke of Hereford. What other title would he soon add?

'I had heard that was the case,' he answered breathlessly. How he longed to be with him in his army. How he longed to know just what was transpiring along the road. Were Richard's men laying siege to Henry's strongholds? Was it to be civil war? For he could not entirely believe the few brief tidings that came through: that Henry was offered no resistance; that his troops moved unimpeded throughout the countryside. It seemed too good to be true. And what was Richard doing all this time? Was he still treated as the king?

Was he still the king?

'Please, Your Excellency. I long to know. What is the news? Is there to be war?'

'The news is strange, Master Guest. There has been little by way of resistance to his forces. City after city has submitted to him without so much as an arrow loosed. And . . . London has already sent emissaries to submit to him.'

Crispin blinked, unable to parse his thoughts. 'I don't understand . . .'

'Have you ever been to the shore, Master Guest? To the coast? Have you ever seen the tide coming in, the crashing of waves drawing closer and closer up the beach, licking at the rugged coastline, taking bits of it with its inexorable march? Then . . . this is what appears to be happening. Lancaster moves relentlessly forward without so much as drawing a sword or razing a village. And he gathers more eddies to his overarching wave, growing stronger as he goes. The men of England have seemed to have decided. And they have turned away from Richard for the hope of Henry.'

'But . . . when did all this happen? Yes, I've heard the disgruntlement here and there, but this is always so, no matter who governs.'

Braybrooke's brows clenched and furrowed as he surveyed the many writs and missives before him. 'It has been advancing for some years. You recall when Lancaster headed the lords who forced Richard to better judgment?'

Of course he remembered! That, too, was a distressing time. A delegation of lords led by Henry came to correct Richard's mistakes and took charge of the realm as stewards for two years. They even briefly had Richard in the Tower. Many of the lords – even Henry's own uncle – wondered if Henry would relinquish the throne to his cousin. And then he did, and the country breathed again. But this time?

'Yes, my lord. How could I forget?'

'That was plainly his intention this time as well, to serve as steward over Richard. And to regain his inheritance.'

'But this time feels different.'

Braybrooke nodded. 'It is, Master Guest.'

'Indeed. For you have not liked me, my lord, and now you seem to treat me with more deference. Is there a reason?'

His gaze was steady on Crispin, but not angry. 'You have proved yourself, Guest. Over the years and by your deeds. You have become the man you were always meant to be. If, in the past, I did not treat you as a son of the Church then, well, I apologize for that short-sightedness.'

Crispin flicked a glance at Jack before he straightened his shoulders. 'I thank you for that, my lord.'

'I want you to have a care, Guest. I want you to listen to good advice and to keep your head down.'

'I am now in my middle years, my lord. I am not the young and brash knight of days gone by, with no discretion, leaping to great deeds. I'd like to think I am more cautious these days.' He looked to Jack to confirm it, but Jack's face was blank with fear.

'Well,' said Braybrooke, seeming embarrassed by his admonishment. He gathered his parchments and shuffled them together, adjusting a ribbon here, a leather strap with a wax seal there. 'I had hoped you had grown a little.'

'I will not jeopardize my family nor Henry by making myself visible to the court.'

'A family? I had not heard that, Master Guest.'

Crispin shuffled his feet. 'Not *my* family, my lord. But that of my . . . my apprentice here. They are . . . important to me.'

'I see.' His eyes raked over Jack, perhaps trying to discern something he had missed before. 'You have been valuable to London, sir. And I didn't want any impetuosity to endanger that.'

'I'm flattered that you have followed my career, Your Excellency.'

'One can scarcely avoid it.' That was the Braybrooke Crispin remembered. 'And now, Guest. Another matter.' The bishop took another missive from his pile and clutched it. 'I understand that you are friends with the Walcotes of Mercery Lane.'

The non sequitur took him off guard again. 'Yes, my lord?'

'I have received this letter. Perhaps it would be a kindness if *you* were to go to them, to tell them—'

But the bishop was cut off because of a sudden loud exclamation in the streets, pouring in from the open windows. The people were shouting. He and Jack ran to the window and looked out.

The streets were filled with people. They were moving in one direction and their voices lifted together in adulation: 'Long live the Duke of Lancaster!' they cried.

Without taking his leave of the bishop, Crispin ran for the door and joined the throng outside, his heart clattering in his chest like a drumbeat.

TWENTY-FIVE

Crispin pushed his way through the crowd, hoping to see him, when, abruptly, someone grabbed him and pulled him forward and encased him in strong arms. It took Crispin mere moments to guess who it was . . . as he eyed the armor-clad men surrounding him.

Henry, Duke of Lancaster, pushed Crispin back. Tears were on his face and he turned to his companion, whose hand was ready at his sword hilt. 'Hotspur! Do you not know this man? This is Crispin Guest. I told you of him.'

Hotspur? Crispin knew who the lord was: Henry Percy, Earl of Northumberland. He tried to give the man a respectful bow but Henry manhandled him again, shaking his arm.

'Crispin,' Henry went on. 'This is Harry Percy.'

Crispin was finally allowed to bow low with great dignity. 'My lord.'

Henry seemed giddy, like the young man he had known. 'I can't believe I have found you. That you were *right* here. God has smiled upon me!'

'I have so many questions,' Crispin began, but he shut his lips, knowing well that there was no time for him to be indulged with answers.

Northumberland glanced toward their men and huffed an impatient sigh. 'Your Grace,' he said, 'we must see the bishop . . .'

'Only a moment, Hotspur. Crispin, will you march in my company?'

Crispin's heart burned and the words came stickily to his lips. 'I . . . I swore an oath to Richard.'

Henry seemed surprised. 'But . . . you broke that oath twenty years ago.'

'No, my lord. It was *three* years ago. When the good queen died.'

Henry paused, taken aback. 'You swore an oath to a traitor?'

Crispin lowered his face. At the time, it seemed the sensible thing to do. Richard was grieving and had just confessed his love of Crispin, that he had looked up to him, that he had felt more than betrayed by his treason. It pierced to the heart then as it did now.

'You were in the right the first time, Crispin,' he said loftily. 'You had sworn an oath to a prince who could never be princely; to a king who would never be a proper king. My father *should* have been king . . .' He calmed suddenly, licking the spittle from his lips, took a breath, and, aware again of his very public surroundings, lowered his voice. 'He should have been king.'

'I don't know that I can go through it all again, Henry,' he rasped. 'I mean . . . my lord.' He couldn't help darting a glance at Northumberland, standing stoically, albeit impatiently, behind Henry.

'Crispin,' said Henry, 'Richard banished me for no good reason. And when my father died, like any common thief, he *stole* all my lands!'

'I was there. When John died.'

He grabbed Crispin's arm once more. '*You* were there?'

'As I promised. His last thoughts were of you. He loved you.'

Henry's lip trembled. His face contorted, trying to master himself. At last he nodded. 'I'm glad *you* were there. He loved you too.' He straightened, girded himself. 'The past is over. All oaths are wiped away. Pledge a new oath to me and to England. For my father. For the House of Lancaster.'

Crispin stilled. The earlier pain of having to decide had fled. He swallowed and locked eyes with Henry. 'I have never forsworn my fealty to the House of Lancaster.'

Henry laughed and slapped him on the back. 'I knew it! I knew it! Crispin, come with us.'

He wiped his face with a shaky hand. 'With you . . . now?'

'We have business with the bishop, and . . . other business as well to attend to. It will be good if you are there.'

Crispin nodded, even as the suspicious eye of Northumberland narrowed upon him. He told Jack to go on home and await him there.

As it happened, Crispin returned to Braybrooke's lodgings with the rest of them. Their business was a strange conversation about precedent, about history. But Crispin soon understood what Henry wanted from the man. Mostly, the bishop gave Henry his fealty which seemed to please Henry well enough.

Later that day, Henry and Northumberland sat in the Lancaster apartments at Westminster Palace.

Crispin, marshalled with the other men into the room, never said a word, nor did Henry ask for his opinion. In fact, Henry seemed to have forgotten completely that Crispin was there. And why should he remember? It was just another whim of Henry's. Crispin was certainly not one to consult. He'd been out of the court for two decades. He had no cock in this fight. Instead, he stood as a shadow, as far away as possible, getting in no one's way. He knew that at any moment he could be asked to leave, and so he listened with great eagerness to what transpired.

Henry's squires were there in the room, staying close to the walls; Thomas Erpington and John Norbury. Another knight he was not acquainted with, a lord named William Willoughby, and Sir William Thirning, chief justice of the King's Bench, were also there.

The dowager duchess made a brief appearance to speak quietly to Henry, though Crispin was unable to hear what they said to one another. Henry listened solicitously, as he respected the Lady Katherine, and she even bestowed a kiss to his forehead in benediction. She seemed surprised to catch sight of Crispin, and before she left, she made a point of smiling and nodding to him.

'Now that we're here, Henry,' said Northumberland, relieved of the last of his armor and holding a large goblet of wine, 'what *are* we to do?' It seemed to be said more or less in jest because the moment was anything but merry. But it seemed to Crispin that a decision had to be made, and Henry seemed reluctant to make it.

Henry looked about the room. He was sitting in the biggest chair – his father's chair, with all the weight of the state burnished into its grain – and lowered his brows. 'The Earls and Dukes of Lancaster have been stewards of the realm for over a century,' he began, running a finger along the rim of his bejeweled cup. 'And steward I meant to be. But . . .'

His leg swung out wide as if he was still wearing his armor. Crispin well remembered that when one was at war, the lords and knights wore armor every day for weeks on end, and it did sometimes become a second skin. Once removed, you invariably forgot that you were *not* wearing it.

Henry stood and wandered in a leisurely way toward the sideboard. Norbury hurried to serve him more wine when he saw what Henry was about, but Henry waved the man off. He grabbed the silver flagon himself and poured more into his cup. Tipping the rim to his lips, he drank and walked back to his seat. His back was to the fire and he appeared as a demon among the flames.

'I truly meant to just be steward,' he said, looking at Northumberland. 'But I am not a fool.'

'No one said you were, Henry. Of late.' He brought the cup to his lips and smirked.

He smiled briefly at the jest before it faded. 'I, er, sent messages to every abbey I could think of and asked the abbots and chaplains – as I did to Bishop Braybrooke today – to scour the histories about the state of governance since the Conquest. What I need . . . what I *want* is precedence.'

'Precedence . . . for what, my Lord of Lancaster?' The earl seemed to be impatiently waiting for some pronouncement from Henry.

He glared at Northumberland. Had this been an argument between them since the campaign began? Crispin knew that throughout their lives, their relationship had been unsteady. It was on again, it seemed.

Henry expelled a long sigh. 'On the legal matter of . . . setting aside King Richard and of choosing me in his stead . . . and how it is to be done.'

Crispin held his breath. He couldn't believe what he was hearing. But of course, it had to be expected.

'God's legs! At last!' crowed Northumberland, throwing back his head and spilling the wine from his goblet. 'I thought you'd never say it.' He raised the cup. 'Long live King Henry!'

Henry's cheeks burnished a dark red, but he gestured for silence from the others when they took up the call.

'Let us not be premature,' he admonished the room. 'We need to make it legal and longstanding. We need to maintain order when transferring the throne. Richard was anointed under the eyes of God. Even if he resigned his office tomorrow, he could withdraw it by next sennight by benefit of that anointing. We need formal proceedings.'

'The only precedent,' said a dark-eyed knight who, to Crispin's mind, had a familiar look to him, 'is King Edward II.'

'Or Fredrick II,' said Thomas Arundel.

They all stared at him. 'Who the hell is that?' said the earl.

'He was king of Germany and Italy . . . and Holy Roman Emperor. In the thirteenth century.'

'Arundel,' said Percy, somewhat flabbergasted, 'how did you pull that out of your arse?'

He sent a chilly eye toward Percy and adjusted his gown. 'I studied my history. He was deposed by the pope for crimes against the Church and the state. For the "king's insufficiency".'

'The "king's insufficiency",' Henry murmured.

'This is ridiculous,' said Norbury. 'You're a Plantagenet. You *are* heir.' It seemed that Henry had taken up Crispin's habit of allowing underlings the right to speak their minds.

'He's not the *nearest* male heir, Norbury,' said Northumberland. 'Harken; Edmund, Earl of March – and where is he keeping himself through all this?' he asked of the room. 'Edmund, Earl of March, is descended from the female line from Edward III's *second* son. And our dear friend Henry Lancaster here is descended from the *third* son.'

'But not through the *female* line,' Norbury countered.

That brought Crispin up short and he eyed each man as they spoke.

'He may have something there, Henry,' said Percy.

Henry finally turned to the gray-eyed Sir William. 'What of it, Sir William? How do I become closer in descent to Richard?'

The older man – wheat-colored hair thinning on his scalp – put fingers to his lips in thought. 'There was some talk – I know not if there was any truth in it – that Edmund, Earl of Lancaster, had been a crouchback.'

'That's absurd!' piped Norbury.

Henry pointed to him. 'Quiet, Norbury. I wish to hear what our learned colleague has to say.'

Sir William continued. 'Suppose that Edmund was a crouchback. And suppose he had actually been the elder brother rather than the younger of King Edward I, but had been passed over because of this deformity.'

Henry edged forward on his chair. 'Is that true?'

'It is only something I heard,' said Sir William. 'Long ago.'

Crispin longed to whisper to Henry, to tell him not to go down this path, but scanning the men in the firelight, and realizing that Henry had not asked his opinion, he kept his own counsel.

Percy leaned toward Henry and spoke in a harsh and loud whisper. 'It's something that can be spread far and wide. So easily done.'

Crispin bristled, until Henry said, 'I am . . . uneasy about that. What if, instead, I were to claim the throne by Right of Conquest?' He looked to all the anxious faces, until Sir William shook his head.

'I fear that would make men of property anxious about keeping their holdings. Who is to say that the king might not conquer each of them?'

'Or take . . . as Richard has done to me?'

Sir William fell silent and the room was hushed again, as if a soft blanket had been draped upon it.

'I like this crouchback notion,' said the earl, breaking the silence. 'You are descended by the right line of the blood coming from the good King Henry III.'

Henry brooded, saying nothing.

The men talked late into the night. Crispin leaned against the wall, eyes drooping, when Henry was suddenly at his side, whispering to him. 'My men and myself have much to discuss.'

Crispin straightened and nodded. 'Do you . . . wish me to depart?'

'I think it might be best. You are still on the Shambles, are you not?'

'Yes.'

'Then I will send word to you there.' He grasped Crispin's arm briefly. 'I am gladdened to see you again.'

Crispin hesitated. He wanted to offer advice, but on looking at the men surrounding Henry, he didn't think his advice could hold much sway. Better that he was out of it.

He bowed low to Henry, and took his leave.

TWENTY-SIX

Once home, Crispin eased himself into his chair by the hearth, staring at the banked coals for a long time before he noticed Jack taking a knee beside him.

'What happened, sir?' he said softly.

Even as weary as he was, his whole body seemed to buzz with excitement. 'I think . . . I think I've been waiting for this for a long time, Jack. I fear to say aloud what he means to do.'

'Will he . . . will he be king, do you think?'

Crispin nodded disbelievingly.

'Master Crispin, you know I will do anything you command me.'

He smiled. 'Yes, I do. We will stay and await further word. We must be cautious. Though the cries of loyalty to Henry are endearing, it may yet end in war.' The elation he felt walking home turned suddenly to dread. He turned to Isabel, standing beside the hearth. 'Do we have enough stores so that you need not venture into the market?'

'Yes, Master Crispin. It might be a stretch of them, but we can manage.'

'Good. You're a very good seneschal to us, Isabel. But there must be no waste. Keep our meals humble.'

'Yes, sir.'

'And now . . .' He sat back and clutched the chair's arms. 'We wait.'

*   *   *

Crispin expected it to take days. Or longer. After his initial excitement, he began to reason that Henry's time was occupied in a legal way to force Richard from his office and . . . install himself. But just because he had spotted Crispin in such a serendipitous way, didn't mean that he would remember to call for *him* among all the important men he had gathered around him. Indeed, Crispin wondered why Henry had invited him along in their discussions without even asking his council. It pricked him only a little. After all, Crispin had been no one for twenty years. No one, but a fond memory to Henry's mind.

How he wanted to go to the Boar's Tusk! To sit among the fellows there with a cup in his hand and talk of what was transpiring. But he felt rooted to the spot, unwilling to be elsewhere in case Henry's men came for him.

It wasn't days but the *next* day. One of the young knights from the meeting with Henry, wearing a Lancaster badge on his surcoat, brought a missive and awaited Crispin outside the door as he read it.

Jack's face was pensive. 'What does it say, sir?'

Crispin read it over twice. 'I'm to go to the Tower and . . . and guard the prisoner.'

'The . . . prisoner?'

He lowered the parchment and simply breathed for a moment. 'Richard.'

Jack quickly saddled Tobias, and Crispin rode side by side with the Lancaster knight, who kept glancing at him silently until the man couldn't seem to help himself. 'You're that Crispin Guest who was the traitor, are you not?'

Crispin's expression was mild. 'Yes,' was all he said.

The knight nodded. 'Well . . . it just could be you were in the right all this time.'

Crispin kept silent . . . but the man's words were strangely satisfying.

They rode through Mercery and there seemed to be some activity around the Walcote estate. He could not tell what it was by the crowds, but neither was he at liberty to stop. He'd have to send a message to find out, and then he vaguely wondered if it had to do with what the Bishop of London was going to say to him. He had quite forgotten about that. Jack would know. Surely *he* could find out.

They took the right-most fork to Lombard Street and thence to Gracechurch Street, then the left at East Cheap until it became Tower Street.

'Have you ever been to the Tower, sir?'

The man's voice startled him, as he had been silent for so much of the journey. 'By the grace of God, I have not.'

'Oh, I see what you mean, sir.'

And of a sudden he was 'sir'. Crispin settled more comfortably on the saddle. 'I spent my traitorous time in Newgate,' he said glibly.

The knight stared at him. He was young – around twenty, Crispin thought. With a fresh face and a well-cultured beard. He again struck Crispin as familiar, but he did not know any men of that age. 'Well, pray God, Master Guest, there will be no more of that for you.'

This has to be a dream, he kept telling himself. He hadn't been treated with this much respect since . . . well. Since before he was purged from court.

They were allowed entry to the courtyard of the Tower and, truth to tell, Crispin *did* feel mildly uncomfortable.

Their horses were taken by grooms and they walked together into the precincts of the Tower, where they met the master of the guard in the gatehouse, a close room with a hearth on one side and a sideboard on the other. He sat in a chair with a high back at a long table, with parchments set before him.

'Crispin Guest, eh?' said the man, looking Crispin over before returning his attention to his work. 'So you're the one with friends in high places . . . or enemies, to have sent you to such a post. You are ordered to guard the prisoner in yon Tower apartments.' He gestured out through the window toward the White Tower, where it was said Richard was housed.

'Forgive me, master,' said Crispin. 'But . . . am I to understand that I am guarding . . . Richard Plantagenet?' He was careful not to grant him any honorifics that could be construed as royal.

'Guarding, securing. Whichever suits your definition best. This man will show you to your quarters.'

'I am to be quartered here? For how long?'

'For however long the Duke of Lancaster wishes it. Will you be trouble, Guest?'

'No, good master. Not at all. It is just . . . May I send a message to my apprentice? This news came sudden to me and I am not prepared.'

'Do what you wish. Show him his quarters and then to his duty.'

Crispin's escort gestured for him to follow. Crispin eyed the corridors, the windows, the entire precincts he could see when they took a stairway that brought him to another gatehouse with several modest rooms. They looked to be guards' rooms. The knight stood before one with an open door. 'Yours, Master Guest.'

He bowed. 'I thank you.'

'There is parchment, ink, and quill there,' he said, pointing to a table within the mean chamber. 'Write out your missive and I will have someone run it to your apprentice.'

With a bow, Crispin entered the chamber. He saw a cold hearth with wood beside it and a tinder box on the mantel, a modest bed with linens and a pot beneath it, a basin and jug, a bucket for fetching water, and a candle in an iron holder sitting on the table, which had one chair pulled up to it. The place smelled of old fires and mustiness. The cobwebs in the upper corners proved that it hadn't been recently inhabited. He sat and wrote a hasty note to Jack before folding the parchment and using his nail to crease it tight.

He left the chamber and handed it to the knight, who tucked it into his belt. 'Come,' he said.

Crispin rested his hand on the hilt of his sword. He was glad to have that, at least. He wouldn't need to be issued one from the arms stores. He was sufficiently ranked that his sword would do. At least he used to be. Only foot soldiers bore pikes.

He supposed Henry thought this would be a great honor for Crispin, or perhaps vengeance for his banishment from court life, but it had been too long ago. He didn't feel the need for vengeance any longer. After all, Crispin had *been* guilty of treason.

They climbed a stair and found the apartments, a grand door studded with iron nails.

'Am I . . .' Crispin glanced back at the elaborate ironwork of the hinges and door latch. 'Am I to be in possession of a key?'

'It is not locked, Master Guest. But the prisoner is not allowed to leave. He may have guests, particularly that Frenchman Jean Creton who is in there now. He's harmless. A mere chronicler from the French court. And from time to time you will no doubt see his other guards, Thomas of Gloucester and Thomas Arundel.'

Crispin squared his shoulders. 'They will not be pleased to see me.'

'Maybe not. But if Lancaster says so, they will *learn* to be pleased.' The man turned away, having acquitted his duty, but Crispin stopped him.

'Sir. I do not know your name. I wish to thank you and remember your kindness in my prayers.'

He smiled. 'Thomas Beaufort. You . . . er, left the late Duke of Lancaster's service the year I was born to Katherine Swynford.'

'Thomas,' he breathed. He looked the man over anew. Little wonder he looked familiar. His aspect was a bit of John of Gaunt and a bit of Lady Katherine. Born a bastard, he had regained his legitimacy after John and Katherine married, and he and his other siblings had been given the surname Beaufort. 'I . . . I had naturally heard of you, but . . .'

'You should have been part of our household. I always wished you were. I heard such stories, you see, from my father. But they were always tempered by a cautionary note. "See what can happen if you are not prudent" was the moral of that story. But I think that was the wrong message. It should have been likened to the tortoise and the hare: slow and steady wins the race. For some of the naysayers are in their graves, aren't they? And . . . well. Here you are.'

Here I am, he thought. *From the fat to the fire.*

'God keep you, Crispin Guest. We shall meet again.' He patted the missive he'd tucked into his belt. 'And I shall send this directly.'

'Thank you, my lord.'

Crispin watched him disappear down the steps and he spent a good long moment thinking about that bastard child – and then his own – before the door behind him opened.

And there was Richard, or rather, the *ghost* of Richard, for he looked nothing like the man when he'd last seen him. He was always pale and effete, but now he looked drawn and far older than his years. Richard was . . . thirty-two now, he reckoned. But oh. These last months had aged him. His cheeks were hollowed, his eyes haunted, and his skin sallow. His hair, always meticulously coiffed with a cultivated inward curl at the ends, simply hung there. His beard, which had been equally cared for and sculpted to his delicate jaw, was now mere wisps of mousy-brown hair.

Crispin, his training too inculcated, bowed. 'Sire,' passed his lips, before he could pull the word back.

Richard raised a brow. 'Crispin Guest. We never expected to see you here. But why not? Everything is in full circle, isn't it?'

'I . . . have no answer for that . . . my lord.'

'Arundel and Gloucester we expected. And now Lancaster throws another traitor into our face.'

'That was not *my* intention, my lord. I am here merely in obedience.'

'To *Lancaster*,' he growled.

It took a moment for Crispin to realize that this man could no longer harm him. He raised his chin. 'I have *always* been a Lancaster man.'

Richard nodded. 'So we see. Look here, Jean.' He turned back into the chamber from his place in the doorway. He pushed the door wider and Crispin spied a man in French-style clothing. This must be that chronicler about whom he had been told. 'Look, Maître Creton. This is the man I told you of. Crispin Guest. He was convicted of this same treachery some twenty-two years ago. He was part of a plot to take us, the rightful king, from the throne, and place his mentor the Duke of Lancaster in our stead. The elder Lancaster, that is. And now . . . history repeats itself.'

Crispin gave a nod. 'Maître Creton.'

Jean Creton bowed cautiously to Crispin, never taking his eyes from him.

'There's no need to add me to your chronicle, Maître. I am but a mere brief note in any history.'

'Every man may play a part in history that he knows not of,' answered the man in heavily accented English.

'True. But my story is done as far as the English court is concerned.'

Creton said nothing to this. The both of them – king and chronicler – merely stared at Crispin from their doorway.

'Well, my lords,' said Crispin uncomfortably. 'I am to begin my duty to guard you, so I am not able to ask if there is anything you want, for I may not leave my post.'

'Guard us,' spat Richard. 'That would imply you are protecting us.'

'And so I am, my lord.'

Richard frowned. 'And so you are. There has been no general uproar that we are treated thus. There are no champions to rescue us. We are surrounded by enemies. So it *is* meet that you protect us, Guest. You, of all people.'

'Surely you know by now, my lord, that I will always do what is right and not what is expected.'

Richard made a sound that could have been a laugh. 'So I should. But I do recall your swearing an oath to me, Guest. An oath that you would be loyal to *us*.'

And he recalled it too. It was at the death of the queen as she lay in Saint Stephen's Chapel at Westminster Palace. Crispin was on his knees to Richard, wondering if he was to live past the encounter, when Richard's softened voice said the impossible, that he loved Crispin and had wanted him at court at his side before his betrayal.

'Time . . . changes circumstances.'

Richard laughed bitterly. 'How convenient is Time. When it can make men forswear themselves over and over again.'

Crispin took a breath. 'I fear none of my answers will satisfy, my lord.'

'And you called us "sire" at first, Guest. Well . . . I suppose you have realized the new conditions. And you're right. You are not my friend either.'

'But *I* am your friend, Your Majesty.'

Crispin turned . . . and couldn't quite believe what he was seeing. It was Edward Grafton, and his sword was drawn.

TWENTY-SEVEN

'Edward, for Christ's sake, sheath your weapon.'

'Master Crispin, I am deeply sorry that it is you here, guarding our king. But that cannot be helped. Step aside.'

Crispin drew his blade. 'Edward, you will never make it out of the Tower alive.'

'I owe everything to King Richard. He took me in when no one would. And it was all your fault.'

'I know. And I am truly sorry for it. But they will cut you down if you try to escape with him.'

'Will you stand in my way? How many times can you forswear your oaths?'

'As many times as necessary!' he spat through clenched teeth. He truly had meant to keep his oath to Richard this time. But when a better man – a Lancaster! – had taken stewardship of the realm, there simply was no other option. 'Now step back, Edward. I don't want to kill you.'

Grafton seemed surprised at his vehemence. His blade lowered slightly. 'You'd kill me?'

'As you seem prepared to do to me.'

'Time and circumstances,' chirped Richard. 'It comes in many colors, Master Guest. Time to reap the consequences.'

'Get back into your chamber!' growled Crispin. He flicked a glance over his shoulder with a sneering, 'My *lord*.'

Richard, furious at the slight, stepped back within and slammed the door.

Crispin adjusted his grip on his sword hilt and inhaled sharply. 'I give you one last warning, Edward.'

'It is *Sir* Edward.'

'Truly? That's the way you want it. Very well. *Edward*.' His reluctance fled. He swung outward to slash at the man's ankles, but Edward's blade was there to block him.

'You forget, Crispin, that you taught me everything you know of swordsmanship.'

Damn. He hadn't reckoned on that. 'I am predictable, am I? Then I shall have to be *un*predictable.' He suddenly brought up the sword with a snap toward the squire's face. Edward barely blocked it in time. Crispin grinned.

'You're an old man, Guest. You can't keep this up.'

'We'll see.'

Crispin held his blade high behind his neck and swiveled, using the momentum of his coiled body to swing the blade quickly and with strength. As expected, Edward pressed forward, tilting himself off balance to meet the blade, and struck Crispin's out of the way. But he couldn't recover his balance in time when Crispin followed through on his pivot and brought his left arm up and down until he trapped Edward's blade by the hilt under his armpit and slammed the flat of his own sword into Edward's face.

Edward stumbled back, his nose bloodied and his sword barely still within his grasp.

'I never taught you that one,' said Crispin, trying not to show how winded he was.

The former squire wiped the blood from his mouth, then spat it onto the stone floor between them. 'So there's some fight left in you, old man.'

'Old man? There *is* fight in me. Know you not who gave me this blade?'

'Who would be such a fool as to give a traitor a sword?'

'So *there's* the man I suspected you'd become,' he rumbled, disappointed. 'What fool? What fool indeed, other than Henry, Duke of Lancaster.'

Edward's eyes widened only slightly. He readied himself again. Crispin wondered how long he *could* last in a fight. Though he practiced regularly now with Jack and Christopher, he was not as fit as he had been in his younger days of daily practice.

He'd hesitated too long. Hadn't he told Jack and Christopher over and over not to give one's opponent an opportunity to strategize? And here he was, defending a blow – a strong one – from Edward's vicious back-handed swing.

Crispin desperately wanted to shake out his hand. It buzzed from the pain of it. But he didn't dare show a weakness that Edward could exploit.

This time, as they slowly circled one another, Crispin started with his sword in a low position and brought it up with a snap, and just as Edward's sword met his with a clang and a spark, Crispin whipped his wrist around and chopped at Edward's arm, turning the blade over his wrist to stab it into the squire's right shoulder.

Edward scrabbled out of the way, and quickly looked down at his houppelande; at the sleeve and the shoulder blooming with red.

By the look on his face, he didn't seem to quite believe Crispin would do him harm. His emotions appeared to pass over his eyes like a shadow and suddenly his expression hardened.

God's blood. Crispin bounced on one foot then the other. Edward was angry now. And an angry fighter was far more dangerous. Crispin had taught Edward years ago to never give way to his emotions when fighting. Fatal mistakes could be made. But what he didn't tell him was that it could also be an advantage. An angry man took chances. And if Edward was lucky, those chances could win him the day.

Crispin couldn't afford that. He took several steps back. He could smell his own sweat infuse his chemise beneath his cote-hardie.

Footsteps approaching down the corridor.

He did not dare look. He couldn't take his gaze away for one moment while Edward faced off with him.

He saw Edward thinking. He couldn't allow him to. Crispin lunged forward and slammed up the blade into the squire's elbow . . . and drew back from the charge immediately.

The squire was bloody in three places now, while Crispin was only winded.

He hated this. He was ashamed of Edward for his faithless reversal, but he didn't want to kill the man. All he could see before him was the boy he had been, how he had trained him, the merry times they had had together, much like he and Jack. But unlike Edward, Jack never took his position for granted. Jack's hard life had taught him that even a scrap of bread could be taken from him by an oppressor. Jack's gratitude put him in better stead in a fight, because he knew how much more he could lose. Edward had had only a small taste of it, but in the end, his blood, his name prevailed and Richard himself had taken him in. Perhaps to spite Crispin. Edward hadn't truly learned the lesson. And it saddened Crispin with a dull ache in his heart.

A cry from Edward's throat, and Crispin snapped up his attention and met him again, blade for blade. While their swords were entangled, Crispin raised his leg and kicked hard, landing the blow to Edward's chest.

Edward stumbled back but, by then, more knights had arrived and surrounded them, and Crispin was spared more swordplay. He heaved a sigh of relief.

'Sir Edward!' cried the Tower knight in a green surcoat. 'What is the meaning of this?'

'What is the meaning?' Edward's wild eyes took in the surrounding knights and guards, for more arrived and still more were on their way. 'I could ask the same of you! What treason is here that imprisons the rightful King of England?'

'Come, Sir Edward. The writing is on the wall. He is the prisoner. There is no other title needed.'

'Says you. And you. And the traitor Crispin Guest here.'

'Edward,' Crispin offered softly. 'Edward. It is over.'

'It is *not* over!' He raised his sword again.

But the knight in the green surcoat struck down on his wrist, disarming him. Edward's sword clattered to the stone floor. He lunged for it, but the other knights grappled him.

'You will come with us,' said the green knight.

Edward sneered once at Crispin, fighting with his captors until he was forcibly hauled away. What would become of him? Crispin wondered. He'd be imprisoned somewhere, no doubt. A traitor to the new Crown.

The knights marched away and soon the corridor fell to silence again.

Crispin set his jaw and sheathed his weapon with a snap. He cast a glance at the closed door that barred him from Richard, and, satisfied that it remained shut, took up his place, arms folded over his chest, in front of the door.

TWENTY-EIGHT

While Crispin guarded, twice Henry came to Richard to ask for his resignation, and twice, after much bellowing on Henry's part, he left, dissatisfied.

On the third time, when he walked into Richard's lodgings in the Tower with a delegation of men, Crispin stepped into the doorway and watched, saying nothing. It certainly wasn't his place to speak.

Henry stood before Richard, who was garbed in a silken gown as if he were to address the court. He wore his crown.

Henry looked tired. Crispin knew that he had the weight of all

England on his shoulders and still hadn't called himself king yet. 'I am here, cousin. As requested. Are you willing to resign?'

Richard pressed his hands together before him. 'We have considered this proposal carefully, dear cousin. And we are willing in the interests of your person, but only upon certain conditions—'

'No!' Henry's voice resounded within the vaulted chamber. 'These conditions must cease. You are no longer in a position to ask for conditions. You will resign, simply and without conditions.'

Richard, ever proud, ever the peacock, suddenly seemed to grow smaller in Crispin's eyes. Instead of his gown bringing him a symbol of his power, it made him look like a weakling, as if he were in his dressing gown, like a man who had just stepped out of his bath: vulnerable, taken unawares.

'What a strange land this is,' he said, voice choked and graveled from the pain clearly etched on his face. 'A strange land and fickle, which has exiled, slain, or ruined so many kings and great men, and is ever tainted with strife and envy.' He slowly reached up and grasped the gold circlet on his head, ornamented with its golden leaves and small jewels, and lifted it. His brown hair did not seem to want to relinquish it, holding on to the circlet as it lifted from the royal head until each strand – one by one – fell away, as if also surrendering to the moment.

It was off his head at last and he held it above him like a halo.

All eyes, shining bright, followed it. It hung there like a painting of a saint on a wall. Richard, like Saint Sebastian struck multiple times with arrows, in his agony looked heavenward. The crown, its leafy points, its gems sparkling in the firelight, looked suddenly like an otherworldly thing. Such a simple ornament that embodied so much. The crown. Was it something a man could simply give over to another, like charity? Ought it not be seized by the stronger, the one with the right, with the blessings of God Almighty?

Richard's hands trembled just that much as he lowered it to his thigh. He turned it in his hands, perhaps watching the play of light upon the gold, the way the object shined, the purity of its metal. Then his gaze flicked briefly toward Henry, and for that moment Crispin held his breath. Was he going to hand it over to Henry at last? Was he going to simply bestow it upon his cousin, his enemy – an enemy *he* himself had made?

But no. Richard stepped into the space left between him alone and the men that surrounded him, and he placed it upon the floor like a meal for a dog, as if offering it as a free-for-all. Did he think they'd *all* make a grab for it?

But no one moved. No one breathed.

He stared at it a moment more before he whispered, 'I resign my right to God.'

Northumberland stepped forward at last to break the spell it held over them, and bent to retrieve the crown.

Northumberland held it for so long Crispin wondered if *he* had fancies for a crown. Perhaps every noble, every lord imagined it. But in that particular moment, standing between the weakling Richard and the powerful Henry, a crown seemed to be far more trouble than it was worth.

In the end, the earl must have thought so too, for he pivoted and faced Henry, presenting it to him.

Henry took it in his hands and scrutinized it, turning it, too, in the light, watching it gleam. But he did not put it on his head as Crispin expected him to. Henry wanted it all legally done. He would not stand as the conqueror, much as his men had implored him to do. Instead, he would wait until the Archbishop of Canterbury placed it upon his head right and proper under the vaulting rafters of Westminster Abbey. Only when Henry was anointed in holy oil would it be his.

Crispin stood off to the side, even as Percy loured over Richard. They had papers for Richard to sign to present to Parliament. Percy's knight laid the parchments on the table.

Richard signed one after the other, not bothering to read them at all. And when he had put quill to the last document, he lowered his face and said almost too softly to hear, 'I hope my cousin will be a good lord to me.' Crispin noticed he had dropped the 'we' and 'us' monikers when addressing himself. Something new had passed before them all. Did the others notice? he wondered, eyes scanning their faces. But they were occupied with the parchments themselves, the knight gathering them, adjusting them, and then they all looked to Henry.

And with that, King Richard was no longer royalty. He was now Sir Richard of Bordeaux, an ordinary knight.

TWENTY-NINE

13 October 1399, London

I t had all been such a whirlwind, Crispin did not know how to
assess all that had happened. After Richard had renounced the
throne, Crispin was no longer required to serve as his gaoler.
Other nobles were put in his place and Crispin was obliged to leave
the Tower and return home to the Shambles without so much as a
fare-thee-well. But he did send a letter to Henry, begging for
Edward Grafton's life. Not too long after, he got word from
Henry's chamberlain Hugh Waterton that his former squire had
been released but he was no longer part of the palace's household.
History repeating itself.

But he hadn't heard this from Henry. In fact, he'd heard nothing
from Henry since that day – weeks ago now – he'd been embraced
before St Paul's, and today was his coronation.

Well, that's that. He had hoped . . . well. He shouldn't have. It
was one thing giving Crispin leave to be part of the end of Richard's
reign, but another thing entirely to have a former traitor serve at
the court. No one would ever forget that Crispin had forsworn
himself. And if a man did it once, who was to say he would
never do it again? Which Crispin had. It was fair and wise. He
couldn't begrudge Henry. But he couldn't help the disappointment
stabbing at his heart.

Perhaps that was why Jack looked at him with such sadness
all the time now, even as they moved through the crowd around
Westminster Abbey. Little Gilbert sat on Jack's shoulders and Little
Crispin was on Crispin's. They had left the others at home, especially when Isabel begged off from being jostled by the crowds.

And jostled they were. He was glad they had the boys on their
shoulders. He would otherwise have worried about them lost
among the people.

They all surged forward, for so many pressed on from behind.
For once, he reveled in being part of the rabble, surrounded by the

sweat and stink of humanity. He was one of *them*, and every Englishman could hold his head high to be standing there at this moment.

Garlands of greenery, with what flowers could be had, festooned the houses and shops along the route in great swags, even strung up across the way and hanging over the people's heads. Smoke from the many chimneys of Westminster mingled with the faraway scent of incense drifting out of the open doors of the cathedral. A strange day indeed.

'Jack, what the devil troubles you? Aren't you pleased to have me back home?'

He blinked, seeming to come back to himself from thoughts far away. 'Oh, aye, sir. It's just . . .' He curled the beard at his chin in his fingers.

'You expected I would be welcomed into Westminster?' His eyes scanned up the face of the cathedral, its rose window lit with the candles from within. 'This is Henry's day. He may not wish a traitor by his side.'

'But you were traitor for his father!' He glanced at Little Crispin on so high a perch and listening intently. He lowered his voice. 'I didn't mean that. And anyway, it's for something else. Something I never got a chance to tell you . . .'

But the loud procession on the streets parted the crowd and there was music and shouting as Henry rode by on his horse in regal costume. He seemed draped in ermine and gold and shone like the sun. Crispin eagerly watched him ride past, and he had to admit that his eyes misted over at the sight.

'You're glad,' shouted Jack beside him.

He nodded. He was afraid to speak and betray himself. He clutched tight to the child's legs on his chest.

'We should have brought the horses,' yelled Jack, but Crispin could scarce hear him.

Richard was unseated and a Lancaster was on the throne. It made his heart glad, and, raising his face to the sky and closing his eyes, he gave thanks to the often fickle Lord of them all . . . and sent up an additional prayer for John of Gaunt.

As the soon-to-be-king passed up the steps and through the arched portal, the crowd began to quiet, for now was the holy service that Crispin wished he could see; the orb and scepter, the sword of justice, the anointing of his hands, feet, and head, and then the crown – with arches in the shape of a cross, styled like an empirical crown – would be set upon his head by the newly restored Archbishop of Canterbury. He was to be King Henry IV. 'And to think I had him on my shoulders like Little Crispin here.'

Jack turned to him.

He hadn't meant to say that aloud. But why not? It was an incredible thing. And to think that Crispin had survived to see this day . . .

'That's . . . that's . . .' But Jack couldn't think of the words either and shook his head in amazement. And then . . . 'He won't forget you, will he, Master Crispin?'

Crispin sighed. 'He's a very important man now, Jack. He'll have many other things on his mind. He remembered me enough to have me guard in the Tower. It is enough.'

But was it? Crispin had tried to dismiss his other thoughts, his desires. He hadn't had these thoughts in decades. They were daydreams, wishes. Of not living on the Shambles anymore. Of finding his place again at court. His hopes had run high in these last few weeks. But nothing had come of his time in the Tower. Oh, he had witnessed Richard's relinquishing of the crown, and that was a heady moment that few on this earth had seen. But he had expected . . . more.

It was damnable having his heart trod on again. He shouldn't have allowed himself to hope. It was a deadly poison so insidious that it infected every part of him, even his soul.

He shook it loose. His hands were still on the boy's legs on his shoulders and he felt the warmth of him. A child named after him. How strange. Of course, Philippa had named Christopher – a name she said was as close to Crispin's name as she could get without raising suspicions. And where *was* that boy?

He looked around. 'Crispin,' he said to the child, shaking one of his legs. 'Look about, see if you can detect Christopher Walcote. He's likely here somewhere. Although, his family is important enough that he might be inside.'

He felt the boy twist and turn, scanning the crowd.

'I don't see him, sir.'

Jack looked as if he would say something, but he bit his lip instead and clutched at Gilbert's legs.

They should have got here earlier, Crispin bemoaned. They could have got closer to the door to at least hear the ceremony. But he did hear the first, 'God save King Henry!' And soon the crowd took it up, and Crispin was as full-throated on it as was his fellow citizens. 'God save King Henry!' rang out like a wave, up and down the rabble, and even the young voices of Jack's boys yelled it out with joy, though they little knew why.

Trumpets sounded and the procession left the church. There were courtiers holding a canopy over his head, one at each of the four corners, and there he was, gleaming crown, ermine, and golden cloth. His horse was brought forth and he mounted so that all the crowd could see. And soon his nobles mounted and all around him the resplendent aspect of the court, with cloaks and pennons flickering in the wind. All of Westminster cheered, and Crispin thought that Henry still looked surprised at it. For Richard was no longer in the Tower. He was God knew where. And what was ultimately to be done with him?

Crispin knew. And he knew that Henry seemed in denial of it. But when one has taken the crown of another, one cannot leave an extra king about. The devil was in the details, for how would it happen? How and who would kill the former King of England?

They followed the procession as far as they could as they wended their way through Westminster and toward Westminster Hall. It was time to go back to London. There were two sleepy boys atop their shoulders, after all, and much excitement they had had this day.

It took longer to return to the Shambles than usual, for the streets were crowded. Who knew London was seething with this much humanity? But Isabel was glad to see her boys safe and sound, and she sat them down and fed them as they talked and talked about what they had seen.

Jack clapped Crispin on his shoulder. 'There's to be a celebration at the Boar's Tusk. Shall we go?'

Jack looked in better spirits and Crispin craved it too. He agreed and they managed to squeeze their way through to Gutter Lane and fight to make a path into the Tusk.

'Let that man through!' cried Gilbert's gravelly voice.

All the men crowded into the tavern looked and cheered Crispin. Crispin laughed. Why they were cheering him he didn't know.

Maybe they supposed he could buy a round of drinks. He wished he could.

Raising a hand to Gilbert, the tavernkeeper waved him over. People patted Crispin on the back as he went, as if his loyalty to Lancaster had translated into his personally putting Henry on the throne! He laughed outright at the ludicrous notion.

'I saved you a spot, Crispin. I knew you'd be here.'

'And here I am. It is a happy day.'

'It is indeed. You have been vindicated, I'd say.'

'I suppose.'

Eleanor came trotting in from the kitchens. 'Crispin!' He found himself enclosed in her arms.

'Eleanor,' he chuckled. Their cheer was rubbing off on him, and he ordered wine, but Gilbert had anticipated him and already had a jug and goblets in his hands.

'If you don't mind Crispin and Jack, I should like to join you.'

'And me too!' chirped Eleanor.

'Then this *is* a day to celebrate.'

He happily drank with Jack and Jack's in-laws and Crispin and Jack told them all they had seen at Westminster.

Crispin's head pleasantly hummed with the wine and, in good cheer, he talked with several men who came by to discuss with him their thoughts on the new king. And all of it was the merriest he'd been in decades . . . until two knights entered through the door. All the merry-making – the musicians with their shawm and drum – stopped. The place fell to a hush.

The knights in surcoat with mail beneath were bare-headed when they stood at the portal and looked about. 'Is Crispin Guest here?' cried one.

God's blood. What now? Crispin slowly rose. 'I am Crispin Guest.'

Every head turned to him. His heart battered his chest and his palms were suddenly damp with sweat. He rubbed them surreptitiously down his cote-hardie.

'You're to come with us.'

'Where?' he asked.

The knight who spoke turned to his compatriot. 'He's a saucy fellow, isn't he? Where, he asks. Westminster. And don't dawdle.'

'My man is here. What—'

'Bring him, then.'

Crispin locked eyes with Jack. The man's eyes were wide with terror. He clasped Jack by the arm and made his way through the strangely silent crowd.

His first instinct was to try to ferret out what he'd done. But then his second thought was . . . no. No, best not to even give it thought.

They reached the knights. Crispin didn't recognize them. They were polite and asked if he had horses. Crispin wasn't used to such solicitousness. Usually when knights wanted him, it was to knock him about, push him ahead of them, or let him trail behind their horses, trotting to keep up in order to meet the sheriffs.

He told them he did have horses but they were back on the Shambles. The knights made no fuss and simply followed them until they arrived at the poulterer's. Jack hurried to saddle both horses while Crispin stood stoically by. And when the horses appeared, the knight who had spoken raised his eyebrows at them. Surely, he expected some old nags instead of the fine beasts that Carantok Teague, a Cornish client, had gifted to Crispin some two years ago. 'Fine horses. Your man is efficient.'

'Thank you. There is no finer apprentice in London.'

The man chuckled good-naturedly and waited for them to mount. As they followed through the winding streets of London, Crispin dared to ask: 'Where in Westminster are we going, good sir knight? It's just that . . . I have not expected to be called to such a place on such a day as this is.'

'And well should you wonder. I tried to remember where I'd heard your name, Master Guest. And when I remembered, it was a strange thing indeed.'

Crispin fell silent then, but the other knight finally spoke. 'I'd heard that name associated with the Tracker. And it seems that is you. Living on the Shambles and everything.'

'Eh?' said the first knight. His white surcoat was divided with a vertical stripe of blue in the center.

'Have you never heard of the Tracker of London? That man who makes fools of the sheriffs by solving murders?'

The white and blue knight swiveled hard in his high-backed saddle to look Crispin over. 'The devil you say?'

The second knight, surcoat in gray, turned as well. 'Isn't that right, Master Guest? You are that man?'

Crispin gave a polite nod. 'I am.'

'Well!' said the first knight. 'Blessed saints. I've only vaguely heard of this. And that is you?'

'Your servant,' he said with another bow.

'How do you find out such things? Criminals and such,' asked the second knight. 'It seems an impossible task.'

'Not if you are observant and ask the right questions. And have a very well-trained apprentice at your side.'

Jack gave him a grateful smile.

'And this is your apprentice then?' asked the second knight. He held up his hand. 'No, don't tell me. He's . . . let me think . . . Jack Tucker?'

Surprised, Jack nodded. 'Right, my lord. I'm obliged to you.'

'Oh, nothing of the sort. I've watched both your careers with interest. And, to tell you truly, with just a bit of envy.'

'Don't envy *me*, my lord,' said Crispin with a crooked smile.

The knights fell silent then and faced the road ahead.

They took Fleet Street where it merged with the Strand. They encountered more people along the route than Crispin remembered seeing before on that road. He supposed they were the stragglers from the festivities and perhaps they'd stayed behind in the taverns of Westminster.

They came to Charing Cross where there were still many revelers and kept going until they reached Westminster Abbey, still filled with people, and then on to Westminster Hall and through the Great Gate.

Crispin gave Jack a reassuring smile, but it was a hollow gesture. As they dismounted, a groom took their horses. Crispin had no idea whether they were to see the beasts again. What part was he expected to play now?

As they neared the entrance to Westminster Hall, they heard reveling and music and much chatter. They followed the knights up the steps and through the arched entry. The place was set up as he remembered it from better days in the court of King Edward. The pennons of all the lords were displayed near the clerestory windows high along the walls. All the chivalry of England. Crispin's family colors used to be there among them . . . until they had been removed. Because of him.

A banquet of the most sumptuous manner was underway. A long

table across the head of the hall held Henry and his closest courtiers, including his wife and sons. Then, facing outward, were many other tables set up perpendicular to the head, for the rest of the feasting courtiers, aldermen, the two newest sheriffs, William Waldern and William Hyde, and the new lord mayor, Thomas Knowles.

Servants there were aplenty, scurrying here and there to serve their patrons, cut their meat, and pour wine into their goblets.

If Crispin had not felt so alarmed, he would have been glad to see it. He and Jack still stood in the doorway between the two knights, when Henry's chamberlain, Hugh Waterton, approached. The knight in white and blue told him to announce Crispin Guest.

Snapping his head toward the knight, Crispin stared at him. What was he doing? This was not the time nor the place for the likes of him.

Waterton's stony face looked Crispin over, stood off to the side, and stamped his staff of office on the tiled floor. In a loud, ringing voice he cried to the open rafters, 'Crispin Guest!'

The musicians were silenced. The courtiers turned to look. And Henry, feasting along with his family, slowly rose at his place.

My God, my knees are knocking. Please, Lord, don't let me look like a fool. Crispin swallowed, squared his shoulders, and gestured for Jack to follow him. The knights flanked him on either side. Were they there to make certain he did not escape?

He walked the long length of the hall in silence. All eyes followed his interminable progress. He listened to each squeak of his shoes, each soft slapping of his sword at his hip, and the loud drumbeat of his heart in his chest.

He came to the last table, standing perpendicular to the head table on its dais. At the same time, the king made his way from his seat at the center to the edge and stood looking down at Crispin for a long time. He didn't know how he held the king's gaze, but Crispin did. He told himself that to faint now would be very bad manners indeed. Instead, he bowed low.

Henry leapt down, strode up to him, and just as he had upon seeing him in the streets of London, he embraced him. Crispin inhaled the sweet aroma of the balsam with which he had been anointed only hours before, the fur trim of his houppelande, the rosewater of his hair . . . and closed his eyes, thinking that maybe it had all been worth it. Maybe.

Slowly, Henry let him go and held his shoulders at arm's length. He turned him toward the crowd. 'This is Crispin Guest of the Shambles. But most of you know him from his time here in court. Master Guest raised me in my father's household. And, more recently, he saved my life.' The crowd gasped and murmured. Henry nodded. 'Yes, if not for this man, I would not this day be standing before you as your king. This man has been a faithful and loyal servant to the House of Lancaster since he was seven years old, when he had come to live in my father's house. Though it was true that he committed a traitorous deed, it was only out of love for my father, the late Duke of Lancaster. He watched over my father as he lay dying while I was banished, unable to attend him. This man – this loyal man – has served the city of London to find murderers and criminals. This man who, above all else, values honor and sacrifice, was himself sacrificed and lived without the mantle of knighthood he had so richly merited. His honor – which the court of Richard had taken from him – was kept dear in his heart and in his deeds. I ask this court, should such a man not reap his rewards at last?'

The crowd burst into cheers.

Breathing hard, Crispin slowly scanned the throng. Wouldn't they have just as easily condemned him again? But Henry's gracious words had filled the crowd with forgiveness and generosity. Where before they had jeered and called for his head, they now called for his reconciliation and honor.

But more than that. The words seeped into Crispin's soul, choked his breath, pricked his eyes, and fed his weary heart.

When Crispin turned toward Henry again, the king was smiling. 'Kneel, Crispin.'

He couldn't breathe, couldn't speak, couldn't think. He could barely see through his damp eyes. Yet, he got down on one knee and bowed his head.

Henry withdrew his sword, the now 'Sword of Lancaster' – the sword he first drew when he had landed again in England at Ravenspur – and held it up. 'Crispin Guest, I, Henry, King of England, declare that you are restored to yourself . . .' Crispin bit his lip, afraid he might openly sob. *I mustn't, I mustn't.* '. . . *Sir* Crispin, Baron of Sheen, knight and lord of the realm . . .' He closed his eyes and felt the light tap of the sword blade once to each shoulder. '. . . House of Guest, never again to be removed from the panoply of lords of England. Arise, Sir Crispin, and face the court. You are of the Shambles no more.'

Trembling and feeling light – so light – he struggled to rise, but there was Jack with his strong hand under Crispin's arm, lifting him and sobbing like a fool.

He turned to face the court, though he could not help the tears filling his own eyes. The court cheered, and there were some wet faces out there too, much to his amazement. During the cheers and applause, Henry leaned toward him and whispered, 'Were you afraid you were brought here to be punished? Forget what you think you know.'

He stared at Henry. The words! The fateful words the dying Abbot Nicholas spoke to him. *Forget what you think you know.* But Henry had left off the last part: *Beware of what you find.*

And yet. Nothing, but nothing could change the elation he felt. His soul soared higher than the hammerbeam ceiling, higher than the roof, nearly as high as Heaven.

THIRTY

Sir Crispin Guest, Baron of Sheen

October 1399, London

They celebrated long into the night and sat with the knights that had escorted him from the Boar's Tusk, and he discovered that their names were Sir Reginald (with the surcoat in white and blue), and Sir Herbert, both household knights to King Henry. They talked of the things they admired about Crispin and Crispin replied in a daze. The new sheriffs even came by to pay their respects and, for once, they didn't call him 'Guest' in that snarling way, but bowed and called him 'Lord Crispin' and 'my lord.' Even the lord mayor of London greeted him with a bow. He could scarce believe it.

But the time was late, and Henry lifted himself from his chair and bid his courtiers good night.

Crispin rose and looked down at himself. He looked no different, and yet . . . how different he felt!

He gathered a tipsy Jack and made his farewells. Grooms brought their horses and they were to make a cold and long ride back to the Shambles. 'Not *of* the Shambles anymore,' he told himself. As it was explained to him, Henry had given him back his family lands at Sheen. But the manor house was no more and it would take some funds to restore it. He hadn't any expectation that Henry's largesse extended that far. But at least there was rent from the tenants now. That, and a small stipend Henry had bestowed. And instantly, it was true. He didn't have to stay on the Shambles any longer.

Even as he cheered at *that* thought, Tucker made another undignified sob.

'Jack, you mustn't carry on so.' The Strand stretched out long before them, a blue ribbon of a road, until he could detect the few candle lights in windows at the edge of London.

'But sir.' Jack dragged a drunken hand under his soggy nose. 'I will miss you. Terribly.'

'What the devil are you talking about?'

'Well . . . you're a lord again. And God bless you, sir, and God save King Henry!'

'Keep your voice down. People are abed.'

'And you being a lord and all, well. You'll have your own household and . . . and . . .' He burst into another sob.

Crispin glared at him. 'You're a fool, Tucker.'

'But sir!'

'Close your mouth and don't speak until I tell you to do so.' Crispin adjusted his seat. His damned eyes were pricking again. 'Have I not told you many a time that I have never met a more loyal man than you? God's blood, Tucker! I can't get along without you now. I expect that you will continue to serve me as my steward. And if you can keep your fool head on, as my squire. And eventually a knight.'

A thud beside him told Crispin that Jack had fallen from his horse.

Crispin threw the reins aside and slipped off his mount. 'Jack, are you all right?'

'Sir?' He rubbed his head. The fall seemed to have sobered him and he sat on his backside, his knees up. '*What* did you say?'

Crispin bent and lifted Jack to his feet, sliding his arm around his shoulders and leaning against the warm flank of Seb, Jack's horse. 'I *said* that I would be pleased if you continued to serve me as my household steward and squire. And in due time, I will knight you myself.'

Even in the dark, Jack's widened eyes shone. 'You can't mean it, Master Crispin. I'm nobody. I've got no name.'

'I know well what it means to be a nobody, Jack. But you now serve a knight of the realm, *Baron* of Sheen, I might remind you, though there is little left of it. That makes *you* somebody. You are Jack Tucker of London. And let no one naysay you ever again.'

When they arrived home, Isabel startled awake in her seat by the fire. 'Bless me, look at the two of you. I was worried sick. When those knights came here looking for you . . . I prayed hard for you, Master Crispin, most of the night.'

Jack gathered her up in his arms and kissed her soundly, even as her wide eyes looked desperately toward Crispin. Jack finally pulled away from her with a loud sucking sound. 'You must have more respect, my love. That isn't "Master Crispin" no more. That there is *Sir* Crispin, Baron of Sheen. The king himself knighted him in front of all the court. Gave him back his title and his lands, and . . . and . . .' He broke into another sob and hugged her tight.

Her astonished face was rather pleasing, Crispin had to admit. 'He speaks the truth, Isabel. And what he can't seem to say is that I have made him my squire. And I hope you and your brood will accompany me from this place at last and we can find a proper manor house for all of us. If you will come. Please say you will.'

'Master Crispin! I mean *Sir* Crispin.' She pushed away from the still sobbing Jack and curtseyed. 'Lord bless me. My own children will slay me if I told you no, for they love you so. And . . .' She put her hands to her cheeks. 'Oh my! I hardly know what to think.'

'Well, think about taking this man to his bed. We have celebrated mightily at court. Come to think of it, I was surprised not to see Clarence Walcote and Christopher there. There were other mercers and aldermen.'

Jack raised his head suddenly and dragged his whole arm across his face. He exchanged a worried glance with his wife. 'You go on up, Isabel. I must talk with Master . . . *Sir* Crispin first.'

She kissed Jack on the cheek, and curtseyed again to Crispin with a, 'God bless you, sir,' before she gathered her fur around her shoulders and climbed the stairs.

Jack wiped his face again and stood with his back to the warming fire. 'Sir,' he began when he'd controlled himself. 'I couldn't tell you amid all . . .' He gestured to the world at large. 'This! First you were guarding the king . . . I mean Sir Richard of Bordeaux . . . and then there was other things and, well. It wasn't ever a fit time to tell you.'

By the look on the man's face and by his words, a heavy stone began to form in Crispin's stomach. 'What? What is it, Jack?'

'It was a few weeks ago. Just at the time King Henry rode into London. It was the message Bishop Braybrooke would have had you take to the Walcotes, sir. He sent it here, sir. You see, Master Clarence . . . he was on a buying journey and he . . . well. He died, sir. And the message had reached the bishop first, Clarence Walcote being such an important man and all. And they conveyed his body back to London. They buried him a sennight ago, sir. That's why they weren't at the feast.'

Crispin couldn't quite focus his eyes. He'd had too many shocks today. And too much wine, truth to tell. He pinched his fingers into his eyes and then shook his head. 'I can't believe it.'

'It took him sudden like, sir. There was naught anyone could do, so the letter said.'

'Oh God. Poor Christopher.'

'Yes, sir. I sent your condolences and explained why you couldn't be there at the funeral.'

'You should have told me, Jack.'

'But you were serving your king, sir. That . . . was more important.'

'I know but . . .'

'Did I . . . did I do wrong, sir?'

Crispin ran his hand over his chin. Stubble was sprouting again. 'No. You thought it out and did the proper thing. Precisely what a steward would do for his lord. I do not fault you.'

'In the morning, sir, best pay your respects.'

'Yes. Yes, I will.'

'To bed now, sir. It's been a hell of a day.'

Jack offered a weak grin again, and Crispin couldn't help but smile back. 'By God, it has been.' Jack had put an arm under him, but Crispin slipped out of it and slung his arm around Jack, squeezing, and they trudged up to prepare him for rest.

Crispin lay in his bed. He had been tired before, but now he was wide awake. The whole world had suddenly opened to him. He could leave the Shambles, he could begin his journey to be a rich man again, *and* he was a lord, restoring the family name that he had sullied.

And . . . Philippa was free . . .

He crossed himself, staring at the ceiling. How did he dare think such thoughts so soon after Clarence Walcote had died, barely cold in the ground!

But God help him, he couldn't *stop* thinking of it.

A thud on his chest and he saw two glowing eyes staring at him in the dark. 'Gyb, you wayward feline. Where have you been?'

The cat merely looked at him and settled down on his chest, waiting to be petted.

He lifted his hand to absently stroke the soft fur. It gave him something to do as he thought about Philippa. Would she want him? Had it all been a game, this wanting, yearning . . . but safe, while Clarence still lived?

And dear, dear Clarence. He had known about Philippa and Crispin. He had known that Christopher was Crispin's child. And he'd never said a word. He had loved the boy as his own, and that was how it should be.

But everything was different now. When all was said and done, would she want to associate with Crispin, when Christopher looked so much like him, when everyone could plainly see he was Crispin's bastard?

Beware of what you find, indeed, he thought, his hand petting the cat's fur. The creature began to purr in a soothing rumble.

Too many thoughts. Too many roads ahead. Not enough sleep.

Yet sleep he did, because, astonished that he *had* slept, he awoke to a sun streaking through the narrow space between the shutters, and the cat, as usual, was already gone.

Jack tended to his fire with water for his shave. In fact, the knave was looking over his shoulder at Crispin and smiling from ear to ear. 'Good morn . . . *Lord* Crispin.'

He had to admit that he was smiling too. Until he remembered that he had to face Christopher today.

He haunted Mercery. He paced back and forth. And everyone who passed him seemed already to know of his new status. They gave him a bow, with a 'God keep you, my lord' and a 'Bless you, Sir Crispin.' People he knew well. People whom he barely knew at all. Word traveled fast in London.

'This is passing strange,' he muttered, leaning against the shop across from the Walcote estate. The whole of it was strange. It sometimes seemed like a dream. He saw it as a patchwork of images: Richard taking the crown off his head and placing it onto the floor; Henry wearing his own crown coming out of Westminster Abbey; Henry knighting Crispin and restoring his titles. The next time he was at Westminster – and he'd be there as much as he liked, he suddenly realized – his family's colors would hang with the others in the hall. Just as they used to do. Just as they had . . . before he had lost it all.

'Talking to yourself?'

Crispin startled and found himself face to face with Christopher. The boy was looking at him quizzically, head cocked to one side.

'Christopher.' He bowed to the boy, hand on his chest. "I am so sorry about your father.'

Christopher's jovial expression stilled and then seemed to melt away from his face. 'You mean Clarence Walcote?' A wrinkle formed between his eyes. 'I'm sorry too. He was a good man. I shall truly miss him, his wisdom, and his humor.'

Crispin didn't quite know what else to say. He looked down at his hands and found himself looking at his family ring, the one thing left from his former life. Now he was sorry he'd sold the one belonging to his father. Except it had bought the furniture and the rent for their landlord Nigellus Cobmartin. But of course, he could soon afford to make another ring for Christopher. If the boy wanted it.

'Christopher—'

'It's all over London. The news. That the king knighted you, gave you back your title and lands.'

Crispin couldn't help but smile and nodded.

'What will you do now?'

Crispin leaned back against the wall again and shrugged. 'I don't honestly know. It will take funds to restore my manor house in Sheen. It . . . burned to the ground . . .' And he could still remember that fateful night when he and Jack watched it burn while they huddled in the snow. 'I have the rents from the tenants. King Henry has promised me a stipend for being a household knight, but the wealth that Richard took from me will never be recovered.'

'That's a shame.'

'Some would say I deserved it.'

'I don't think they will say that now.'

He offered a sad smile. 'You are generous.'

'No. It's just that those in London have come to appreciate and respect you.' He rested his thumbs in his belt . . . as Crispin often did. 'Will you . . . will you still be the Tracker, I wonder?'

'I don't know, Christopher.'

After a time, they both turned their attention to the Walcote manor. It stood quiet and somewhat lonely on the wet street, with its walls and gatehouse shining from the morning rain.

'Did you ever find the stolen relics, sir?'

Crispin lifted his foot and rested it against the wall. 'Only one. The girdle. All the others are lost.'

'Why the girdle?'

'It was old and well used. The purchaser became suspicious and enquired of St Frideswide Priory himself. He gladly returned it.' Crispin remembered the moment when he had held the girdle in his hands and offered it to the new prioress, Dame Petronella. He had felt that familiar tingle in his fingers that told him the relic was authentic, that it had, indeed, belonged to Saint Frideswide. Was it that he in particular was endowed with such a gift, an ability to sense the validity of a relic, or was it something all the faithful were blessed with? In truth, he didn't want to know.

They fell silent again. Crispin snatched a surreptitious glance at his son before dropping his gaze again.

Without turning toward him, Christopher said softly, 'You should go to her.'

Crispin stiffened. 'I . . .'

'You . . . you should . . . marry her.'

Crispin slowly faced him and measured his expression. It was somewhat neutral, but there was still something of a glint in his eye. 'Oh, I should, should I?'

He smiled, a little sadly, Crispin thought. Perhaps he was thinking of Clarence. Or perhaps lost opportunities. 'Yes. You should. *Sir Crispin.*'

'Is that why? Because of who I am now, a knight and lord?'

Christopher's merry expression sobered. 'No. Never that. For she told me not long ago that she would have married you as you were, on the Shambles. And that it was *you* who had refused *her.*'

'Ever to my shame and damnation,' he muttered. 'It was the sin of pride, Christopher. I still thought of myself as better than her, and I could never marry a scullion. Now she is a great lady.'

'And you are a great lord.'

'A penniless lord. By comparison.'

'What do you care of that?'

He didn't. He would have taken her back years ago if he could have. How he hated that his good fortune would come by way of a dead merchant.

His eyes wandered back to the sullen exterior of the Walcote manor. 'If I do ask her and if I am blessed with her affirmation, would you – God's blood!' He hated that his voice trembled. 'To all the world you are the son of the proud mercer family, the Walcotes. You are well known as Christopher Walcote. Well respected for it. I hold no ill will for you for that name. It belonged to a gentle and wise man. But. You are *my* son, and it would give me no end of pleasure to bestow upon you the fine and ancient name of Guest. It is a Welsh name and given its title and honors by King Henry II. Perhaps I did not value it as much as I should have, but it has always been mine and the titles and the honor go with it once more. Yet . . . to claim this name, you would – unfortunately – have to be declared a bastard first. Do you understand the implications? It would bring down shame upon you and your mother. It must be your decision.'

'You would adopt me?'

'Not so much adopt you as *claim* you. I would never have said a word before in order to prevent this very dishonor upon you. But now that my name has worth again, well . . .'

'It's . . . a huge decision.'

'Yes, it is. I don't wish to diminish the role that Clarence Walcote played in your life. I am grateful to him for giving you the life I could not. And for . . . for keeping your secret. For in the end, he did know about you.'

Christopher's mouth sagged open. His eyes shone with moisture suddenly. 'He did?' he whispered.

Crispin nodded fondly at his son. 'He did. But vowed never to speak of it. Do you understand the great sacrifice he made? In order to keep your honor, he said nothing. He could easily have denounced you. It takes a courageous man to do such a thing as he did. A loving man. For he loved you well.'

Lowering his head, Christopher wiped the tears from his eyes. 'I will always honor him with prayers and masses.'

Crispin's spirits lifted timidly. 'Does that mean . . . you might consider it? That you could someday call me "Father"?'

Christopher's face, still wet with tears, broke into a lopsided grin. 'I loved and will continue to honor the name of Clarence Walcote. *But*. One need only look upon this face. Clearly, Sir Crispin . . . I mean . . . *Father* . . . how could I ever avoid it?'

EPILOGUE

A knock at the door and Steward Jack Tucker tapped the shoulder of the footman. Jack would get the door, he indicated silently, letting the man go on to his duties.

It had been a good six months since his master had regained all that he had lost, and had married, and had elevated Jack to the superior position of steward and squire, positions that he – even in his wildest dreams – could never have imagined aspiring to. His clothes no longer had patches or repairs. They were new and numerous. Good wool, and even some with fancy embroidery; floral spirals and masculine suns. The proudest of them all were the cote-hardies with an embroidered patch on his breast with the arms of Guest. The Guest name was restored and now Jack was part of that history.

With coins in his purse at last – and no meager amounts either! – he could afford to garb his wife in the finery she deserved. His children, though still as rambunctious and as muddy as always, wore far better garments, even as they wore through the stockings at the knee with the rapidity of the old ones. They had proper tutors, too – even the girls – so they could all read and write and learn history.

The mistress of the house, Madam Walcote . . . *No.* He shook his head. *Lady* Philippa, he corrected – as she now was – doted on Jack's children as if they were her own. In fact, Isabel was now her personal maid. Though she was more like Lady Philippa's fast friend, gossiping and chattering as they did, falling to silence when Jack came into the room and smirking the whole time.

He raised his eyes to the high ceilings of the former Walcote manor – now the Guest manor – scarcely believing he was responsible for all of it, for every servant was now under *him*, along with the grounds, the maintenance, and the sarding bookkeeping!

Yes, Jack Tucker, former scullion and scrappy orphan of the streets, was now a squire, with a promised knighthood not far off. Even after six months, he often shook his head in disbelief. Every morning when he woke in his soft bed, under warm, feather-filled comforters, his amazement was rekindled . . . and his thankful prayers recited. He reckoned there was not a man more loyal to another in all England as he was to Master . . . no . . . *Lord* Crispin.

It was a shame that Lord Crispin's estates in Sheen were unfit to live in, having burned down some fourteen years ago. But since King Henry gifted it back to his master, he hoped that someday Lord Crispin could afford to rebuild. At least he received the tenants' rents again. For now, he was content living in the heart of London, Jack could tell. Of course, maybe that sparkle in his eye was from having his love at last, the woman he had been besotted with for those same fifteen years. He was instructed not to call upon his master *too* early in the morning these days. Jack chuckled at it.

He made his way across the tiled floor and reached the front entry. He unlocked the bolts and pulled the door open, fixing his face into polite greeting.

A man – not a lord, by the look of him – turned anxious hands one over the other. He looked up hopefully but warily at Jack. 'Master,' he said, stepping forward, but being careful not to pass the threshold unless invited, clasping his nervous hands together in an attitude of prayer. 'Please. Am I at the right place, sir? I'm looking for Crispin Guest. The Tracker of London. I need his help.'

Jack hesitated. His master was now a knight, a lord, an important man of the court. Even now he was required by the king to attend him, but had begged to stay in London for a little while longer to be with his new wife. And it seemed that King Henry could deny his vassal nothing, acceding to his desires, though Jack knew Crispin would have to go to Westminster soon.

He opened his mouth with the intention of telling the man that the Tracker was no more. But before he could say anything, the man interrupted.

'My wife has been missing for days. And I know . . . I *know* it has to do with our wretched landlord. He's been pawing at her since the moment we moved into his lodgings. Once I caught him cornering her in the kitchens, and her, a face as white as linen. I fear he's stolen her away and done her harm. Please, sir. Please. May I speak to the Tracker?'

The man's distress was written in the droplets of sweat on his upper lip and brow. His eyes darted from here to there. And his throat must have been dry for all the swallowing he was doing.

Jack knew his master well. He knew him better than any man alive, he supposed. There was always a sparkle in his eye when it came to talking of his many adventures as London's Tracker. And he relished the fact that he had retired from such work. Now, he'd sit before the fire with his wife at his side, Christopher sitting in a chair in the corner, and Jack's children gathered around him on the fur laid out on the floor. And they'd beg him to tell his tales. He'd smile indulgently at the children he seemed to love as his own, and he'd tell the stories of him and his courageous apprentice Jack – and he'd always lift his eyes to Jack for a moment and wink – making Jack out to be the hero more often than not, for he seemed to enjoy the look of awe the children had when glancing at their father, a man who surely did not look as heroic when he helped them out of their clothes, or changed their clouts. It was just one more thing to love his master for.

Jack studied the desperate man before him. What was he to tell him? Where was he to go? The sheriffs were just as inept at such things as they always had been. And their serjeants could only be trusted to be as scraping as any thief.

Where was he to go?

Jack bit his lip. 'Sir, this is the house of Lord Crispin Guest, Baron of Sheen.'

'Yes, but . . . he's the Crispin Guest I seek, is he not?'

Jack rubbed absently at his ginger beard and clucked his tongue. 'Aye, that he is . . . or *was*. But he has laid aside his vocation as Tracker to serve the king as a knight, good sir. He hasn't been occupied as Tracker for these last six months . . .'

The man looked on anxiously, desperately, and Jack could do nothing but curse himself as he sighed. 'Well . . . I suppose . . . I can ask, but I tell you, man, it will do no good. He's retired. He's adviser to the king. He don't run about London looking into things no more.' He glanced at the doorway and saw that the rain had begun again. 'No sense in you getting wet, good master. Come into the parlor, at least.' He directed the footman to take the man there as Jack glanced up the stairs. The family was in the solar: Sir Crispin, Lady Philippa, Crispin's son Christopher, Isabel, and all of

Jack's children. He hated to interrupt them. His master deserved this time of contentment.

He girded himself and walked slowly up each riser. As he gained the landing, he walked along the gallery to the open solar door. When he peered in, his heart gladdened at the sight. His wife Isabel was sitting in a chair next to Philippa and they were working on an embroidery together, as close as sisters. Crispin sat in the big chair, while Gyb, the black cat with the white blaze and belly, rested in his arms. His master smiled and absently stroked the cat as he watched his son Christopher telling a story to the children gathered around his feet on the fur. Little Crispin was leaning back against his namesake's leg without a care that he was a cutpurse's son and he was relaxing against a lord of the realm, while Gilbert sat beside him, holding the toddler Genevieve who seemed to be dozing. Helen, the little mother, was gently rocking the week-old babe, Isabel, in her cradle, lying beside the older baby, Johanna.

It was as serene a scene as was painted on any solar wall. A warm and homely room, with fine pillows and many chairs for the suddenly large family inhabiting the place, along with other items of wealth on display – a chandler here, a silver wine jug and silver goblets on a finely carved ambry there . . .

A gold reliquary sat in pride of place in the center of the mantel above the hearth, containing a single thorn from the Crown of Thorns. Jack knew it was authentic. He and his master knew it well. It would have sat beside a carefully framed linen cloth impressed with the faint image of Jesus Himself . . . but that had been burned to ash by Lord Crispin some fifteen years ago.

He crept into the room so no one would notice him, and he leaned over to whisper into Crispin's ear. His master turned his slate gray eyes to him, and his dark brows – some gray hairs now visible within – lowered slightly. He rose, disturbing the cat and Little Crispin's rest, but the boy merely looked up at him and scooted back against his vacated chair, pulling the cat into *his* lap. Neither Lady Philippa nor Jack's wife ever glanced their way.

Crispin stood in the corridor and faced Jack. 'What is it, Jack?'

'As I said, sir. There's a man downstairs who is most distraught. He's desperately looking for the Tracker's help.'

'The Tracker is no longer at home,' he said simply.

'I know that well, sir. But . . . he was so . . . so disturbed. His wife, you see, might have been abducted by a detestable landlord and . . . well, sir. I don't like what might have happened to her.'

'Tucker, we don't investigate crimes any longer. I have a position at court to uphold.'

'Oh, I know, m'lord. How well I know it. A man such as yourself, getting back his own, well . . .' He smacked his thigh. 'Right then. We can't have an important man like you working on the streets as the Tracker no more. It isn't fitting. Besides, I'm certain the sheriffs will help the man. In . . . *some* fashion. Don't fret over it, sir. I will send the man on his way.'

Jack was slow to turn, and even slower descending the stairs. He was waiting for it and, as he reached the second step, he heard it.

'Hold, Jack. You know as well as I do that the sheriffs will do little for this man.' He sighed and grumbled, and at last said, 'I suppose . . . there's no harm in hearing what he has to say.'

Jack smiled all the way down the steps as Sir Crispin Guest, Baron of Sheen, followed him to the parlor to speak to their client.

AFTERWORD

t's been a long, strange journey, me and my medieval detective. He started as an idea, and a way to get myself published at last. The plan was to turn my attention from historical *novels* and write medieval *mysteries* instead. Who should this detective be? He needed to be different from the usual monks and nuns out there on bookshelves. What if the series was more of a noir, with a hardboiled-type detective? And how should this be achieved?

It took two years of just thinking about it. Who he was and how did he get there? And funnily enough, once I *did* figure out how he got there, his whole character and backstory rolled out for me like a carpet.

There's a lot to unpack here in this last tale. There are a lot of real people in it, more than in any other Crispin adventure. And it had to be so.

Henry's conquest of England reads like an exciting and rough-shod ride. He collected supporters along the way so easily. Very few skirmishes, very few killed. It was obvious that Richard was not well liked by his people, and this must have encouraged Henry as he pushed forward with his tale of being wronged. There was one small rebellion from Richard's side, but even those were dispatched by townsfolk who quickly lynched the rebels.

We don't know what Henry first intended when he decided to return to England. We know his first impulse was to get his inheritance back and possibly take up again his role as an appellant lord to correct Richard's faults in governance. It was not chronicled that he ever mentioned taking the crown any earlier than September of 1399. In fact, he purposely never spoke of it when confronting Richard, and swore over and over that he had no such intention. I suppose he hoped it would simply be acclaimed, though that didn't quite happen until he utzed it along himself.

This was not Shakespeare's *Richard II*. Richard resisted every step of the way, sometimes rather churlishly. Jean Creton, who had by sheer coincidence come from King Charles's court in Paris as one of his squires, poets, and historians – a real person – who happened to be at the wrong place at the right time to tell us first-hand his account of what he saw of Richard's deposition, and later wrote his chronicle when he was back in France – and in verse, no less.

Henry 'Hotspur' Percy, the Earl of Northumberland, was not particularly fond of Henry when they first knew each other, but quickly came around to his side when he returned from his banishment, though theirs was a fiery on again/off again relationship.

Jean Froissart was a fourteenth-century French historian living in England who gave us a comprehensive history of the Hundred Years War. Adam of Usk, a fourteenth-century Welsh priest and historian/chronicler, who had accompanied Henry and the exiled Archbishop of Canterbury on their march from Bristol to Chester and chronicled closely these events, gave us a certain withering eye toward Richard in his report. He also met with Richard while the king was in the Tower. Between these three sources and other texts, I was able to figure out what was going on outside Crispin's knowledge of that march from Ravenspur to London, and I tried to the best of my ability to put the actual words into Richard's and Henry's mouths.

Richard's fate was sealed. Perhaps if he hadn't been so proud (which, in the end, was the deadliest sin), and he had been more accepting and accommodating of his abdication, he might have convinced Henry to banish him to live his life simply somewhere else. But it's never a prudent thing to have a deposed king around to raise rebellions. In the end, Richard was never going to be allowed to live. He ended up at last at John of Gaunt's favorite castle, Pontefract. And there, his gaolers starved him to death. Or perhaps he simply gave up and starved himself. Either way, he was dead. His body was immediately paraded throughout all of England so that people could see him and *know* he was dead. Still, it didn't stop the pretenders from suddenly coming forth and declaring that *they* were Richard of Bordeaux, looking for a life of luxury from patrons of King Richard. One such pretender plied his scheme in Scotland, one Thomas Ward . . . of Trumpington. I kid you not. His lands were confiscated by the crown in 1408 for his deceit.

Don't mistake Crispin's fidelity to Henry as an endorsement by me. Henry, by all observations, wasn't that great a king either.

Crispin, in his loyalty to the Lancasters, couldn't really see the whole picture for himself.

Well, that's the Henry and Richard part. Now for a few notes on the mystery part of the book.

There was indeed, in the 'truth is stranger than fiction' file, a documented case of a real runaway nun who faked her own death. Joan of Leeds was the one who cobbled together a dummy body and a phony burial in her monastery in the early fourteenth century. The Archbishop of York wrote about it in a 1318 letter and explained that 'with the help of numerous of her accomplices, evil doers, with malice aforethought, (Joan of Leeds) crafted a dummy in the likeness of her body in order to mislead the devoted faithful, and she had no shame in procuring its burial in a sacred space amongst the religious of that place.' This letter was sent to the town of Beverley because there had been rumors of her being seen there. He demanded that she be returned and complained that 'she now wanders at large to the notorious peril to her soul and to the scandal she involved herself, irreverently and perverted her path of life arrogantly to the way of carnal lust and away from poverty and obedience.'

Hmm. Which would *you* rather pursue?

It was not known how exactly she handled her freedom from the Church, but, apparently, she lived the rest of her life outside the confines of the convent. Go Joan!

And by the way, don't go looking for it. There is no St Frideswide Priory or Church in London. I made it up.

But we must also talk about another aspect of the mystery, that of the apothecary who supplied the means of abortion. It is a very recent phenomenon to consider abortion as our society currently does. Jewish scholars have maintained that the fetus is not human until it takes its first breath, just as God gave Adam *his* first breath.

Hippocrates, on the other hand, forbade ending pregnancies. In his oath he mentions, 'I will not give to a woman an abortive remedy', but then again, he also stated that the fetus was only viable from the moment its various organs – their forms and structures – can be known, which puts the kibosh on only later abortions. This was also what the famous ancient physician, surgeon, and philosopher Galen (from c. 129 CE) expressed, from which most medieval physicians took their cues. Aristotle viewed abortion as population control for a well-ordered society, but only before the embryo achieved animal life, or was recognizably human.

So much for medieval science.

I had planned out Crispin's journey long ago. I knew how it would end. It could have, even *should* have been more noir, but I just couldn't stand to do that to the fellow after all he's been through. Crispin lives on for me. I have never picked a death date for him, so, for all I know, he's still hanging around London, a 669-year-old man, still grumbling about the sheriffs.

Thank you, thank you, thank you to all the readers out there who have followed his tale and have loved him as I have. I am grateful to you for your years of support, since his launch when he was first published by St. Martin's Minotaur, to the self-published prequel, to the good work the folks at Severn House did making the path smooth to tell his last tale.

Crispin at last gets his well-deserved rest – or does he? You decide. Meanwhile, I work on other things to write, whether paranormal or new historical mysteries. I hope you have enjoyed the series, and if you have, please review. You can follow all my books, and try a few of the new ones, at JeriWesterson.com. Cheers.

21982320348497